DREAMWORKS

SHREK

Do You Know the Muffin Man?

JOE BOOKS LTD

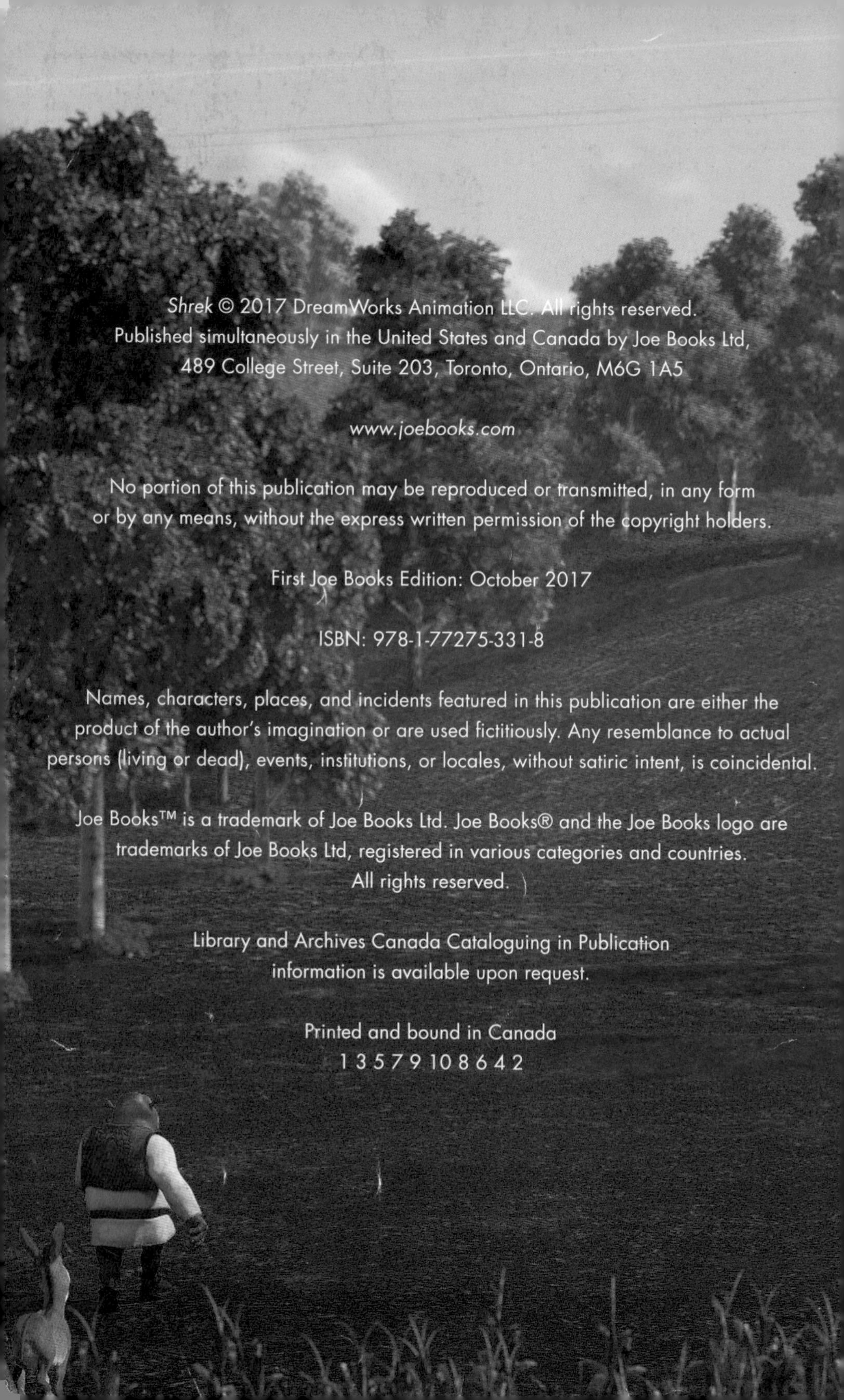

Published simultaneously in the United States and Canada by Joe Books Ltd,
489 College Street, Suite 203, Toronto, Ontario, M6G 1A5

www.joebooks.com

First Joe Books Edition: October 2017

ISBN: 978-1-77275-331-8

Library and Archives Canada Cataloguing in Publication
information is available upon request.

Printed and bound in Canada
1 3 5 7 9 10 8 6 4 2

DreamWorks

SHREK

Do You Know the Muffin Man?

Writer
Patrick Storck

Artists
Glauco Silva (#1-#2)
Salvatore Costanza (#3-#4)

Color Artist
Aikau Oliviera

Letterer
Brandon DeStefano

Editors
Rich Young
Jennifer Hale

Design
Sayre Street Books

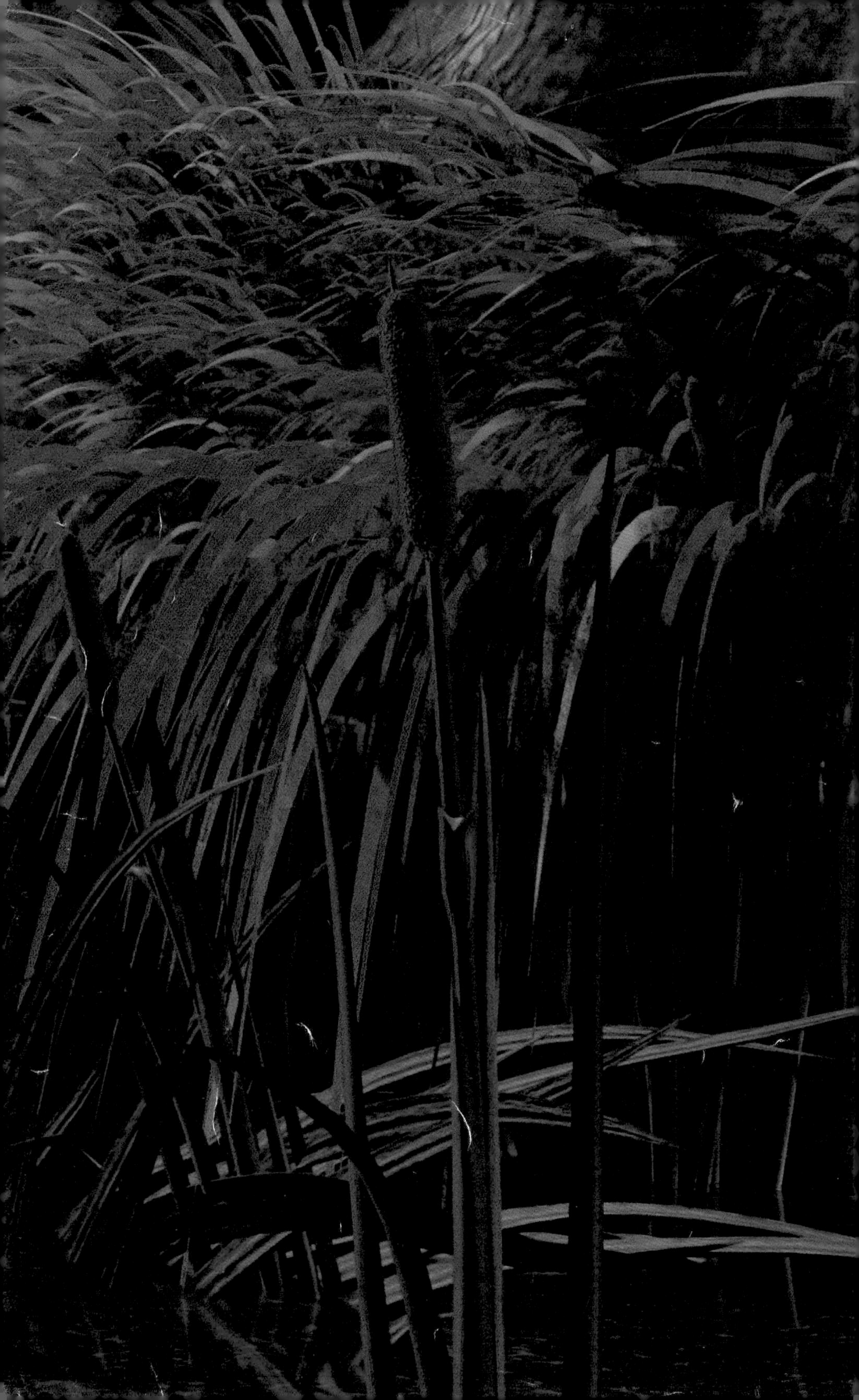

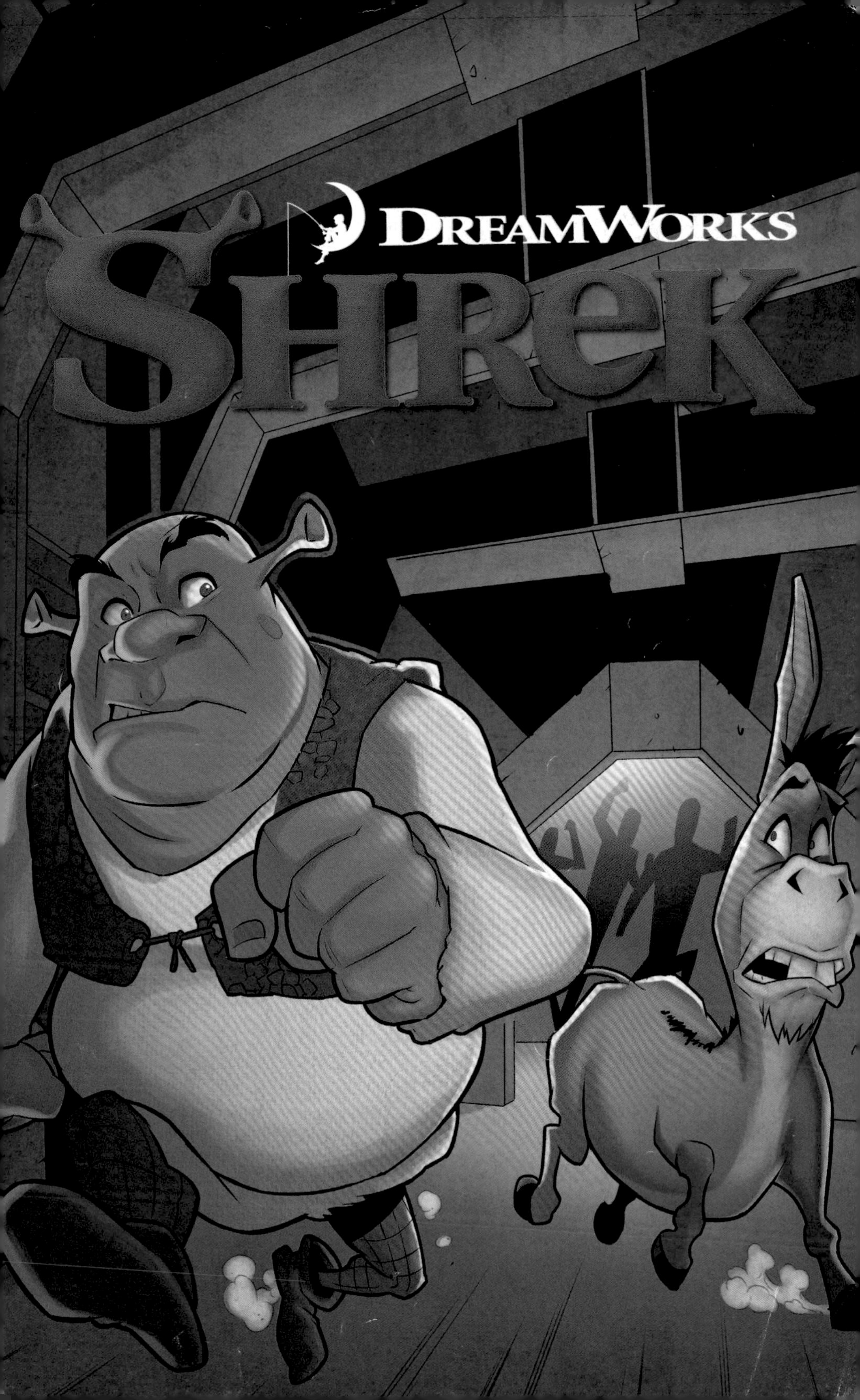
DreamWorks
Shrek

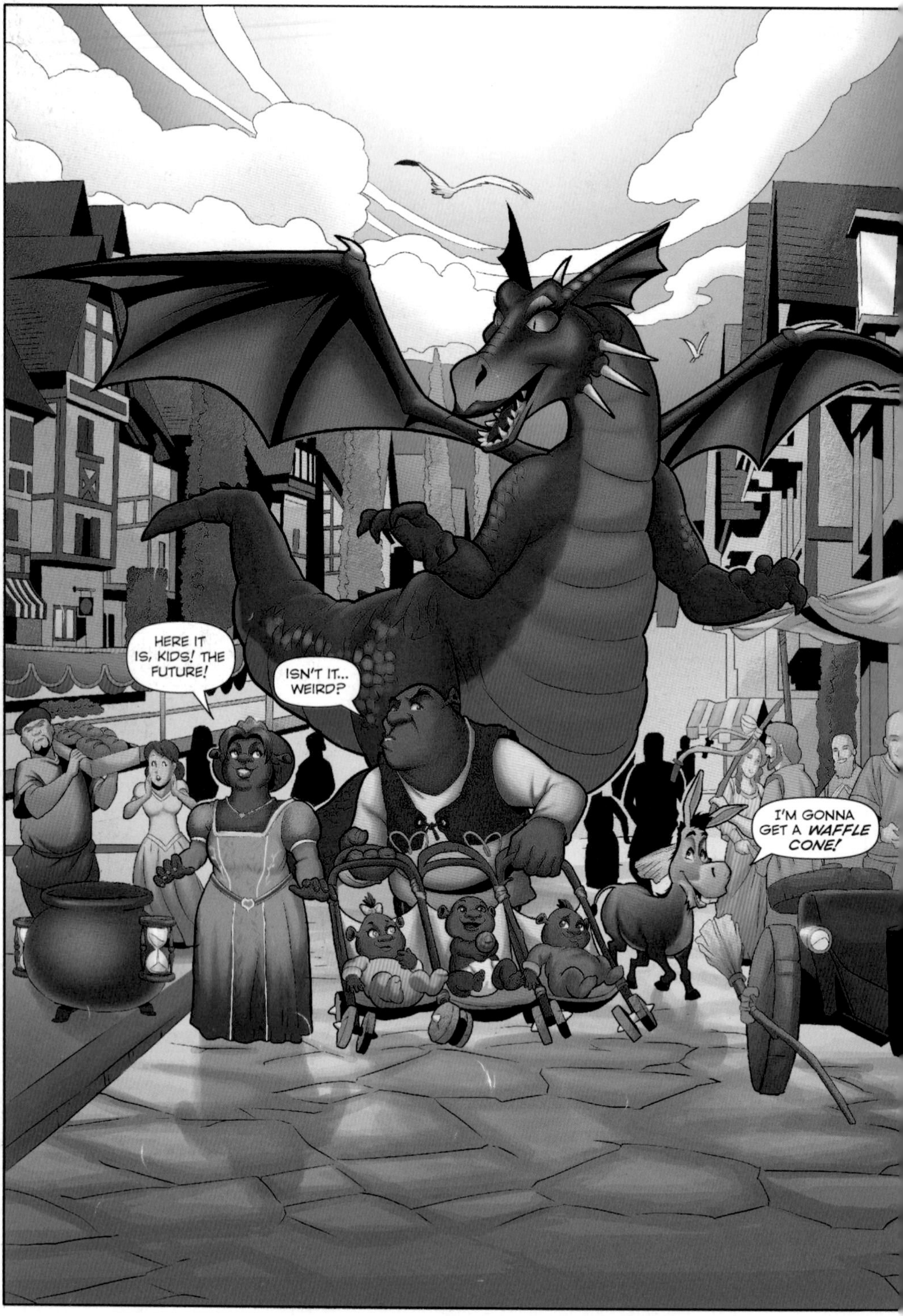
HERE IT IS, KIDS! THE FUTURE!
ISN'T IT... WEIRD?
I'M GONNA GET A *WAFFLE CONE!*

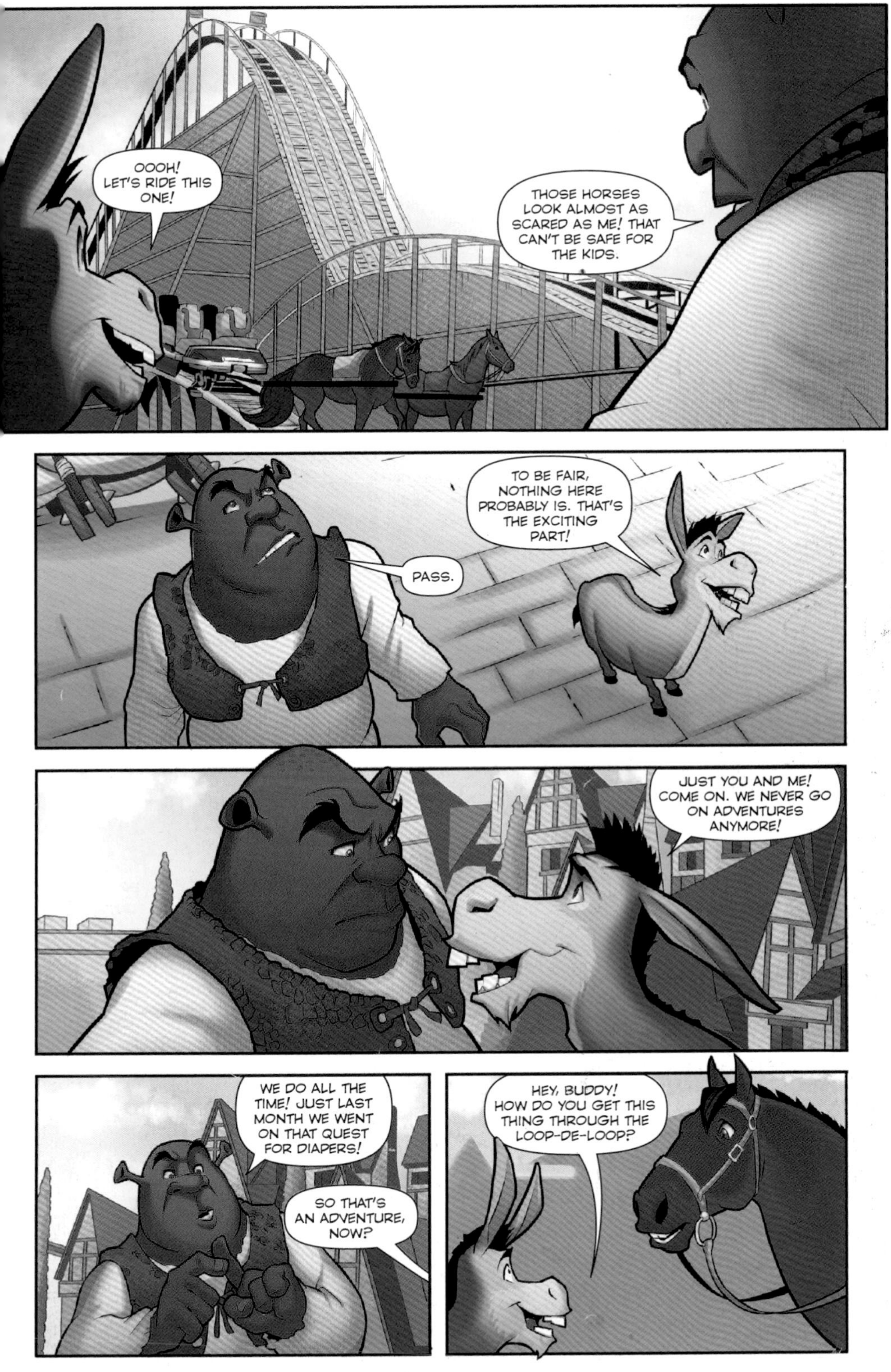
OOOH! LET'S RIDE THIS ONE!
THOSE HORSES LOOK ALMOST AS SCARED AS ME! THAT CAN'T BE SAFE FOR THE KIDS.
TO BE FAIR, NOTHING HERE PROBABLY IS. THAT'S THE EXCITING PART!
PASS.
JUST YOU AND ME! COME ON. WE NEVER GO ON ADVENTURES ANYMORE!
WE DO ALL THE TIME! JUST LAST MONTH WE WENT ON THAT QUEST FOR DIAPERS!
SO THAT'S AN ADVENTURE, NOW?
HEY, BUDDY! HOW DO YOU GET THIS THING THROUGH THE LOOP-DE-LOOP?

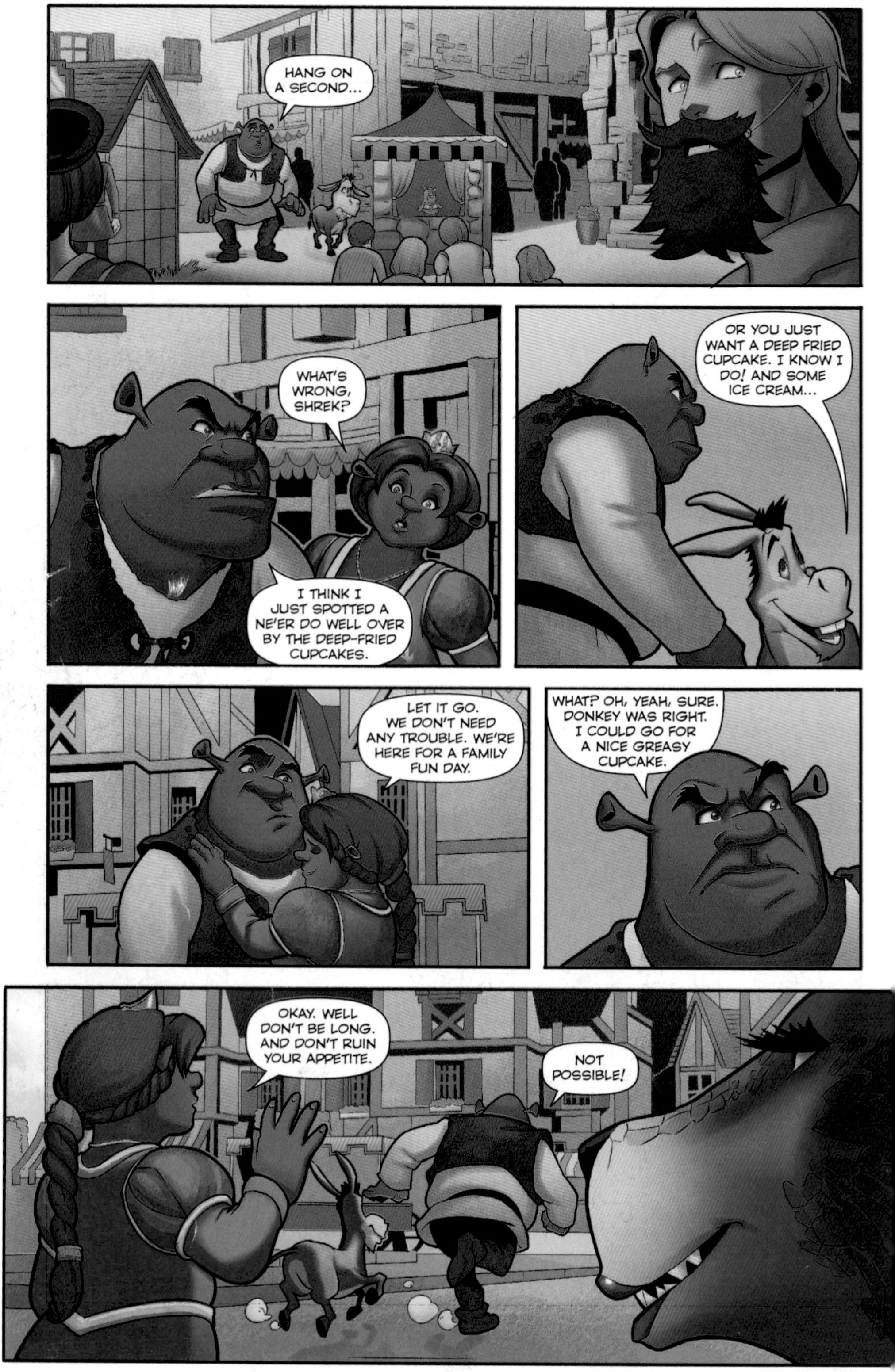
HANG ON A SECOND...
WHAT'S WRONG, SHREK?
I THINK I JUST SPOTTED A NE'ER DO WELL OVER BY THE DEEP-FRIED CUPCAKES.
OR YOU JUST WANT A DEEP FRIED CUPCAKE. I KNOW I DO! AND SOME ICE CREAM...
LET IT GO. WE DON'T NEED ANY TROUBLE. WE'RE HERE FOR A FAMILY FUN DAY.
WHAT? OH, YEAH, SURE. DONKEY WAS RIGHT. I COULD GO FOR A NICE GREASY CUPCAKE.
OKAY. WELL DON'T BE LONG. AND DON'T RUIN YOUR APPETITE.
NOT POSSIBLE!

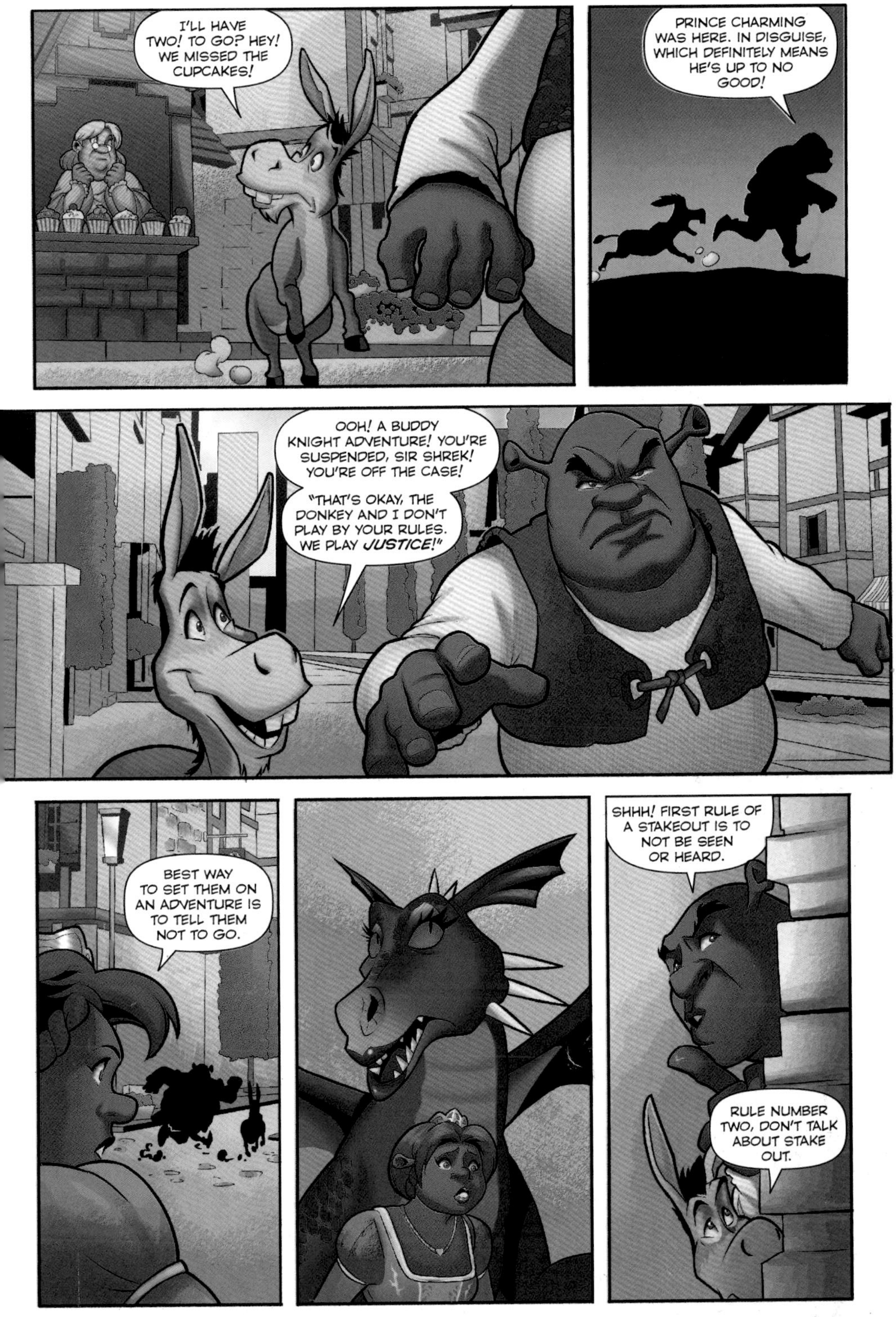
I'LL HAVE TWO! TO GO? HEY! WE MISSED THE CUPCAKES!
PRINCE CHARMING WAS HERE. IN DISGUISE, WHICH DEFINITELY MEANS HE'S UP TO NO GOOD!
OOH! A BUDDY KNIGHT ADVENTURE! YOU'RE SUSPENDED, SIR SHREK! YOU'RE OFF THE CASE!
"THAT'S OKAY, THE DONKEY AND I DON'T PLAY BY YOUR RULES. WE PLAY *JUSTICE!*"
BEST WAY TO SET THEM ON AN ADVENTURE IS TO TELL THEM NOT TO GO.
SHHH! FIRST RULE OF A STAKEOUT IS TO NOT BE SEEN OR HEARD.
RULE NUMBER TWO, DON'T TALK ABOUT STAKE OUT.

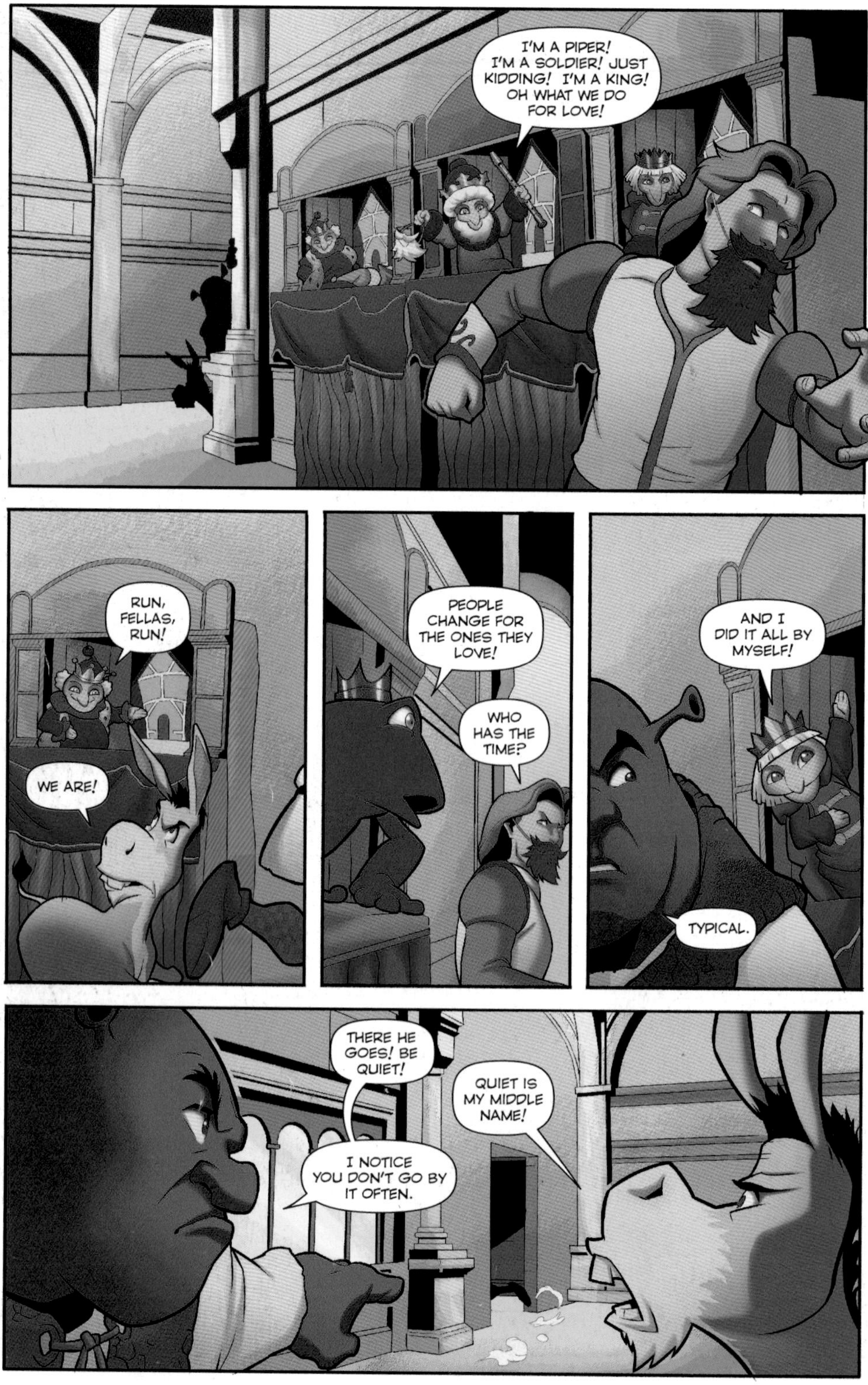
I'M A PIPER! I'M A SOLDIER! JUST KIDDING! I'M A KING! OH WHAT WE DO FOR LOVE!
RUN, FELLAS, RUN!
WE ARE!
PEOPLE CHANGE FOR THE ONES THEY LOVE!
WHO HAS THE TIME?
AND I DID IT ALL BY MYSELF!
TYPICAL.
THERE HE GOES! BE QUIET!
QUIET IS MY MIDDLE NAME!
I NOTICE YOU DON'T GO BY IT OFTEN.

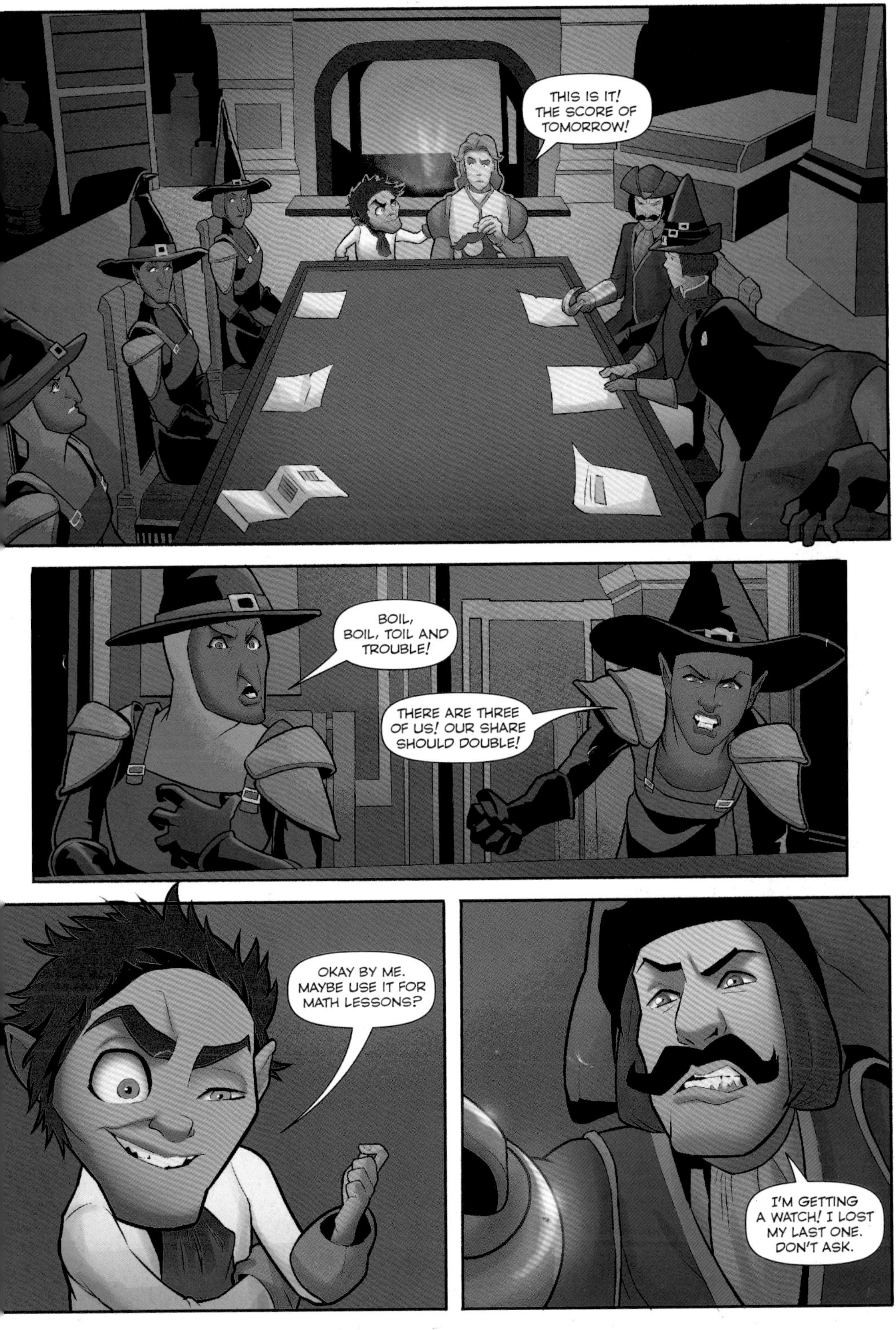
THIS IS IT! THE SCORE OF TOMORROW!
BOIL, BOIL, TOIL AND TROUBLE!
THERE ARE THREE OF US! OUR SHARE SHOULD DOUBLE!
OKAY BY ME. MAYBE USE IT FOR MATH LESSONS?
I'M GETTING A WATCH! I LOST MY LAST ONE. DON'T ASK.

WE KNOW THAT ALL OF THE CASH IS COLLECTED EVERY HOUR AND TAKEN HERE, TO THE MAIN TENT.

HE KNOWS SO MUCH ABOUT THESE THINGS!

WE LEAD EVERYONE AWAY SO THERE'S MORE ROOM TO MOVE. I HAVE A DISTRACTION IN MIND!

AND I HAVE THE ESCAPE ROUTE! WHO'S READY TO BUCKLE SOME SWASH!

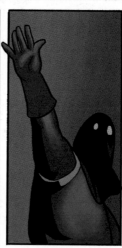

I STILL SAY WE BREAK OVER THE BACK WALL.

}HEE{ }HEE{ }HEE{ }HEE{

THAT'LL NEVER WORK WITHOUT A GRAPPLING HOOK AND A CATAPULT!

OH! HI! WE'RE ON YOUR SIDE! DOUBLE AGENTS. GO ON. YOU WERE SAYING?

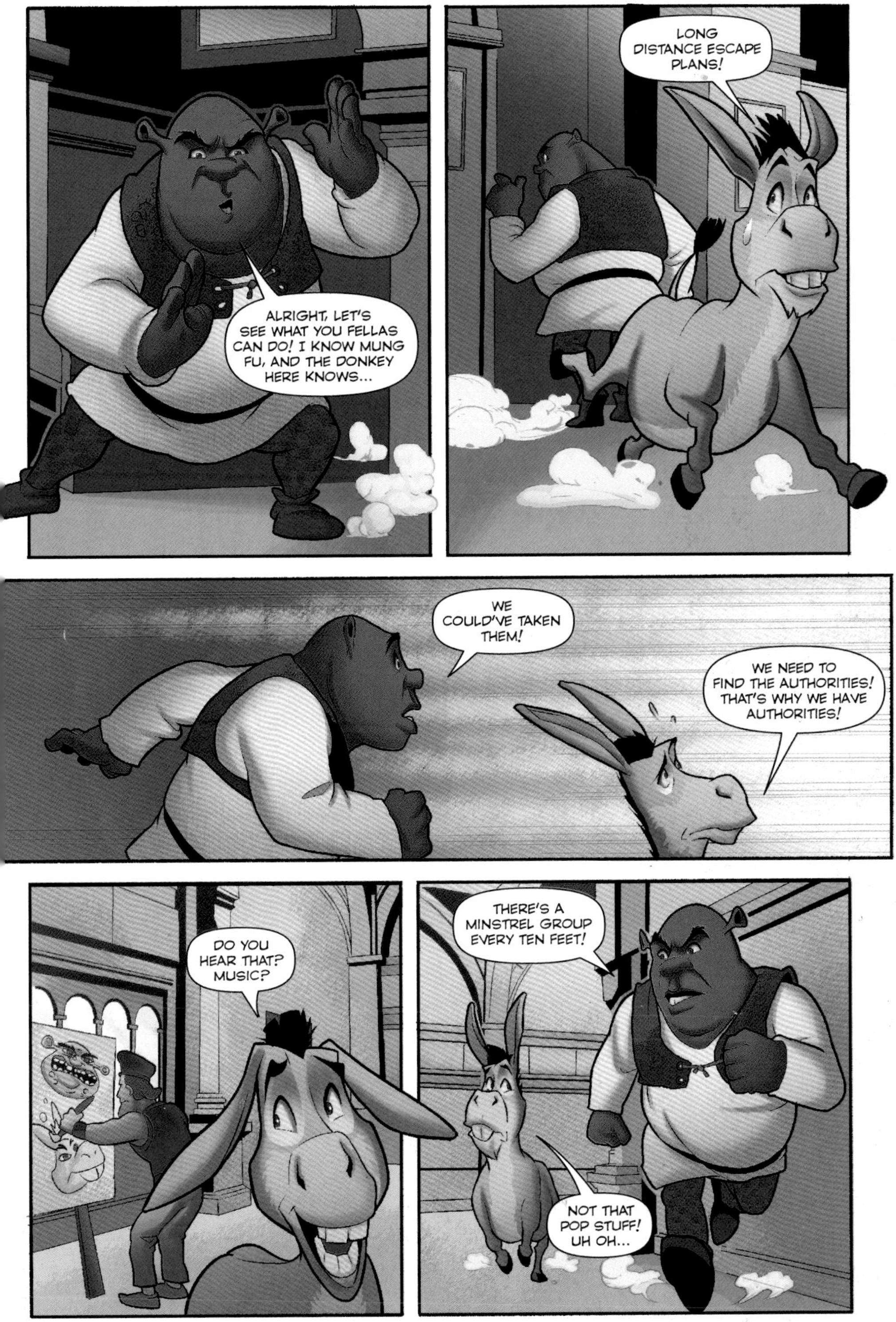
ALRIGHT, LET'S SEE WHAT YOU FELLAS CAN DO! I KNOW MUNG FU, AND THE DONKEY HERE KNOWS...
LONG DISTANCE ESCAPE PLANS!
WE COULD'VE TAKEN THEM!
WE NEED TO FIND THE AUTHORITIES! THAT'S WHY WE HAVE AUTHORITIES!
DO YOU HEAR THAT? MUSIC?
THERE'S A MINSTREL GROUP EVERY TEN FEET!
NOT THAT POP STUFF! UH OH...

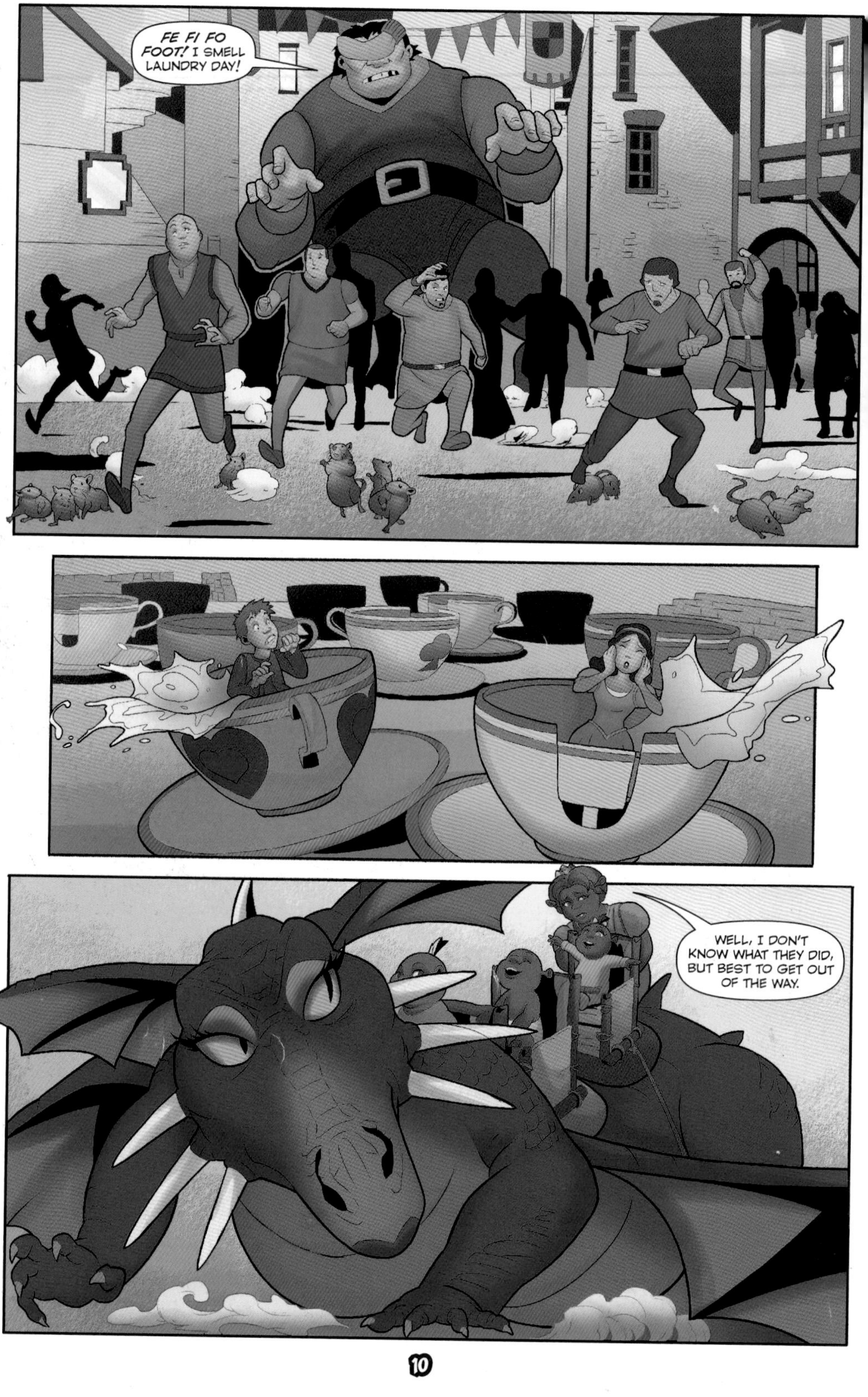
FE FI FO FOOT! I SMELL LAUNDRY DAY!
WELL, I DON'T KNOW WHAT THEY DID, BUT BEST TO GET OUT OF THE WAY.

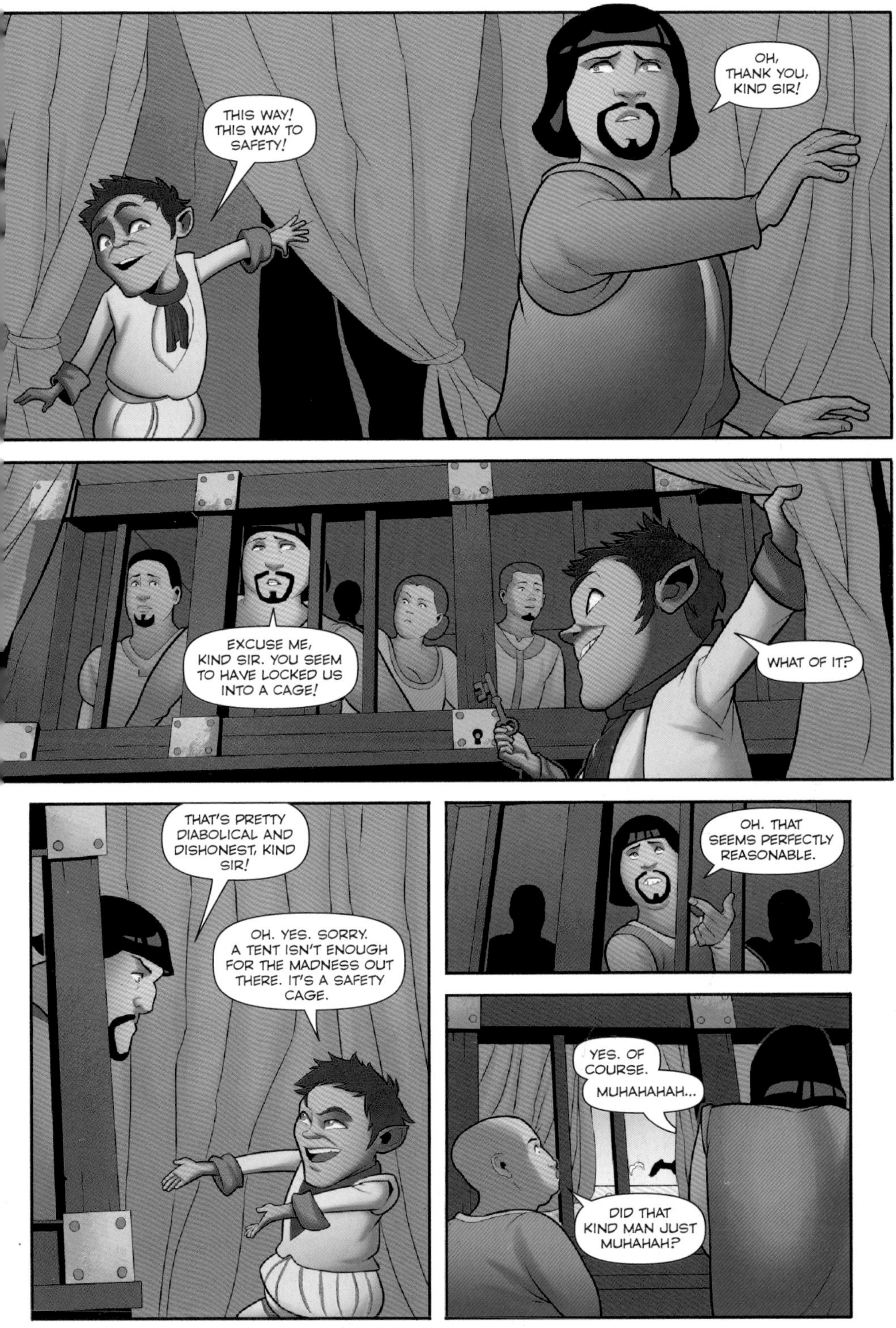
THIS WAY! THIS WAY TO SAFETY!
OH, THANK YOU, KIND SIR!
EXCUSE ME, KIND SIR. YOU SEEM TO HAVE LOCKED US INTO A CAGE!
WHAT OF IT?
THAT'S PRETTY DIABOLICAL AND DISHONEST, KIND SIR!
OH. YES. SORRY. A TENT ISN'T ENOUGH FOR THE MADNESS OUT THERE. IT'S A SAFETY CAGE.
OH. THAT SEEMS PERFECTLY REASONABLE.
YES. OF COURSE.
MUHAHAHAH...
DID THAT KIND MAN JUST MUHAHAH?

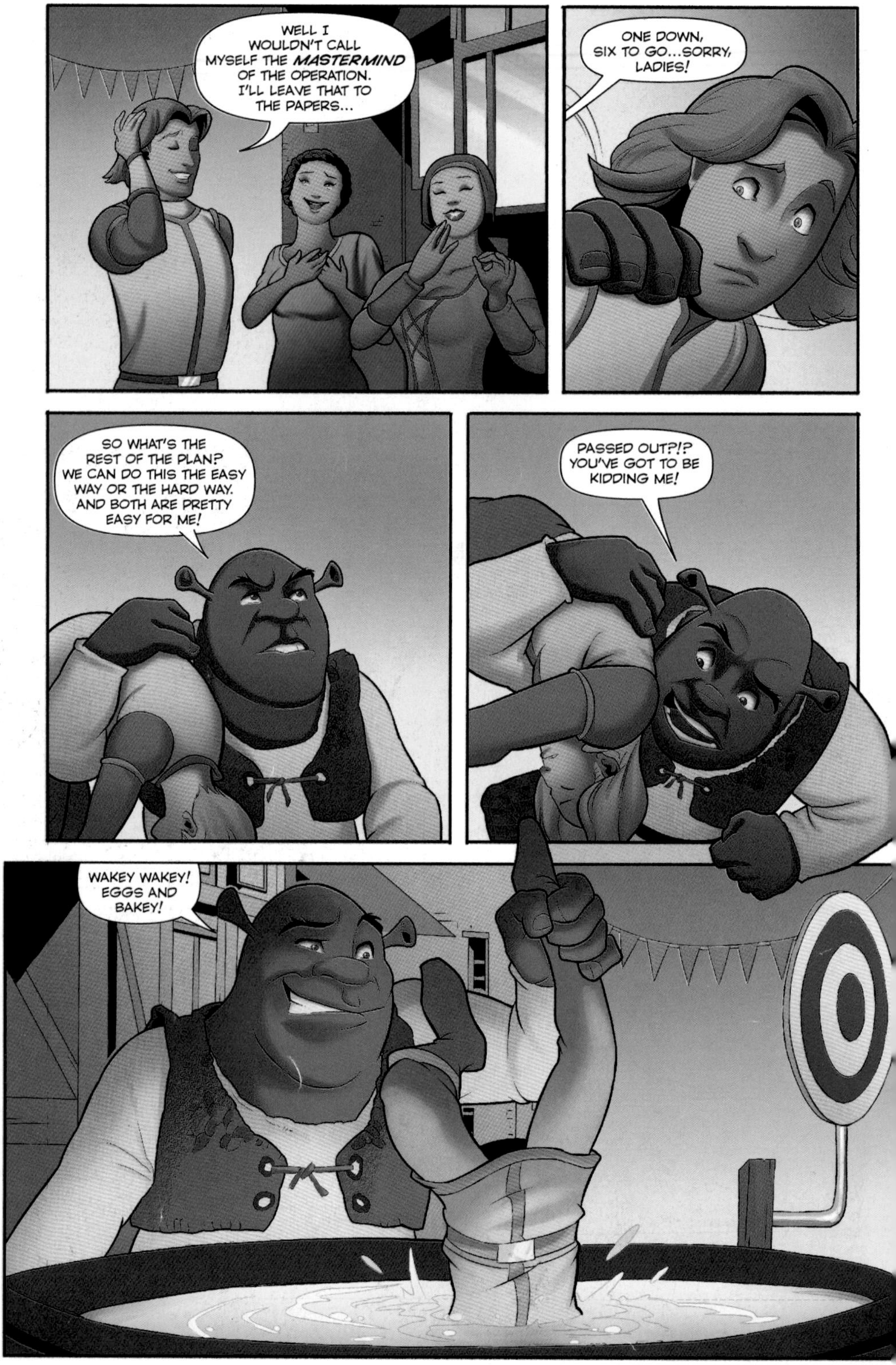
WELL I WOULDN'T CALL MYSELF THE MASTERMIND OF THE OPERATION. I'LL LEAVE THAT TO THE PAPERS...
ONE DOWN, SIX TO GO...SORRY, LADIES!
SO WHAT'S THE REST OF THE PLAN? WE CAN DO THIS THE EASY WAY OR THE HARD WAY. AND BOTH ARE PRETTY EASY FOR ME!
PASSED OUT?!? YOU'VE GOT TO BE KIDDING ME!
WAKEY WAKEY! EGGS AND BAKEY!

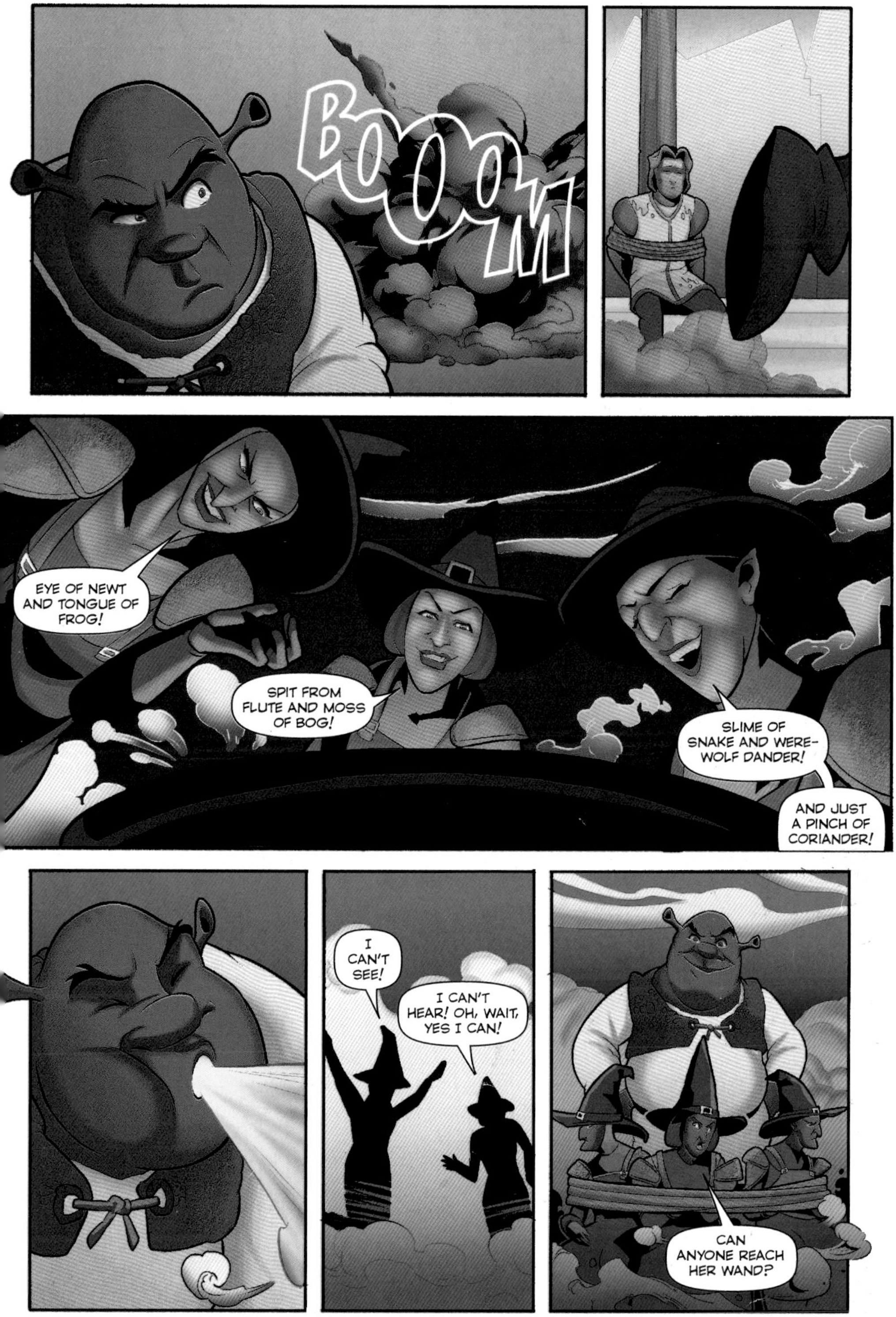
BOOOOM
EYE OF NEWT AND TONGUE OF FROG!
SPIT FROM FLUTE AND MOSS OF BOG!
SLIME OF SNAKE AND WERE-WOLF DANDER!
AND JUST A PINCH OF CORIANDER!
I CAN'T SEE!
I CAN'T HEAR! OH, WAIT, YES I CAN!
CAN ANYONE REACH HER WAND?

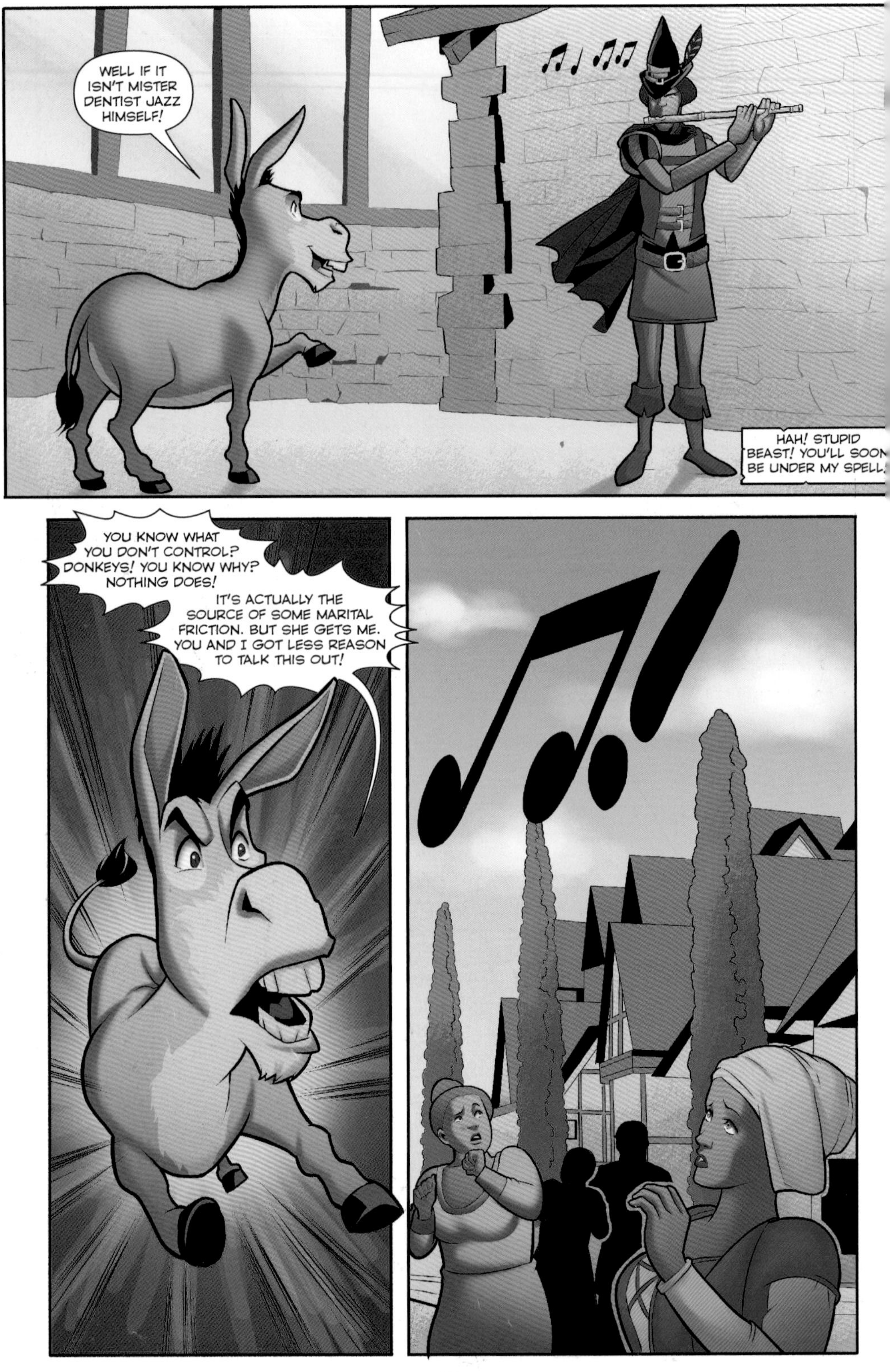
WELL IF IT ISN'T MISTER DENTIST JAZZ HIMSELF!
HAH! STUPID BEAST! YOU'LL SOON BE UNDER MY SPELL!
YOU KNOW WHAT YOU DON'T CONTROL? DONKEYS! YOU KNOW WHY? NOTHING DOES!
IT'S ACTUALLY THE SOURCE OF SOME MARITAL FRICTION. BUT SHE GETS ME. YOU AND I GOT LESS REASON TO TALK THIS OUT!

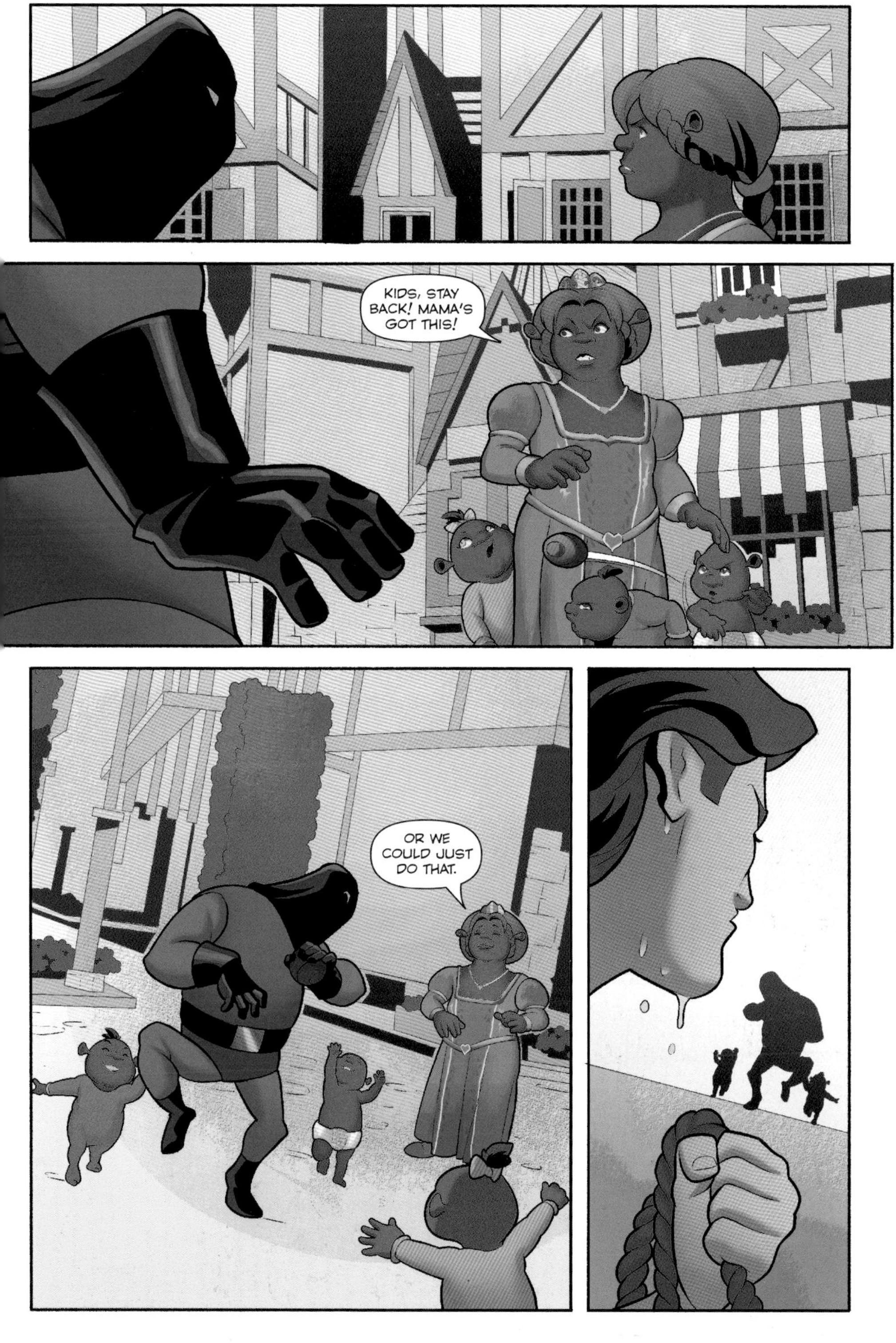
KIDS, STAY BACK! MAMA'S GOT THIS!
OR WE COULD JUST DO THAT.

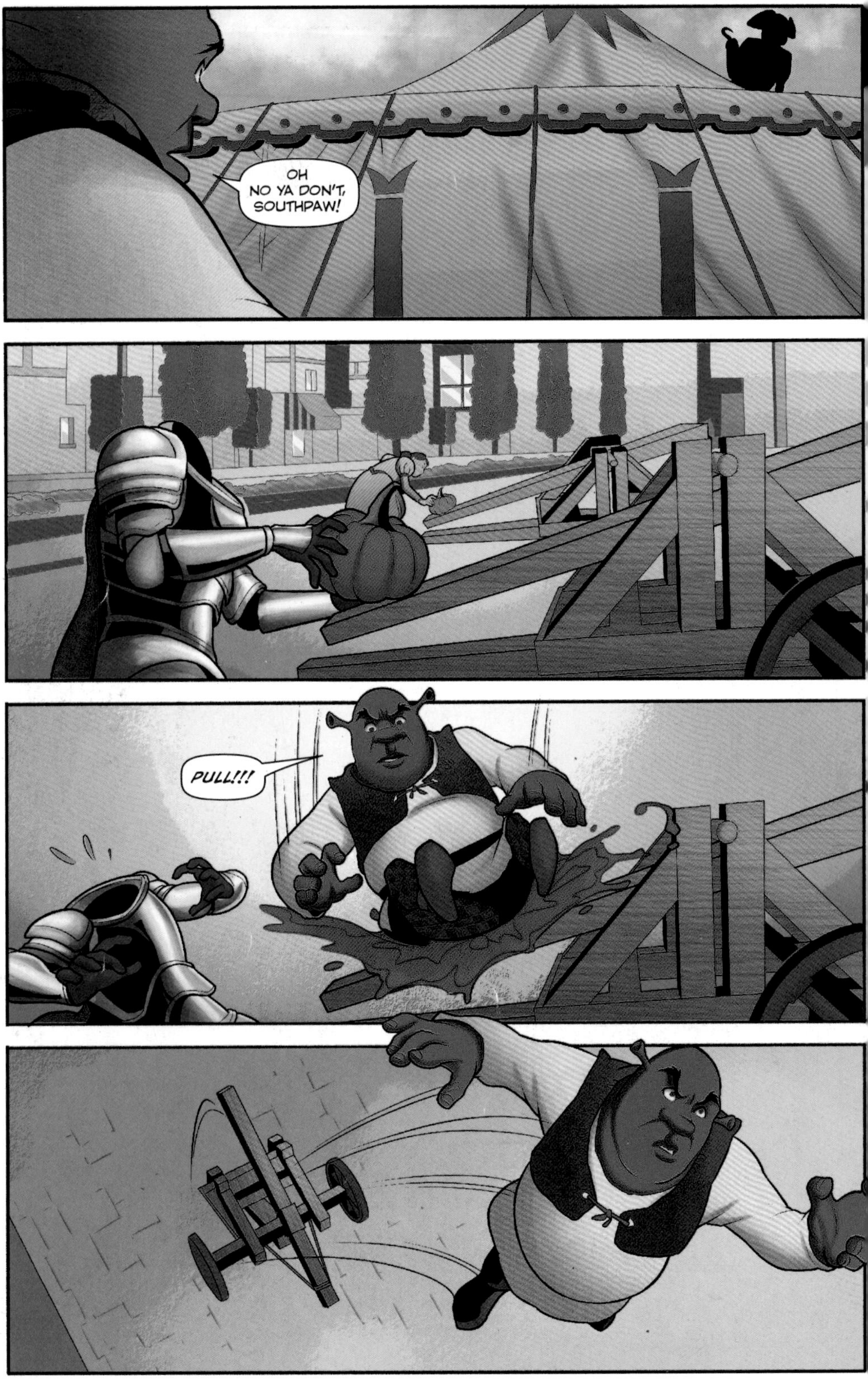
OH NO YA DON'T, SOUTHPAW!
PULL!!!

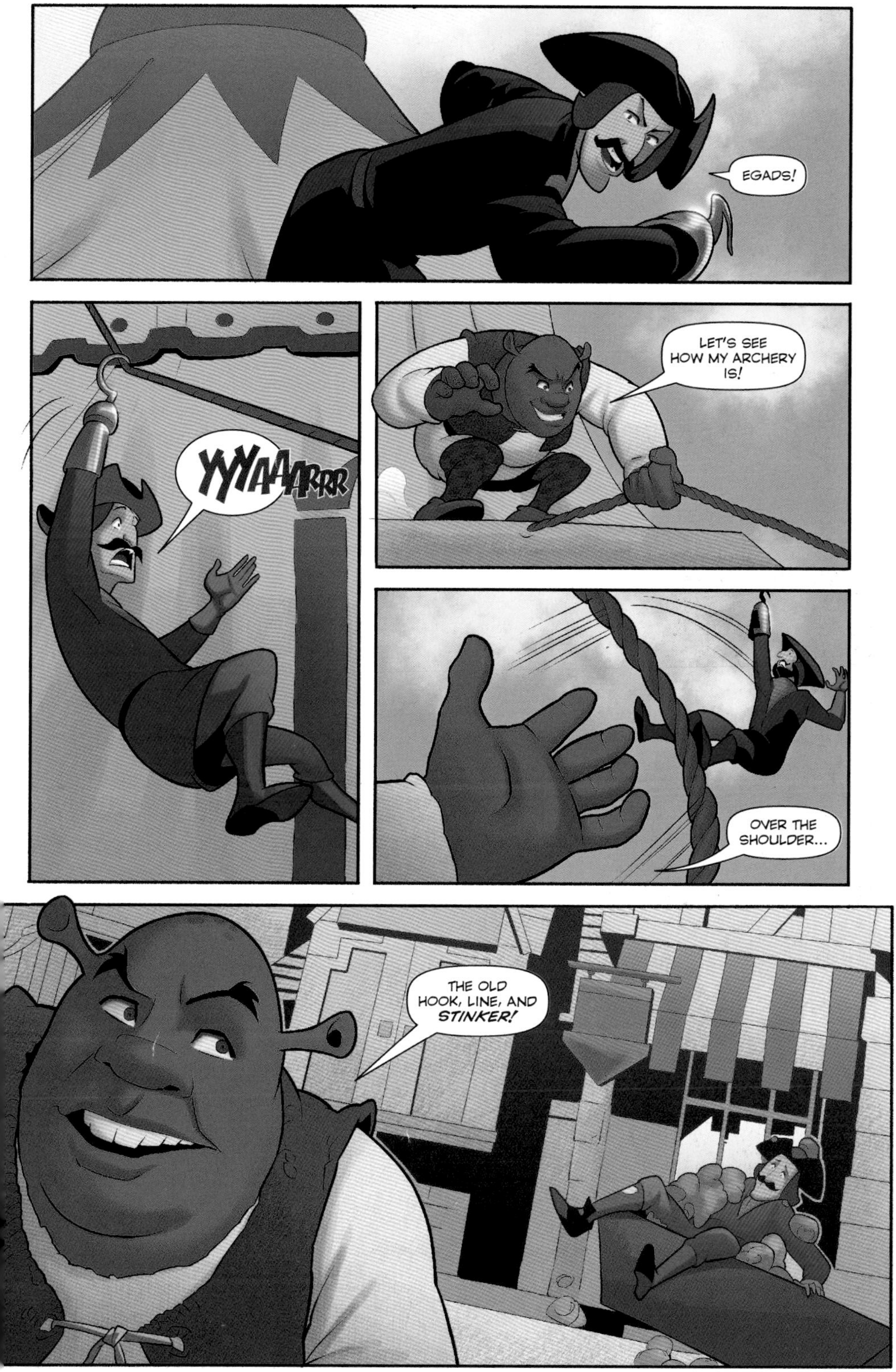
EGADS!
YYYAAARRR
LET'S SEE HOW MY ARCHERY IS!
OVER THE SHOULDER...
THE OLD HOOK, LINE, AND *STINKER!*

WE DID IT! SAVED THE DAY AGAIN! WE'RE HEROES! WHERE'S THE BUFFET? SOMEONE FEED ME SOME GRAPES!

NOT SO FAST. RUMPELWHATSHISNAME IS STILL OUT THERE SOMEWHERE.

IF THEY SAID THE MAIN TENT WAS THE TARGET, WHY WASN'T HE THERE?

MAYBE HE'S ALREADY ON THE RUN. WEE COWARD...

NO ROPE, NO SHOE PRINTS ON THE WALL...THE TRAIL IS COLD. UNLESS...HE'S STILL IN THE PARK!

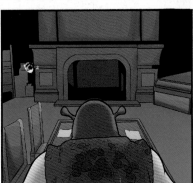

CAN'T SEE ANY-THING! IF ONLY I WAS UP AS HIGH AS... NOPE. NOT GONNA DO IT!

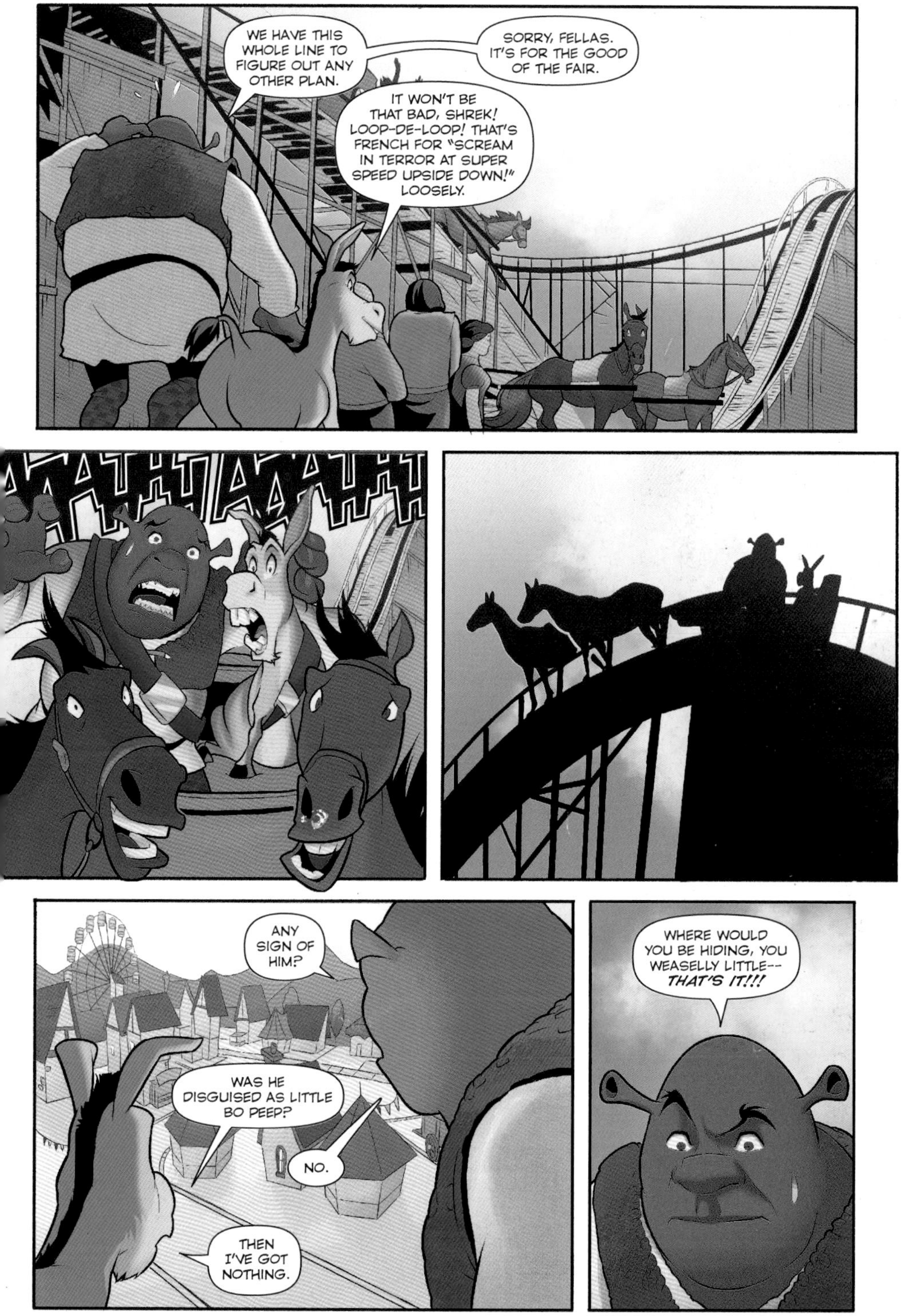
WE HAVE THIS WHOLE LINE TO FIGURE OUT ANY OTHER PLAN.
SORRY, FELLAS. IT'S FOR THE GOOD OF THE FAIR.
IT WON'T BE THAT BAD, SHREK! LOOP-DE-LOOP! THAT'S FRENCH FOR "SCREAM IN TERROR AT SUPER SPEED UPSIDE DOWN!" LOOSELY.
ANY SIGN OF HIM?
WAS HE DISGUISED AS LITTLE BO PEEP?
NO.
THEN I'VE GOT NOTHING.
WHERE WOULD YOU BE HIDING, YOU WEASELLY LITTLE-- *THAT'S IT!!!*

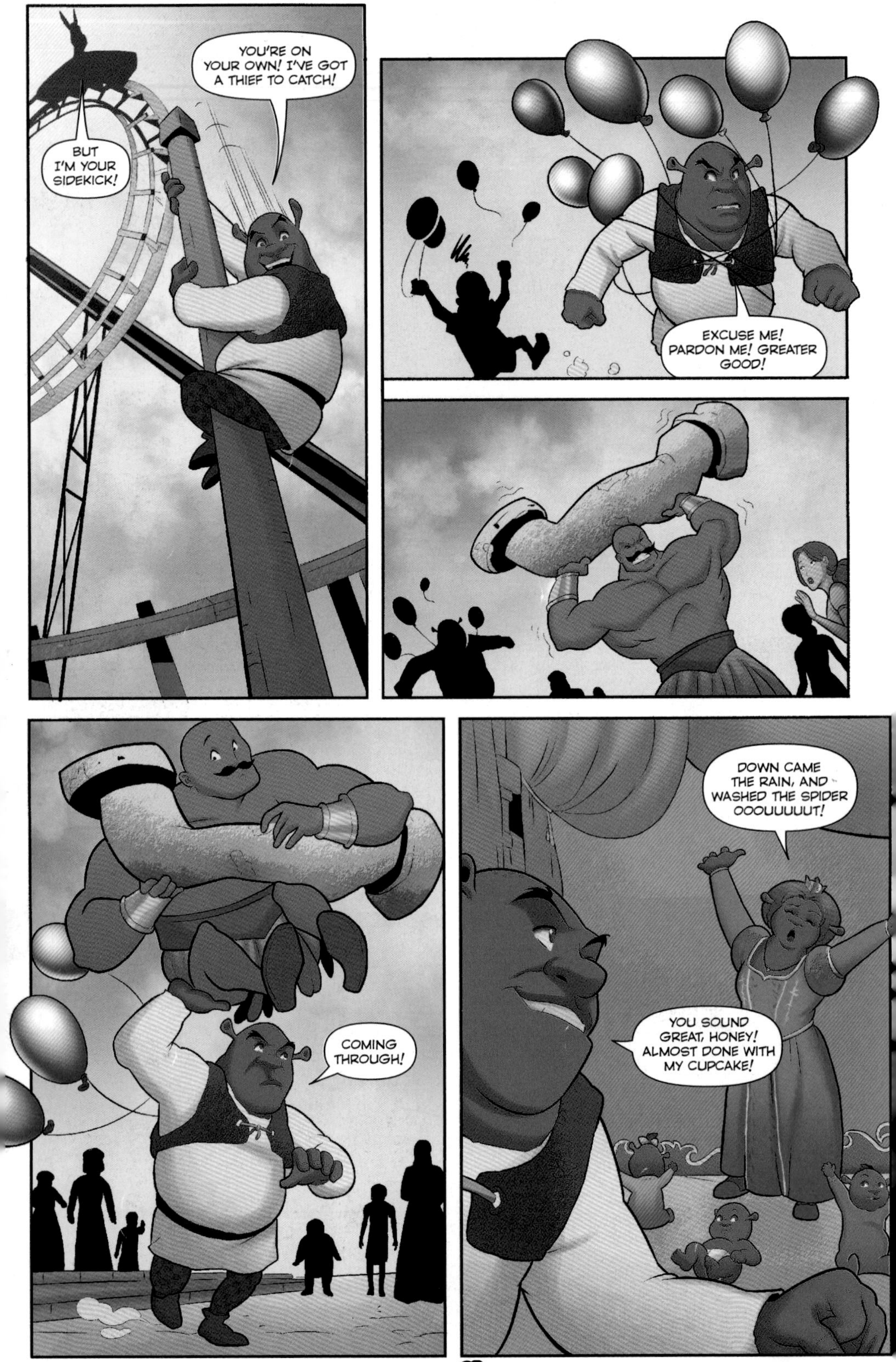
YOU'RE ON YOUR OWN! I'VE GOT A THIEF TO CATCH!
BUT I'M YOUR SIDEKICK!
EXCUSE ME! PARDON ME! GREATER GOOD!
COMING THROUGH!
DOWN CAME THE RAIN, AND WASHED THE SPIDER OOOUUUUUT!
YOU SOUND GREAT, HONEY! ALMOST DONE WITH MY CUPCAKE!

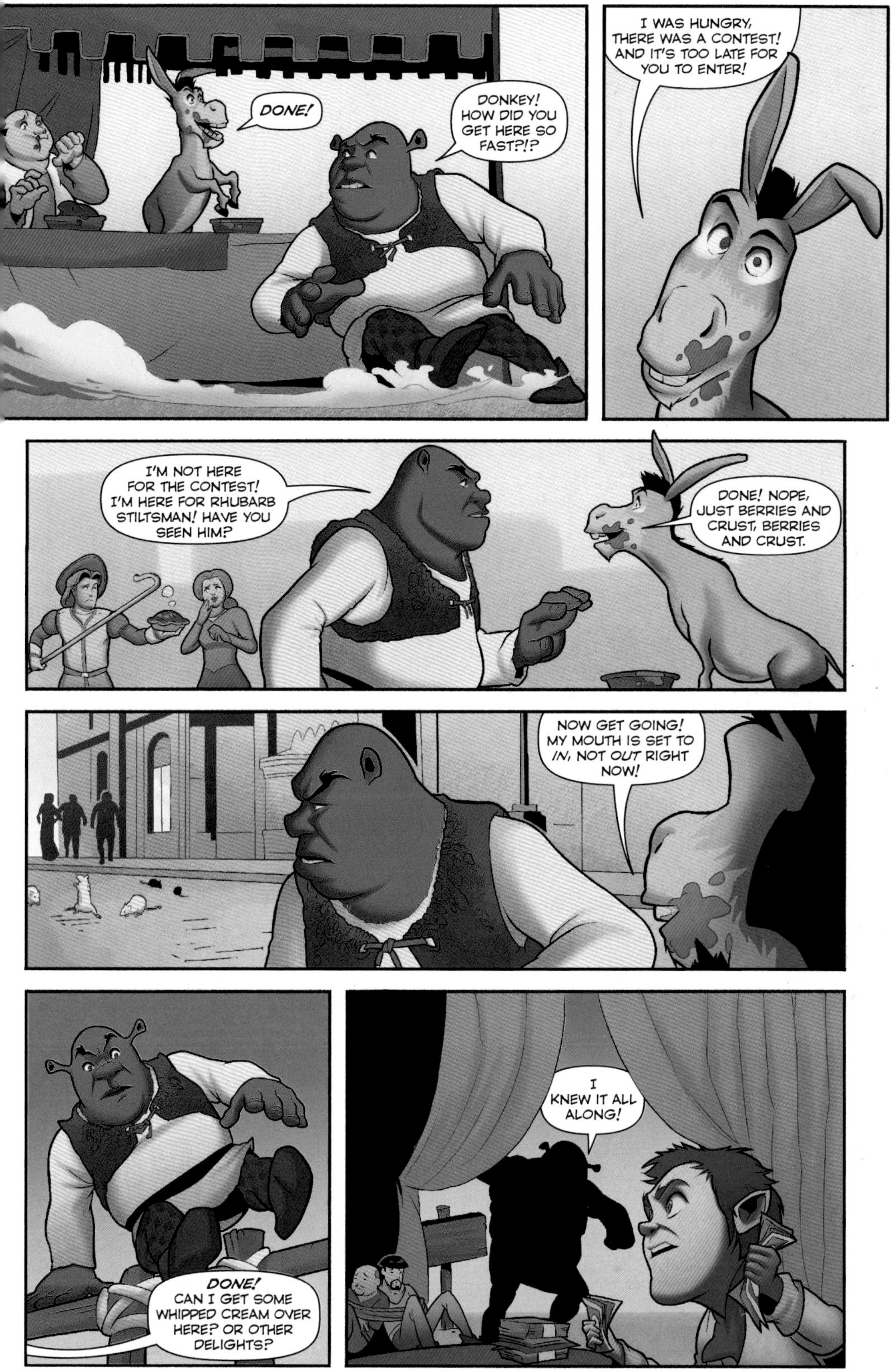
DONE!
DONKEY! HOW DID YOU GET HERE SO FAST?!?
I WAS HUNGRY, THERE WAS A CONTEST! AND IT'S TOO LATE FOR YOU TO ENTER!
I'M NOT HERE FOR THE CONTEST! I'M HERE FOR RHUBARB STILTSMAN! HAVE YOU SEEN HIM?
DONE! NOPE, JUST BERRIES AND CRUST, BERRIES AND CRUST.
NOW GET GOING! MY MOUTH IS SET TO *IN*, NOT *OUT* RIGHT NOW!
DONE! CAN I GET SOME WHIPPED CREAM OVER HERE? OR OTHER DELIGHTS?
I KNEW IT ALL ALONG!

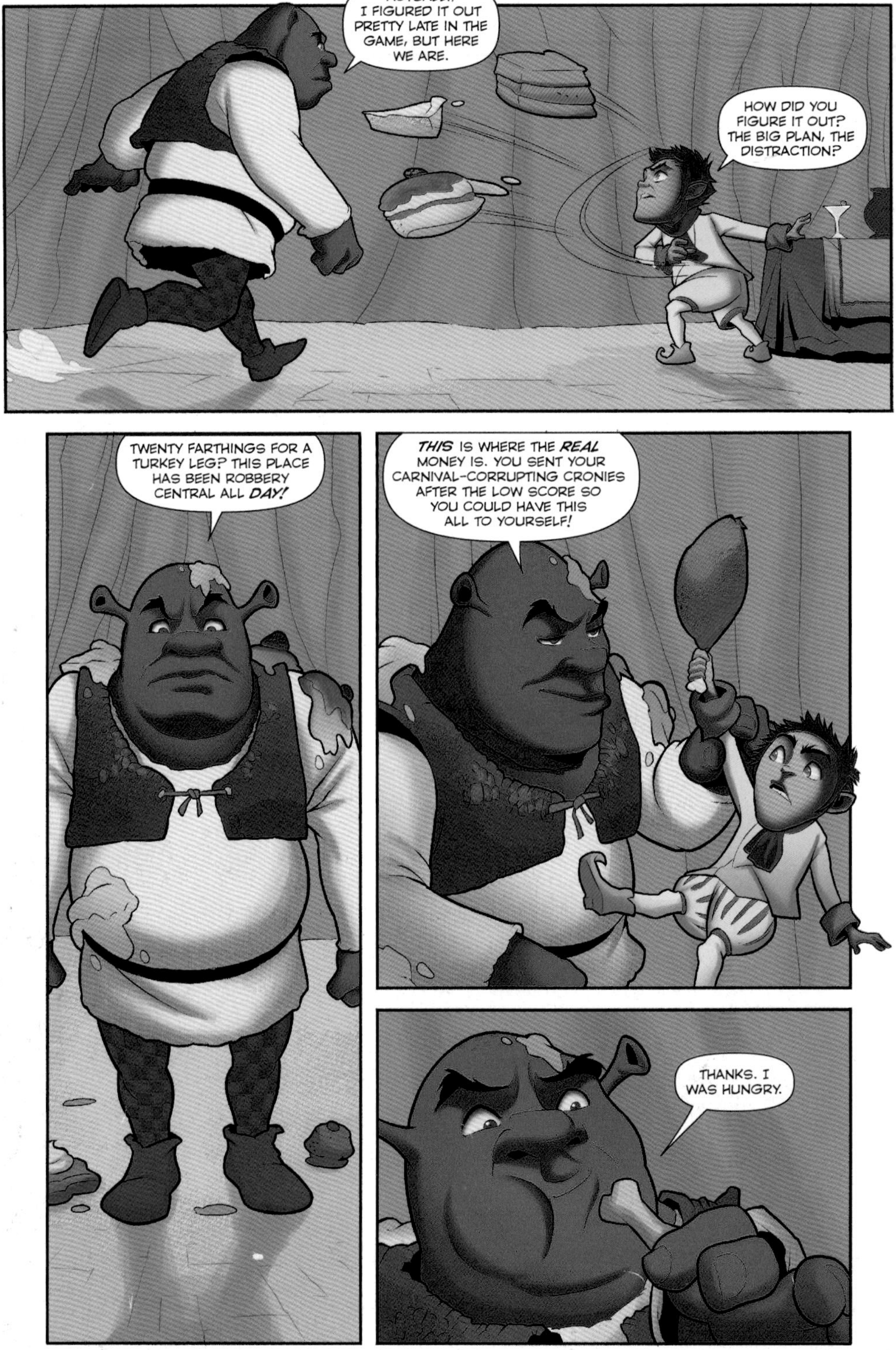
ACTUALLY, I FIGURED IT OUT PRETTY LATE IN THE GAME, BUT HERE WE ARE.
HOW DID YOU FIGURE IT OUT? THE BIG PLAN, THE DISTRACTION?
TWENTY FARTHINGS FOR A TURKEY LEG? THIS PLACE HAS BEEN ROBBERY CENTRAL ALL DAY!
THIS IS WHERE THE REAL MONEY IS. YOU SENT YOUR CARNIVAL-CORRUPTING CRONIES AFTER THE LOW SCORE SO YOU COULD HAVE THIS ALL TO YOURSELF!
THANKS. I WAS HUNGRY.

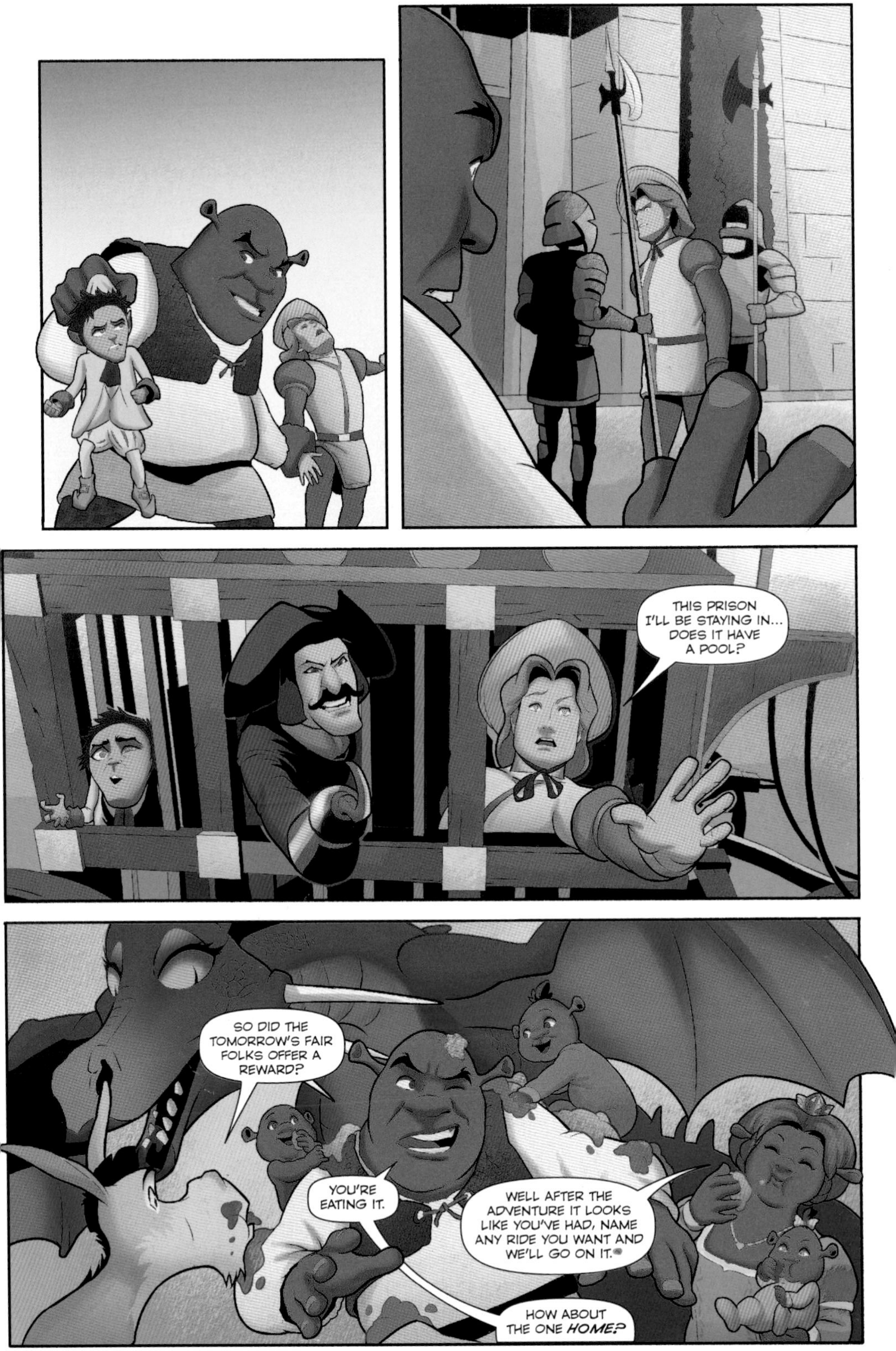
THIS PRISON I'LL BE STAYING IN... DOES IT HAVE A POOL?
SO DID THE TOMORROW'S FAIR FOLKS OFFER A REWARD?
YOU'RE EATING IT.
WELL AFTER THE ADVENTURE IT LOOKS LIKE YOU'VE HAD, NAME ANY RIDE YOU WANT AND WE'LL GO ON IT.
HOW ABOUT THE ONE HOME?

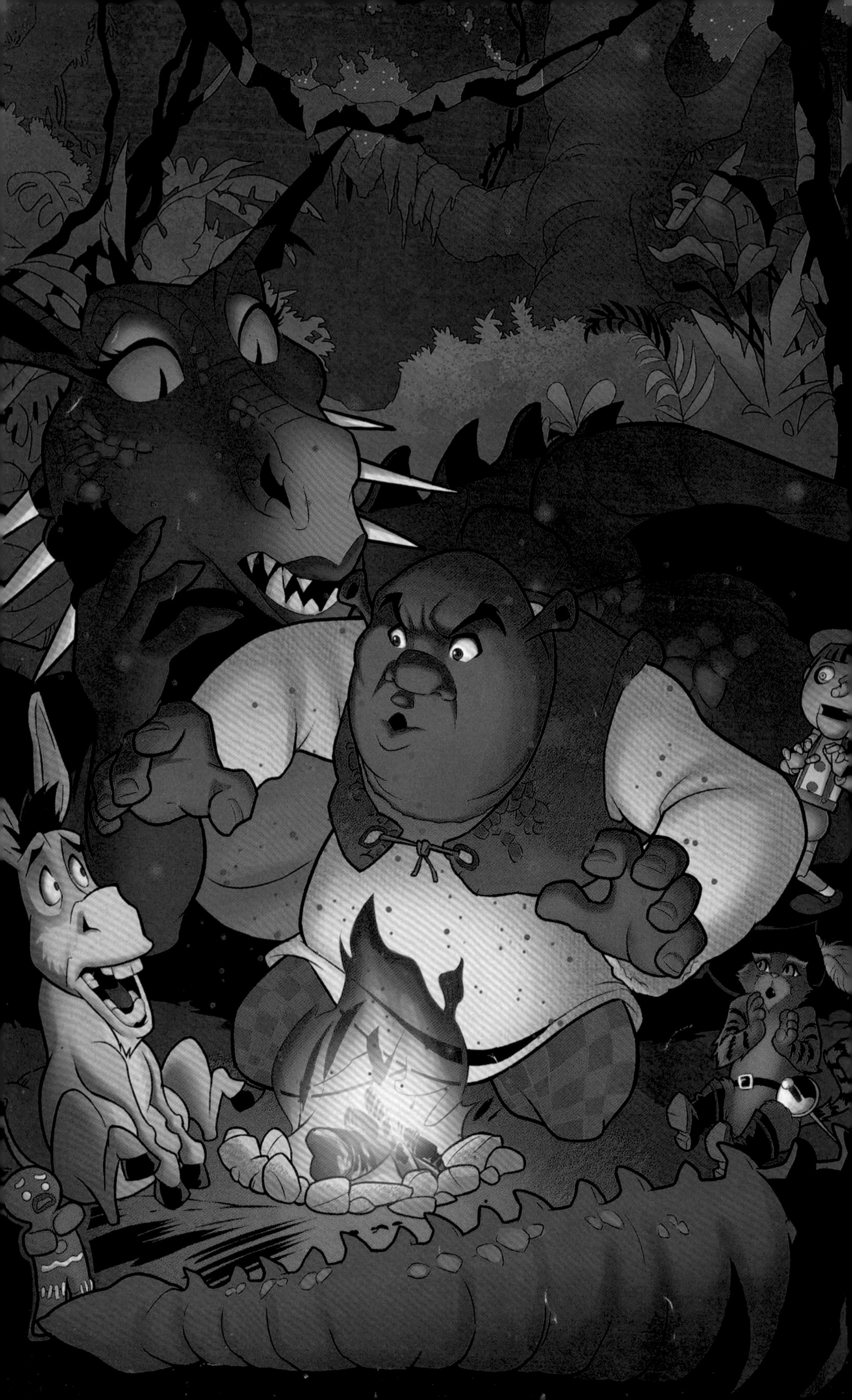

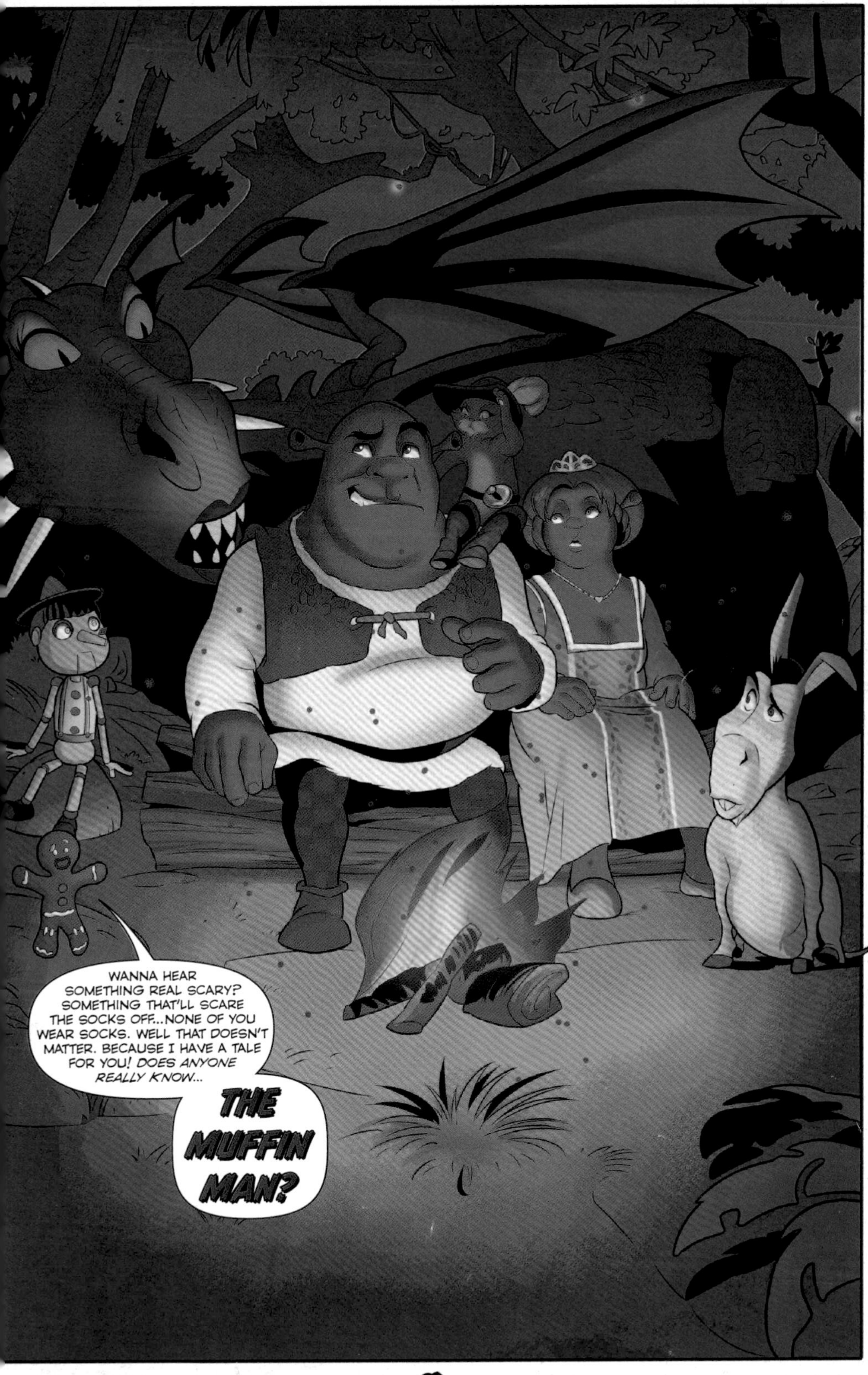
WANNA HEAR SOMETHING REAL SCARY? SOMETHING THAT'LL SCARE THE SOCKS OFF...NONE OF YOU WEAR SOCKS. WELL THAT DOESN'T MATTER. BECAUSE I HAVE A TALE FOR YOU! DOES ANYONE REALLY KNOW...
THE MUFFIN MAN?

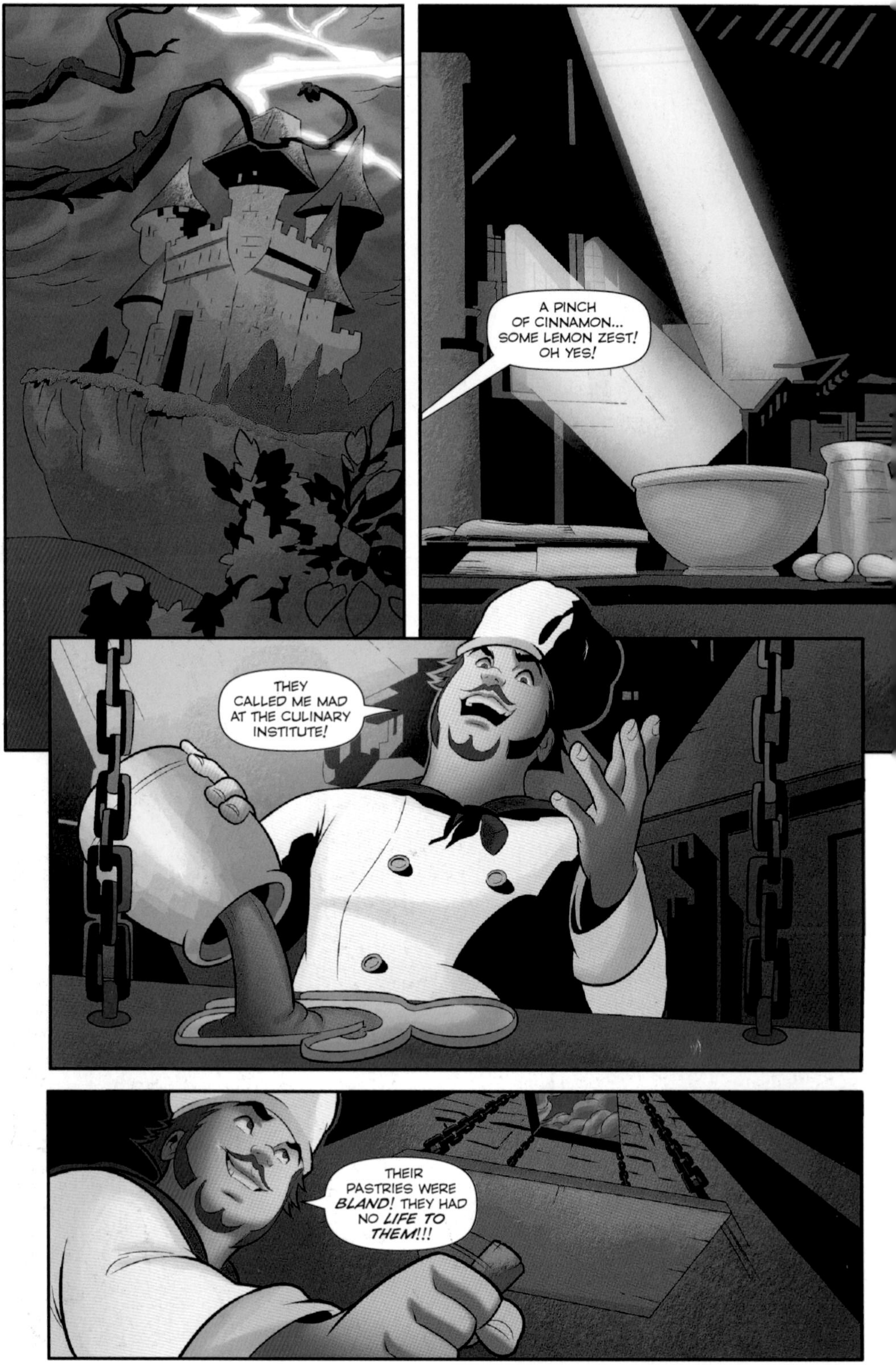
A PINCH OF CINNAMON... SOME LEMON ZEST! OH YES!
THEY CALLED ME MAD AT THE CULINARY INSTITUTE!
THEIR PASTRIES WERE *BLAND!* THEY HAD NO *LIFE TO THEM!!!*

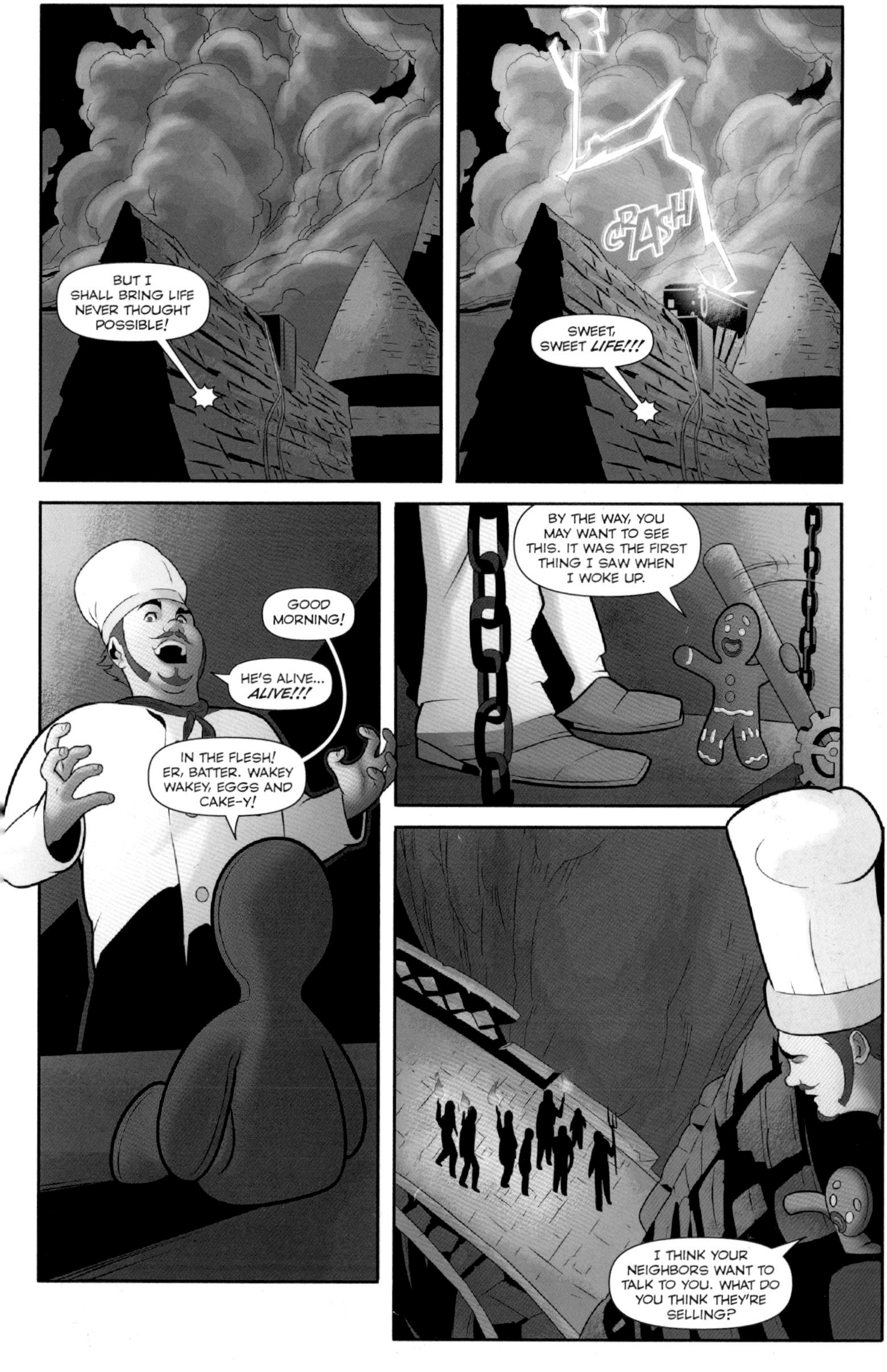
BUT I SHALL BRING LIFE NEVER THOUGHT POSSIBLE!
CRASH!
SWEET, SWEET LIFE!!!
GOOD MORNING!
HE'S ALIVE... ALIVE!!!
IN THE FLESH! ER, BATTER. WAKEY WAKEY, EGGS AND CAKE-Y!
BY THE WAY, YOU MAY WANT TO SEE THIS. IT WAS THE FIRST THING I SAW WHEN I WOKE UP.
I THINK YOUR NEIGHBORS WANT TO TALK TO YOU. WHAT DO YOU THINK THEY'RE SELLING?

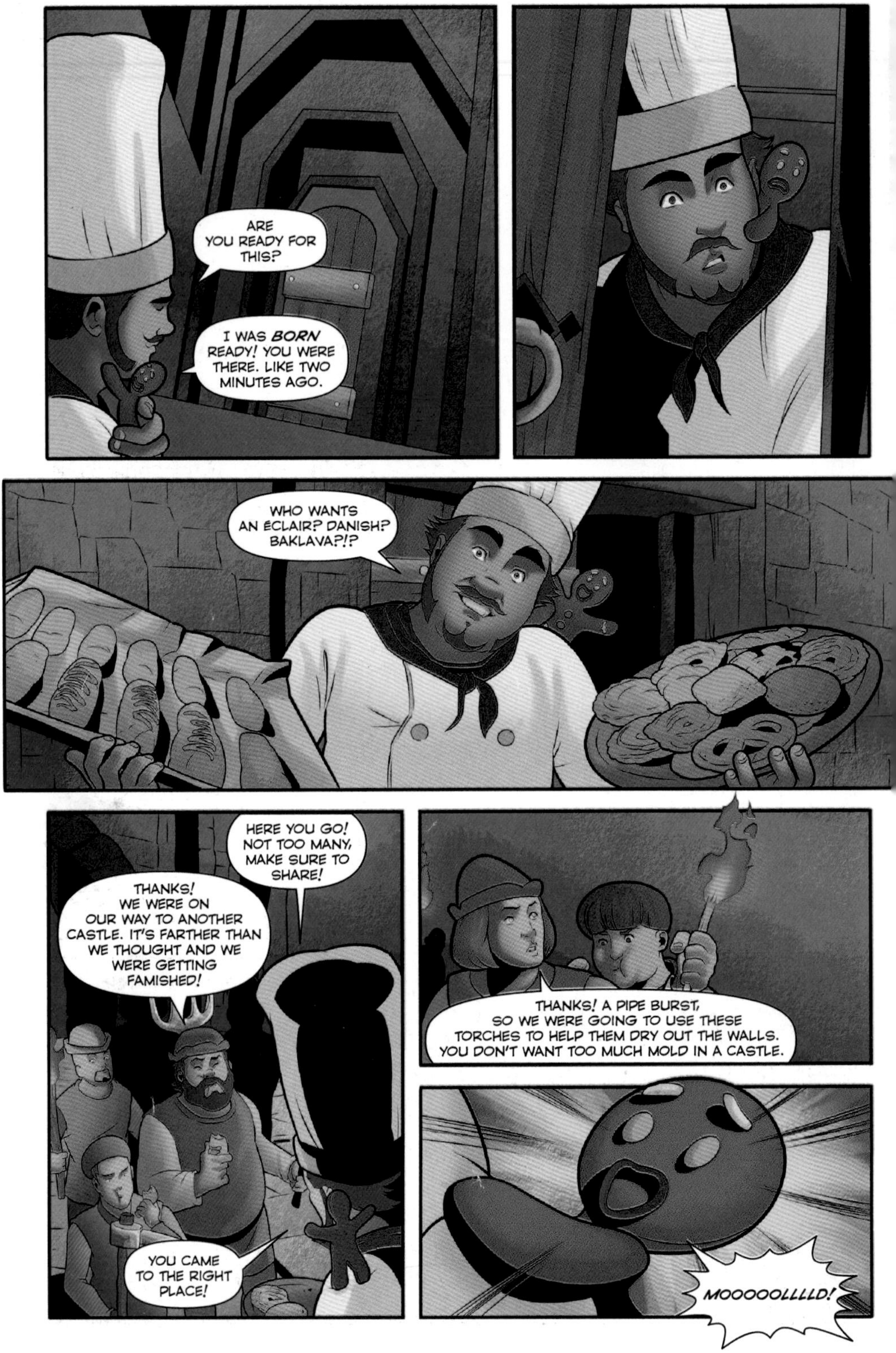
ARE YOU READY FOR THIS?
I WAS BORN READY! YOU WERE THERE. LIKE TWO MINUTES AGO.
WHO WANTS AN ÉCLAIR? DANISH? BAKLAVA?!?
HERE YOU GO! NOT TOO MANY, MAKE SURE TO SHARE!
THANKS! WE WERE ON OUR WAY TO ANOTHER CASTLE. IT'S FARTHER THAN WE THOUGHT AND WE WERE GETTING FAMISHED!
YOU CAME TO THE RIGHT PLACE!
THANKS! A PIPE BURST, SO WE WERE GOING TO USE THESE TORCHES TO HELP THEM DRY OUT THE WALLS. YOU DON'T WANT TOO MUCH MOLD IN A CASTLE.
MOOOOOLLLLD!

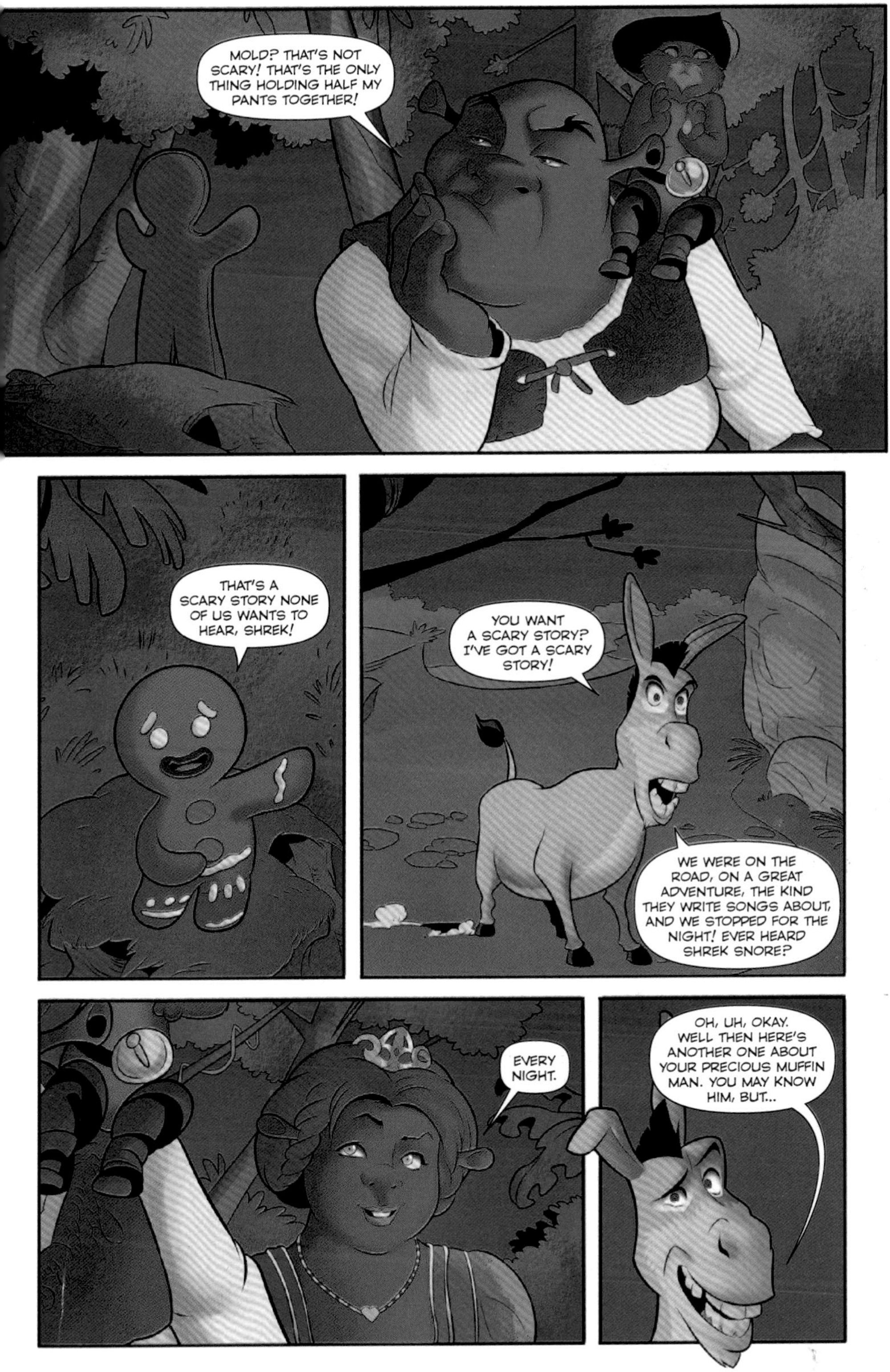
MOLD? THAT'S NOT SCARY! THAT'S THE ONLY THING HOLDING HALF MY PANTS TOGETHER!
THAT'S A SCARY STORY NONE OF US WANTS TO HEAR, SHREK!
YOU WANT A SCARY STORY? I'VE GOT A SCARY STORY!
WE WERE ON THE ROAD, ON A GREAT ADVENTURE, THE KIND THEY WRITE SONGS ABOUT, AND WE STOPPED FOR THE NIGHT! EVER HEARD SHREK SNORE?
EVERY NIGHT.
OH, UH, OKAY. WELL THEN HERE'S ANOTHER ONE ABOUT YOUR PRECIOUS MUFFIN MAN. YOU MAY KNOW HIM, BUT...

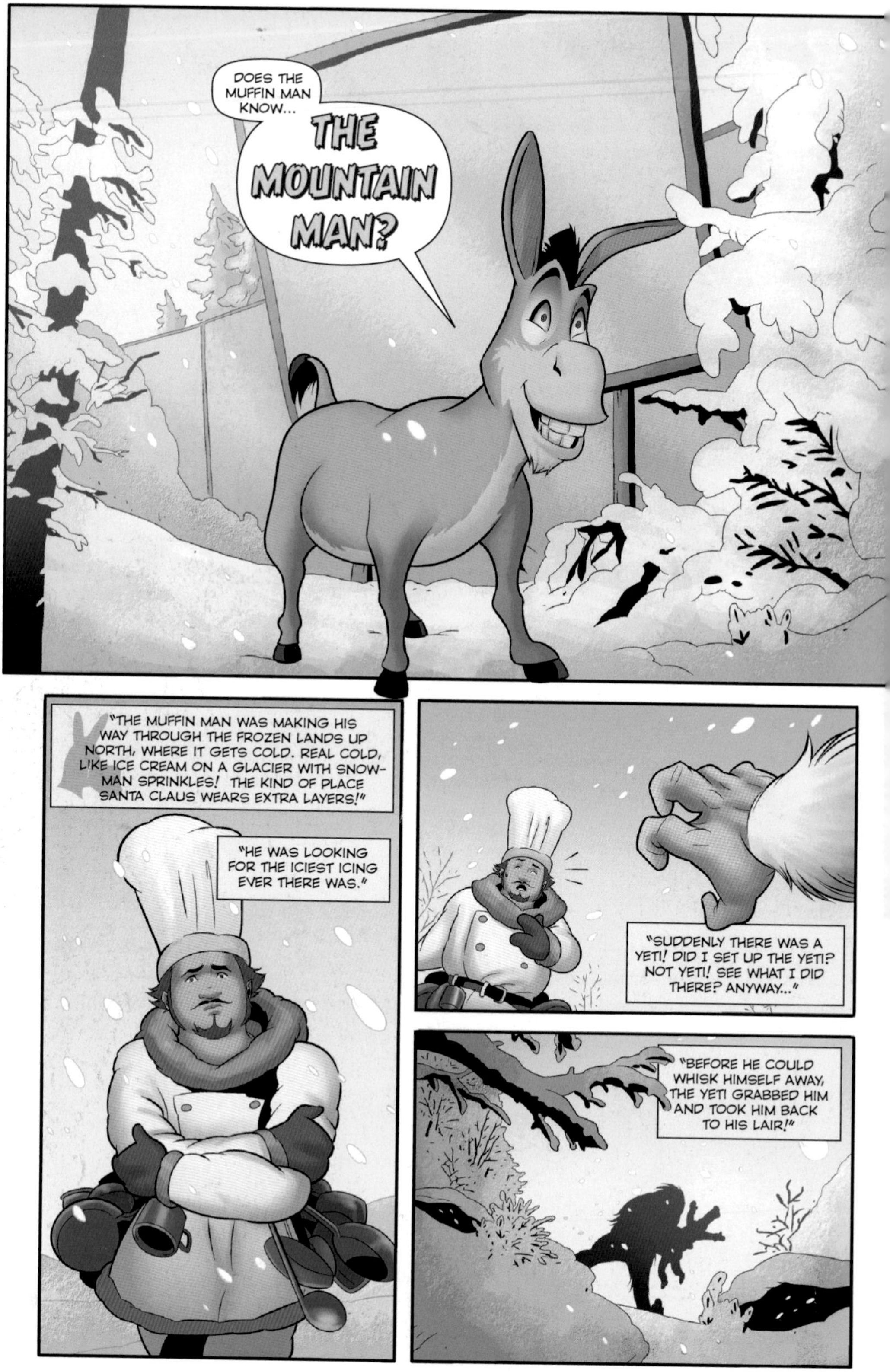
DOES THE MUFFIN MAN KNOW...
THE MOUNTAIN MAN?
"THE MUFFIN MAN WAS MAKING HIS WAY THROUGH THE FROZEN LANDS UP NORTH, WHERE IT GETS COLD. REAL COLD, LIKE ICE CREAM ON A GLACIER WITH SNOW-MAN SPRINKLES! THE KIND OF PLACE SANTA CLAUS WEARS EXTRA LAYERS!"
"HE WAS LOOKING FOR THE ICIEST ICING EVER THERE WAS."
"SUDDENLY THERE WAS A YETI! DID I SET UP THE YETI? NOT YETI! SEE WHAT I DID THERE? ANYWAY..."
"BEFORE HE COULD WHISK HIMSELF AWAY, THE YETI GRABBED HIM AND TOOK HIM BACK TO HIS LAIR!"

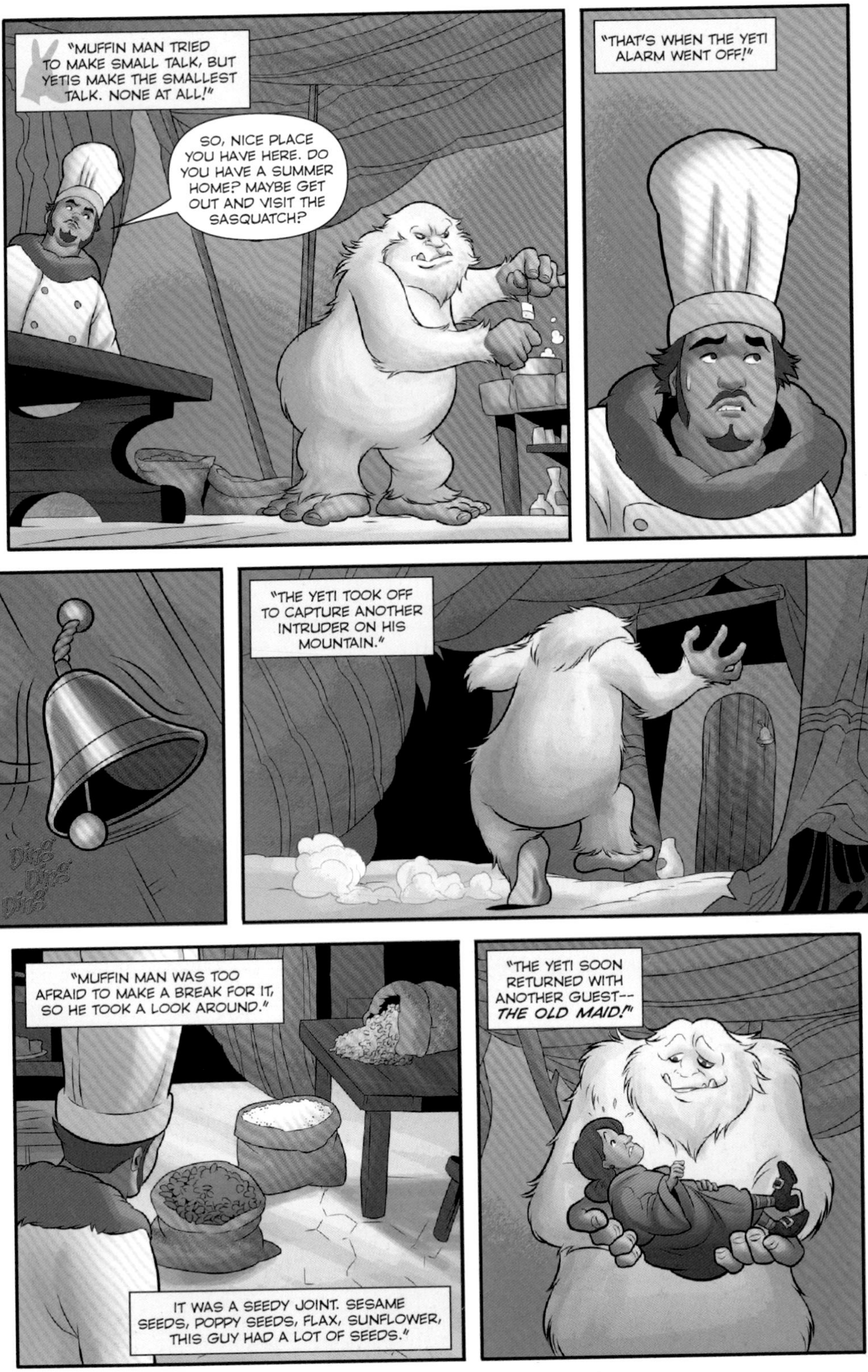
"MUFFIN MAN TRIED TO MAKE SMALL TALK, BUT YETIS MAKE THE SMALLEST TALK. NONE AT ALL!"
SO, NICE PLACE YOU HAVE HERE. DO YOU HAVE A SUMMER HOME? MAYBE GET OUT AND VISIT THE SASQUATCH?
"THAT'S WHEN THE YETI ALARM WENT OFF!"
Ding Ding Ding
"THE YETI TOOK OFF TO CAPTURE ANOTHER INTRUDER ON HIS MOUNTAIN."
"MUFFIN MAN WAS TOO AFRAID TO MAKE A BREAK FOR IT, SO HE TOOK A LOOK AROUND."
IT WAS A SEEDY JOINT. SESAME SEEDS, POPPY SEEDS, FLAX, SUNFLOWER, THIS GUY HAD A LOT OF SEEDS."
"THE YETI SOON RETURNED WITH ANOTHER GUEST-- *THE OLD MAID!*"

"I DON'T KNOW WHY SHE WAS UP THERE. I THINK HE ASKED, TOO."

WHY ARE YOU IN THE MOUNTAINS?

I'M OLD. I GET LOST. AND WITH MY EYES, SNOW LOOKS LIKE BREAD CRUMBS.

"THEY WERE SNOWED-IN CAPTIVES, CAPTIVATED, TRYING TO PASS THE TIME WITH A GIANT SMELLY MONSTER! NO OFFENSE!"

"EXCUSE ME?"

"EXCUSED. SO THE OLD MAID PULLED OUT A DECK OF CARDS TO PLAY, YOU GUESSED IT, OLD MAID!"

OLD MAID
CARD GAME

"THE MUFFIN MAN WAS NOWHERE NEAR AS GOOD AS THE OLD MAID! THE CHOCOLATE CHIPS WERE STACKED AGAINST HIM!"

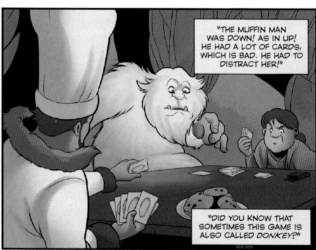

"THE MUFFIN MAN WAS DOWN! AS IN UP! HE HAD A LOT OF CARDS, WHICH IS BAD. HE HAD TO DISTRACT HER!"

"DID YOU KNOW THAT SOMETIMES THIS GAME IS ALSO CALLED DONKEY?"

"THE DONKEY IS A PROUD AND MAJESTIC CREATURE, DOESN'T OFTEN GET THE RESPECT IT DESERVES. THEY ARE QUITE INTELLIGENT, HANDSOME, AND A WELCOME ADDITION TO ANY--"

"GET ON WITH IT!"

"THE OLD MAID!"

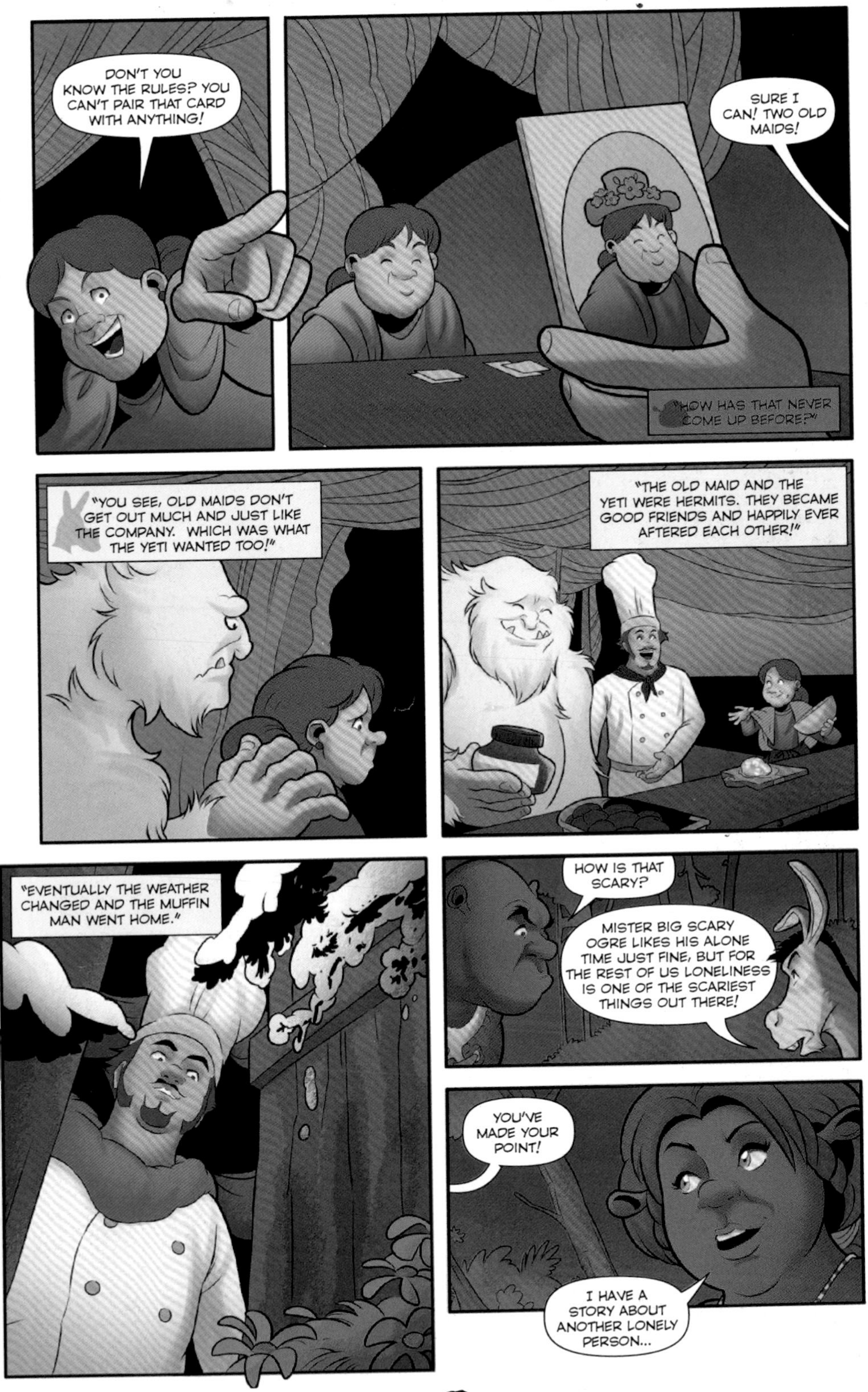
DON'T YOU KNOW THE RULES? YOU CAN'T PAIR THAT CARD WITH ANYTHING!
SURE I CAN! TWO OLD MAIDS!
"HOW HAS THAT NEVER COME UP BEFORE?"
"YOU SEE, OLD MAIDS DON'T GET OUT MUCH AND JUST LIKE THE COMPANY. WHICH WAS WHAT THE YETI WANTED TOO!"
"THE OLD MAID AND THE YETI WERE HERMITS. THEY BECAME GOOD FRIENDS AND HAPPILY EVER AFTERED EACH OTHER!"
"EVENTUALLY THE WEATHER CHANGED AND THE MUFFIN MAN WENT HOME."
HOW IS THAT SCARY?
MISTER BIG SCARY OGRE LIKES HIS ALONE TIME JUST FINE, BUT FOR THE REST OF US LONELINESS IS ONE OF THE SCARIEST THINGS OUT THERE!
YOU'VE MADE YOUR POINT!
I HAVE A STORY ABOUT ANOTHER LONELY PERSON...

Muffin and the Beanstalk

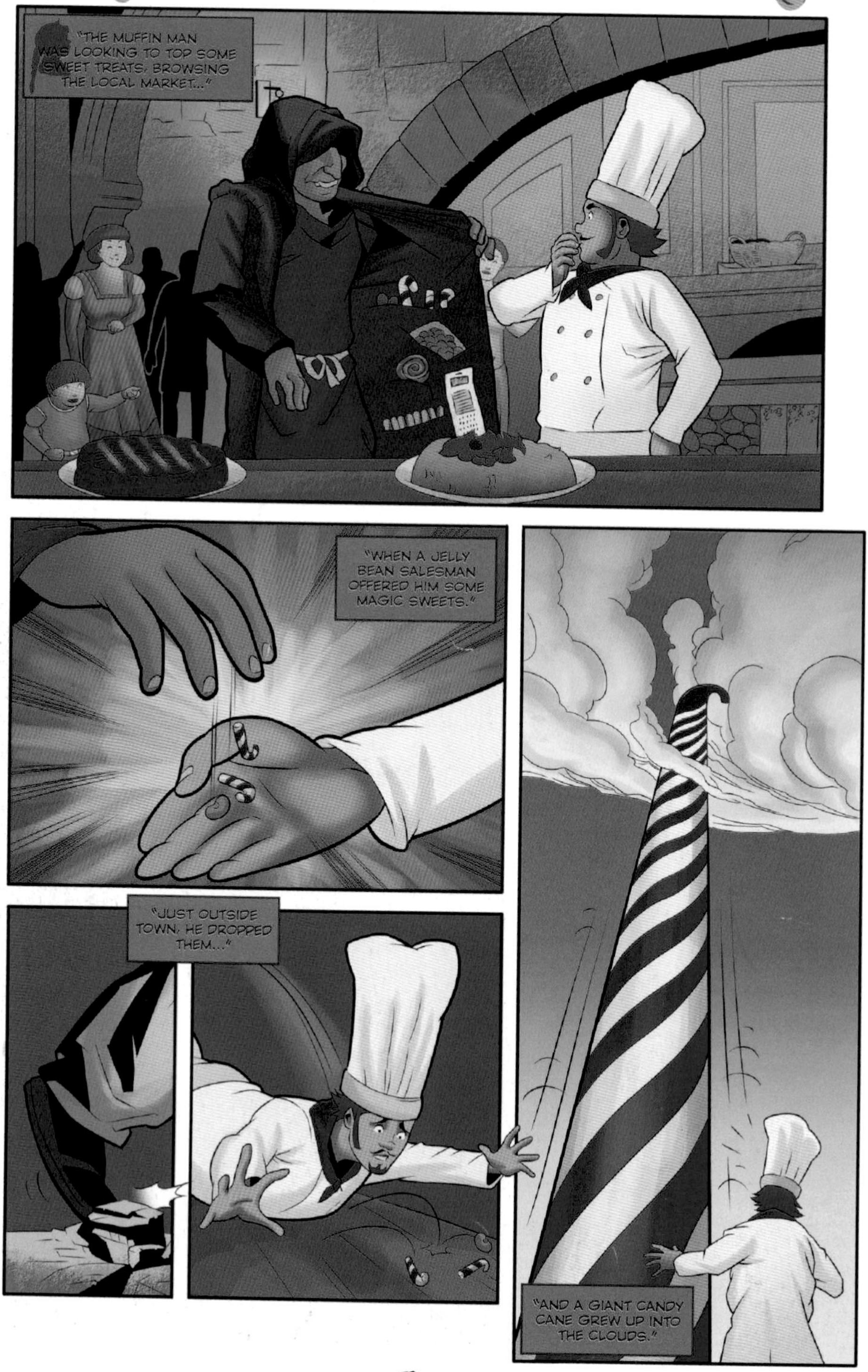
"THE MUFFIN MAN WAS LOOKING TO TOP SOME SWEET TREATS, BROWSING THE LOCAL MARKET..."
"WHEN A JELLY BEAN SALESMAN OFFERED HIM SOME MAGIC SWEETS."
"JUST OUTSIDE TOWN, HE DROPPED THEM..."
"AND A GIANT CANDY CANE GREW UP INTO THE CLOUDS."

"THE MUFFIN MAN CLIMBED!"

"THE CLOUDS WERE MADE OF COTTON CANDY!"

"UP THERE LIVED AN ANGRY GIANT!"

"THE GIANT CHASED THE MUFFIN MAN, THROWING OVER FURNITURE, TIPPING OVER THE DINNER TABLE!"

"HE CHASED THE MUFFIN MAN PAST THE OVERTURNED MEAL!"

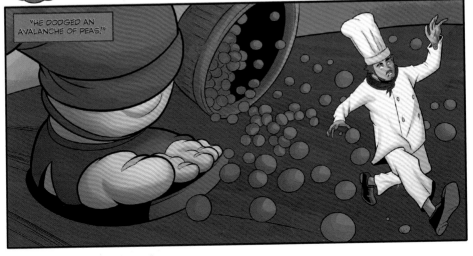

"HE DODGED AN AVALANCHE OF PEAS!"

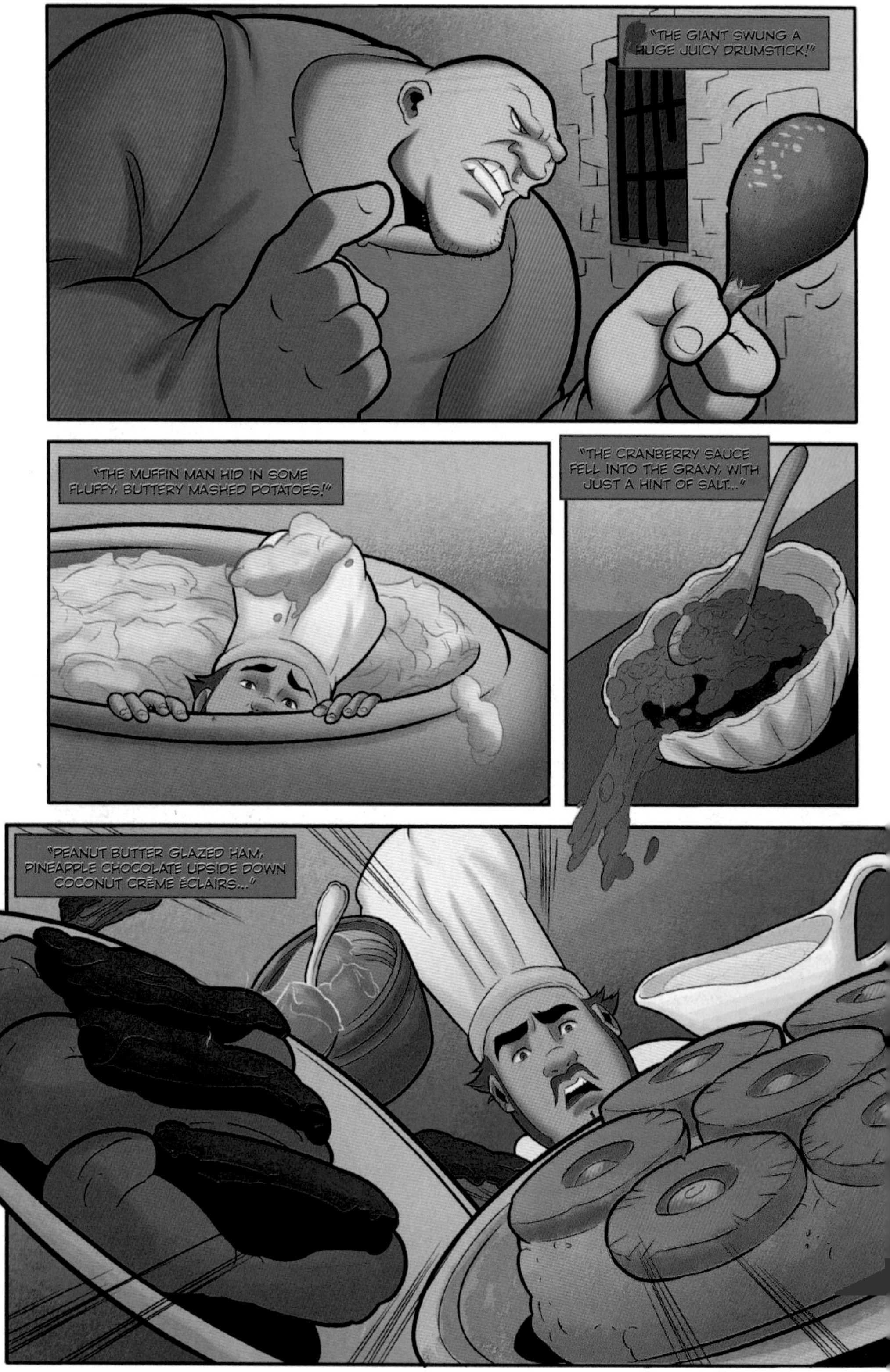
"THE GIANT SWUNG A HUGE JUICY DRUMSTICK!"
"THE MUFFIN MAN HID IN SOME FLUFFY, BUTTERY MASHED POTATOES!"
"THE CRANBERRY SAUCE FELL INTO THE GRAVY, WITH JUST A HINT OF SALT..."
"PEANUT BUTTER GLAZED HAM, PINEAPPLE CHOCOLATE UPSIDE DOWN COCONUT CRÈME ÉCLAIRS..."

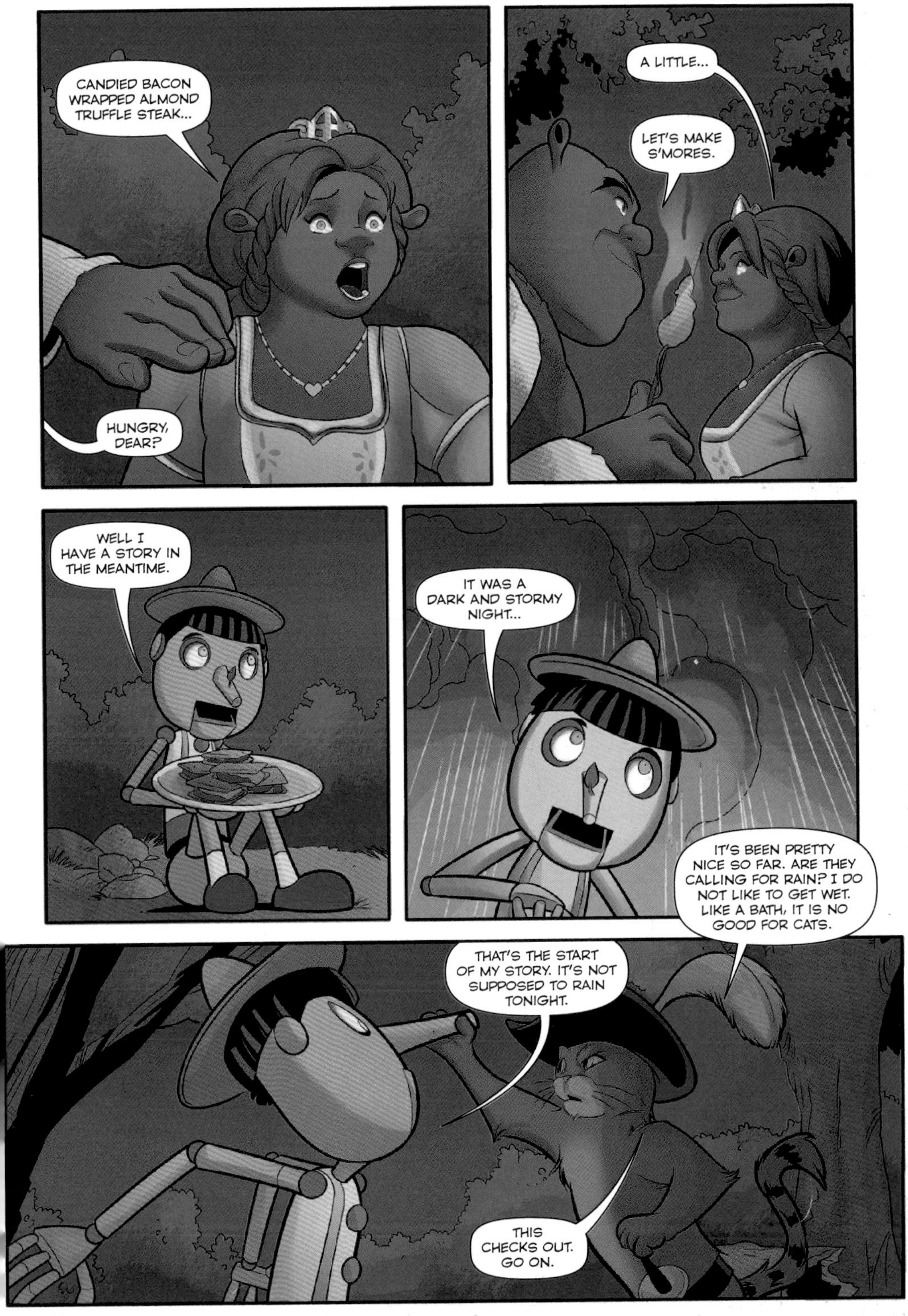
CANDIED BACON WRAPPED ALMOND TRUFFLE STEAK...
HUNGRY, DEAR?
A LITTLE...
LET'S MAKE S'MORES.
WELL I HAVE A STORY IN THE MEANTIME.
IT WAS A DARK AND STORMY NIGHT...
IT'S BEEN PRETTY NICE SO FAR. ARE THEY CALLING FOR RAIN? I DO NOT LIKE TO GET WET. LIKE A BATH, IT IS NO GOOD FOR CATS.
THAT'S THE START OF MY STORY. IT'S NOT SUPPOSED TO RAIN TONIGHT.
THIS CHECKS OUT. GO ON.

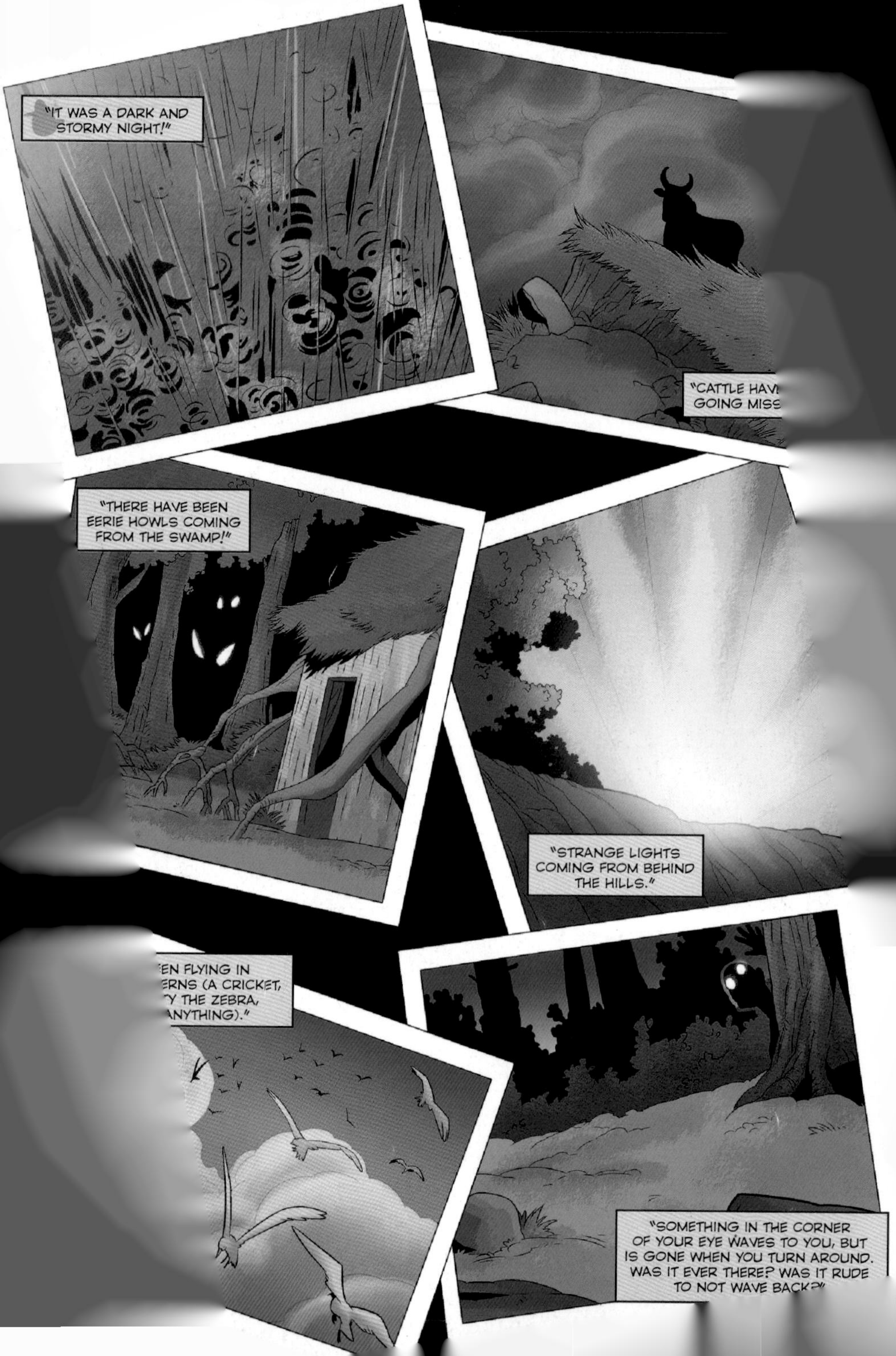
"IT WAS A DARK AND STORMY NIGHT!"
"CATTLE HAV
GOING MISS
"THERE HAVE BEEN EERIE HOWLS COMING FROM THE SWAMP!"
"STRANGE LIGHTS COMING FROM BEHIND THE HILLS."
EN FLYING IN
ERNS (A CRICKET,
TY THE ZEBRA,
ANYTHING)."
"SOMETHING IN THE CORNER OF YOUR EYE WAVES TO YOU, BUT IS GONE WHEN YOU TURN AROUND. WAS IT EVER THERE? WAS IT RUDE TO NOT WAVE BACK?"

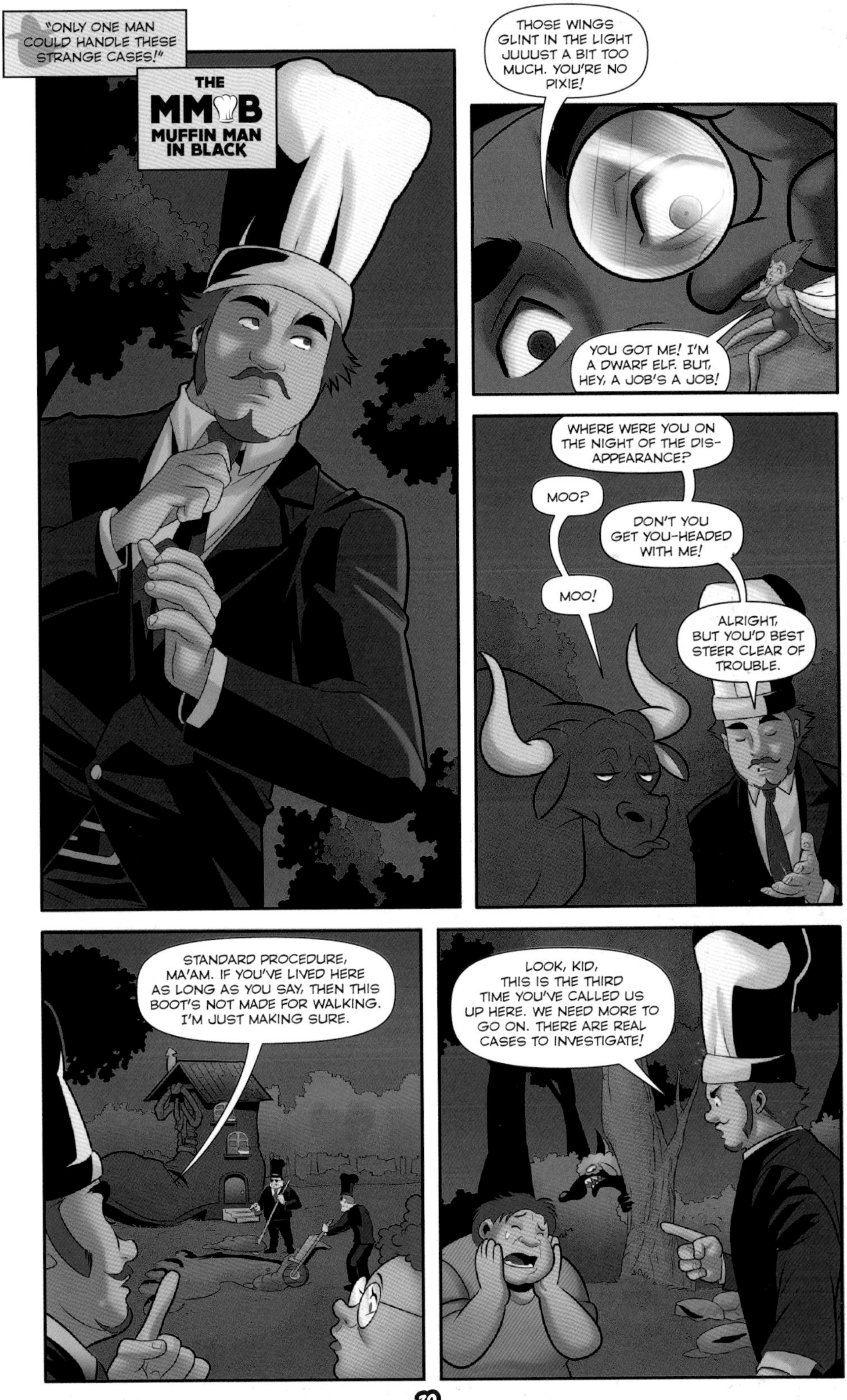
"ONLY ONE MAN COULD HANDLE THESE STRANGE CASES!"
THE MMIB MUFFIN MAN IN BLACK
THOSE WINGS GLINT IN THE LIGHT JUUUST A BIT TOO MUCH. YOU'RE NO PIXIE!
YOU GOT ME! I'M A DWARF ELF. BUT, HEY, A JOB'S A JOB!
WHERE WERE YOU ON THE NIGHT OF THE DIS-APPEARANCE?
MOO?
DON'T YOU GET YOU-HEADED WITH ME!
MOO!
ALRIGHT, BUT YOU'D BEST STEER CLEAR OF TROUBLE.
STANDARD PROCEDURE, MA'AM. IF YOU'VE LIVED HERE AS LONG AS YOU SAY, THEN THIS BOOT'S NOT MADE FOR WALKING. I'M JUST MAKING SURE.
LOOK, KID, THIS IS THE THIRD TIME YOU'VE CALLED US UP HERE. WE NEED MORE TO GO ON. THERE ARE REAL CASES TO INVESTIGATE!

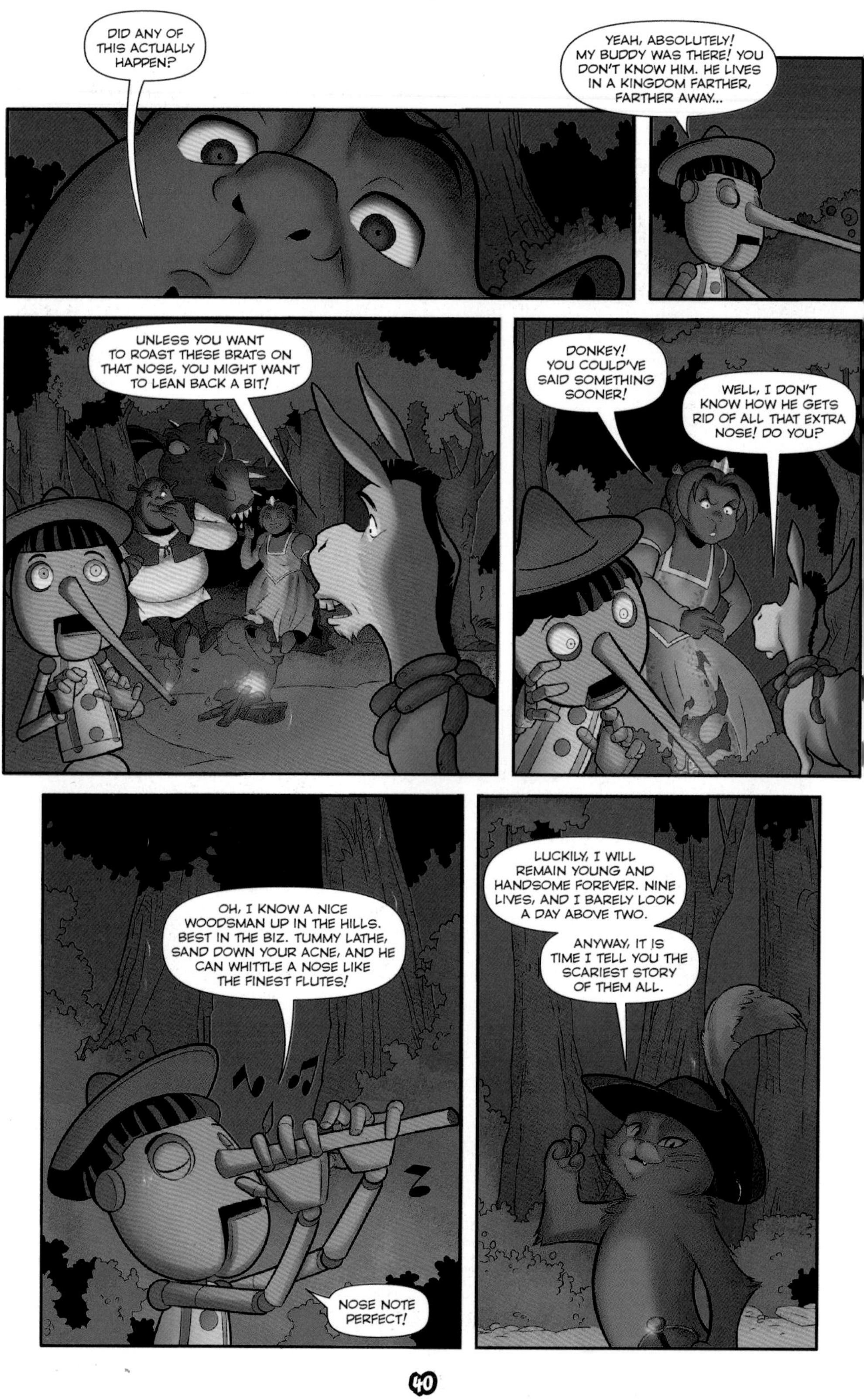
DID ANY OF THIS ACTUALLY HAPPEN?
YEAH, ABSOLUTELY! MY BUDDY WAS THERE! YOU DON'T KNOW HIM. HE LIVES IN A KINGDOM FARTHER, FARTHER AWAY...
UNLESS YOU WANT TO ROAST THESE BRATS ON THAT NOSE, YOU MIGHT WANT TO LEAN BACK A BIT!
DONKEY! YOU COULD'VE SAID SOMETHING SOONER!
WELL, I DON'T KNOW HOW HE GETS RID OF ALL THAT EXTRA NOSE! DO YOU?
OH, I KNOW A NICE WOODSMAN UP IN THE HILLS. BEST IN THE BIZ. TUMMY LATHE, SAND DOWN YOUR ACNE, AND HE CAN WHITTLE A NOSE LIKE THE FINEST FLUTES!
NOSE NOTE PERFECT!
LUCKILY, I WILL REMAIN YOUNG AND HANDSOME FOREVER. NINE LIVES, AND I BARELY LOOK A DAY ABOVE TWO.
ANYWAY, IT IS TIME I TELL YOU THE SCARIEST STORY OF THEM ALL.

HOT CROSSROADS BUNS!

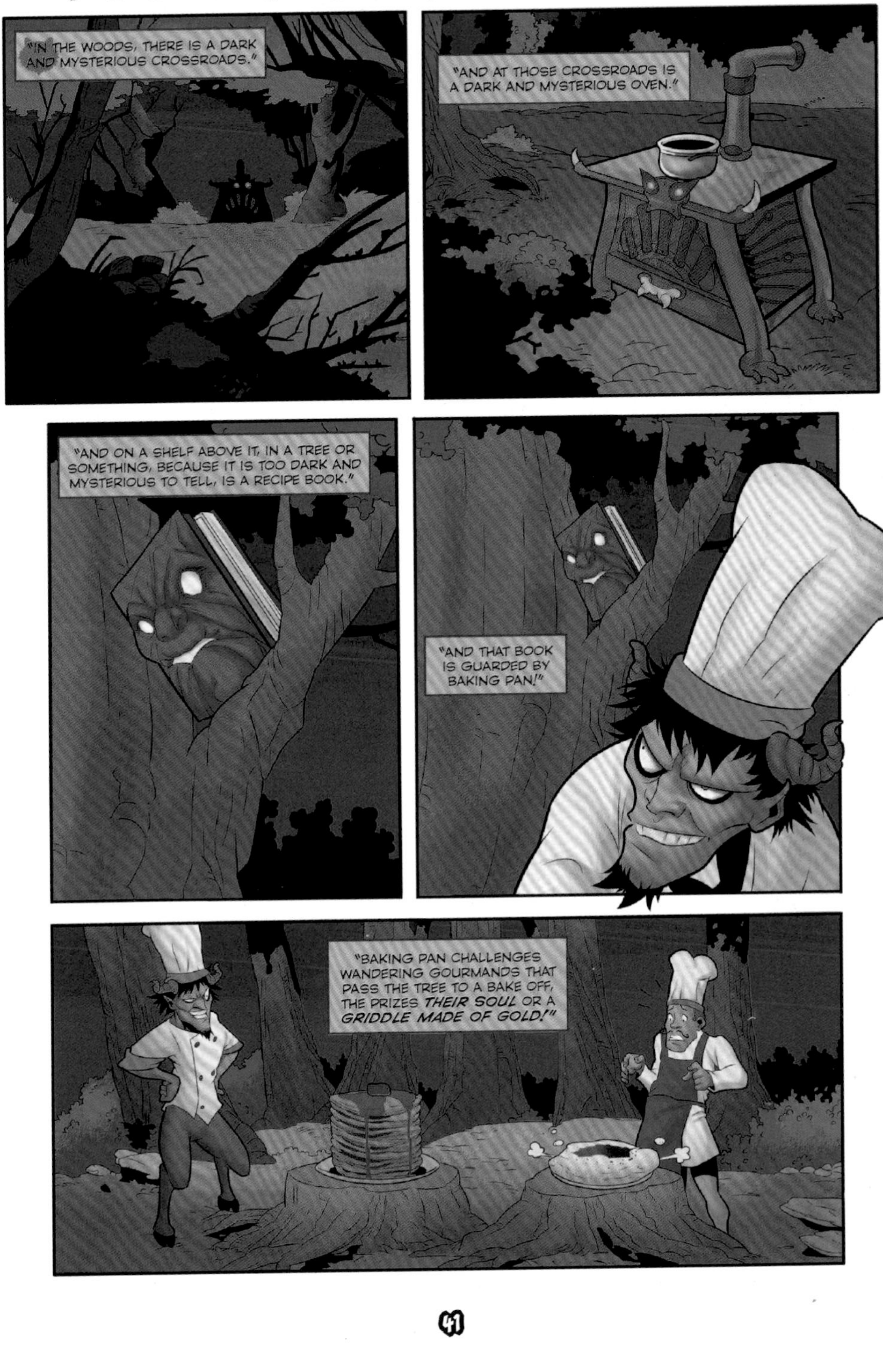
"IN THE WOODS, THERE IS A DARK AND MYSTERIOUS CROSSROADS."
"AND AT THOSE CROSSROADS IS A DARK AND MYSTERIOUS OVEN."
"AND ON A SHELF ABOVE IT, IN A TREE OR SOMETHING, BECAUSE IT IS TOO DARK AND MYSTERIOUS TO TELL, IS A RECIPE BOOK."
"AND THAT BOOK IS GUARDED BY BAKING PAN!"
"BAKING PAN CHALLENGES WANDERING GOURMANDS THAT PASS THE TREE TO A BAKE OFF, THE PRIZES *THEIR SOUL* OR A *GRIDDLE MADE OF GOLD!*"

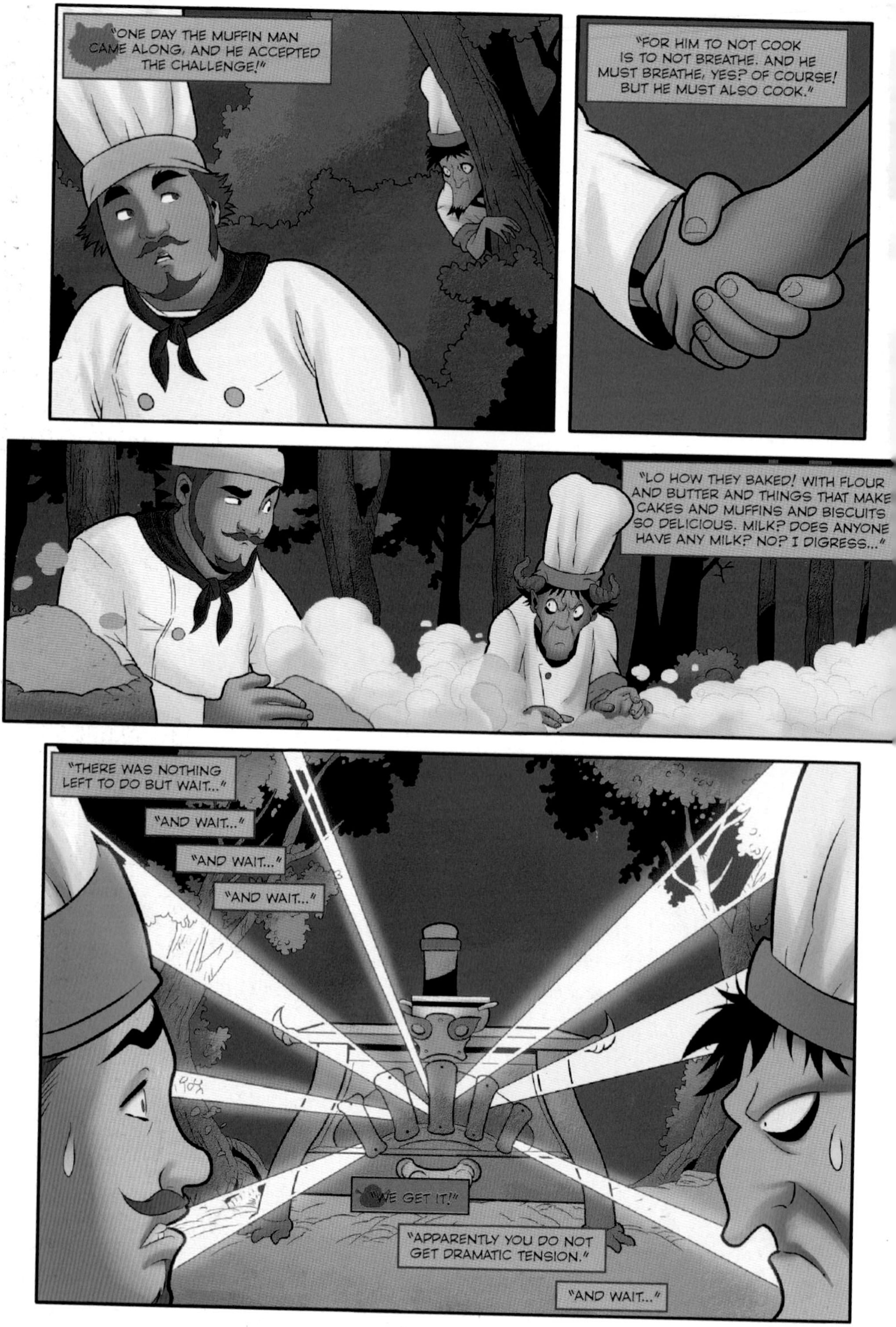
"ONE DAY THE MUFFIN MAN CAME ALONG, AND HE ACCEPTED THE CHALLENGE!"
"FOR HIM TO NOT COOK IS TO NOT BREATHE. AND HE MUST BREATHE, YES? OF COURSE! BUT HE MUST ALSO COOK."
"LO HOW THEY BAKED! WITH FLOUR AND BUTTER AND THINGS THAT MAKE CAKES AND MUFFINS AND BISCUITS SO DELICIOUS. MILK? DOES ANYONE HAVE ANY MILK? NO? I DIGRESS..."
"THERE WAS NOTHING LEFT TO DO BUT WAIT..."
"AND WAIT..."
"AND WAIT..."
"AND WAIT..."
"WE GET IT!"
"APPARENTLY YOU DO NOT GET DRAMATIC TENSION."
"AND WAIT..."

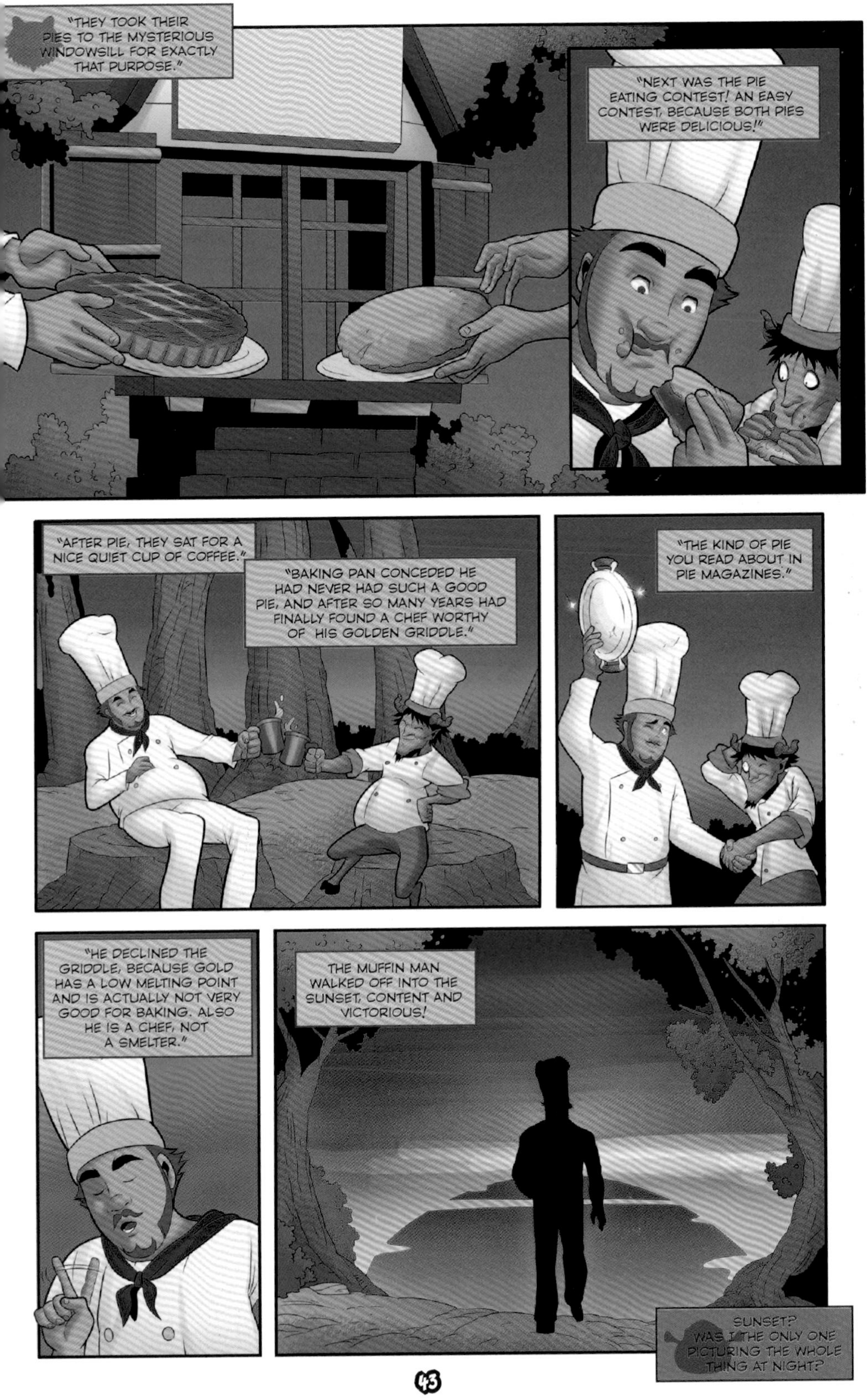
"THEY TOOK THEIR PIES TO THE MYSTERIOUS WINDOWSILL FOR EXACTLY THAT PURPOSE."
"NEXT WAS THE PIE EATING CONTEST! AN EASY CONTEST, BECAUSE BOTH PIES WERE DELICIOUS!"
"AFTER PIE, THEY SAT FOR A NICE QUIET CUP OF COFFEE."
"BAKING PAN CONCEDED HE HAD NEVER HAD SUCH A GOOD PIE, AND AFTER SO MANY YEARS HAD FINALLY FOUND A CHEF WORTHY OF HIS GOLDEN GRIDDLE."
"THE KIND OF PIE YOU READ ABOUT IN PIE MAGAZINES."
"HE DECLINED THE GRIDDLE, BECAUSE GOLD HAS A LOW MELTING POINT AND IS ACTUALLY NOT VERY GOOD FOR BAKING. ALSO HE IS A CHEF, NOT A SMELTER."
THE MUFFIN MAN WALKED OFF INTO THE SUNSET, CONTENT AND VICTORIOUS!
SUNSET? WAS I THE ONLY ONE PICTURING THE WHOLE THING AT NIGHT?

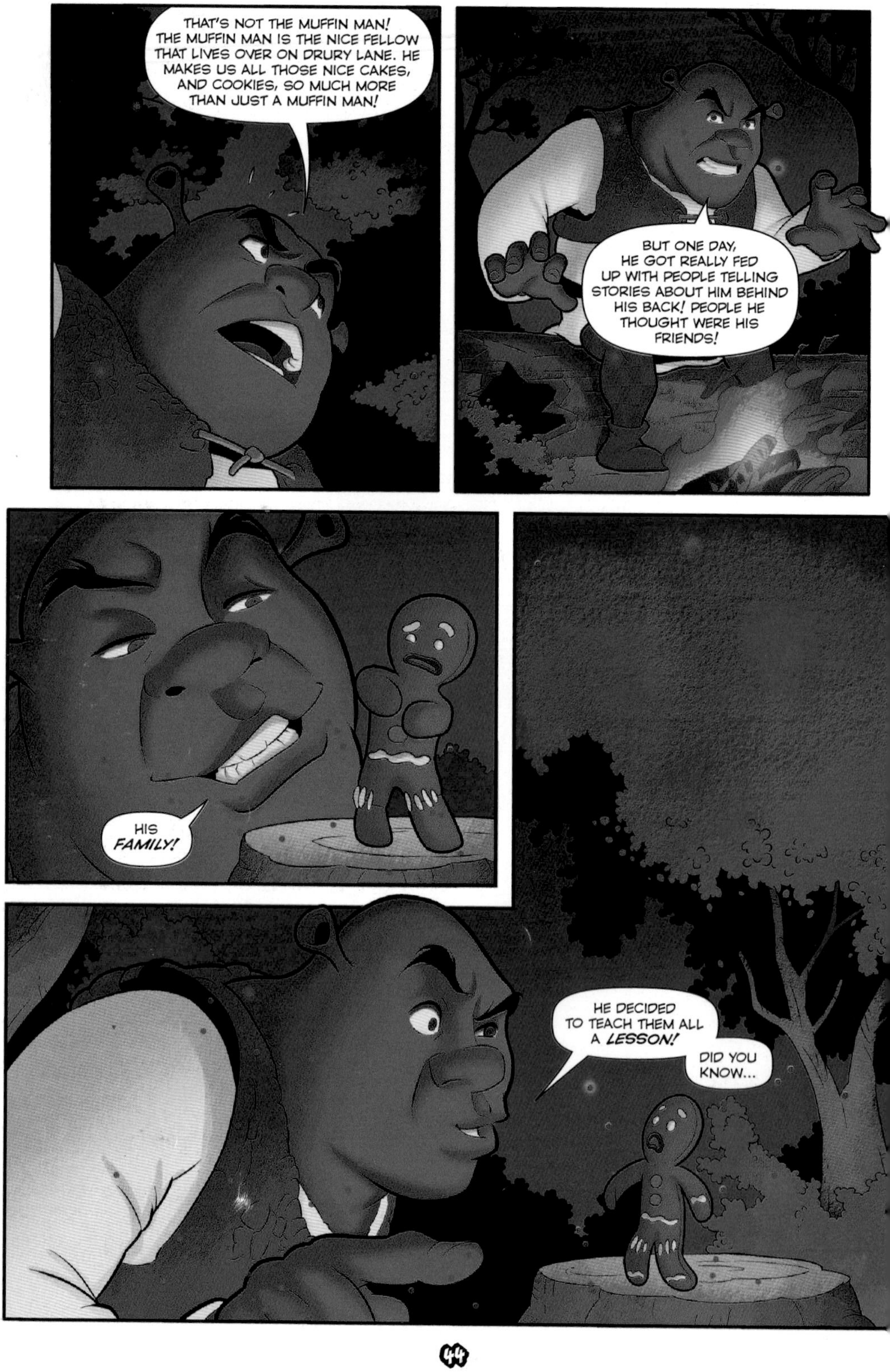
THAT'S NOT THE MUFFIN MAN! THE MUFFIN MAN IS THE NICE FELLOW THAT LIVES OVER ON DRURY LANE. HE MAKES US ALL THOSE NICE CAKES, AND COOKIES, SO MUCH MORE THAN JUST A MUFFIN MAN!
BUT ONE DAY, HE GOT REALLY FED UP WITH PEOPLE TELLING STORIES ABOUT HIM BEHIND HIS BACK! PEOPLE HE THOUGHT WERE HIS FRIENDS!
HIS *FAMILY!*
HE DECIDED TO TEACH THEM ALL A *LESSON!*
DID YOU KNOW...

THE MUFFIN MAN KNOWS YOU!?

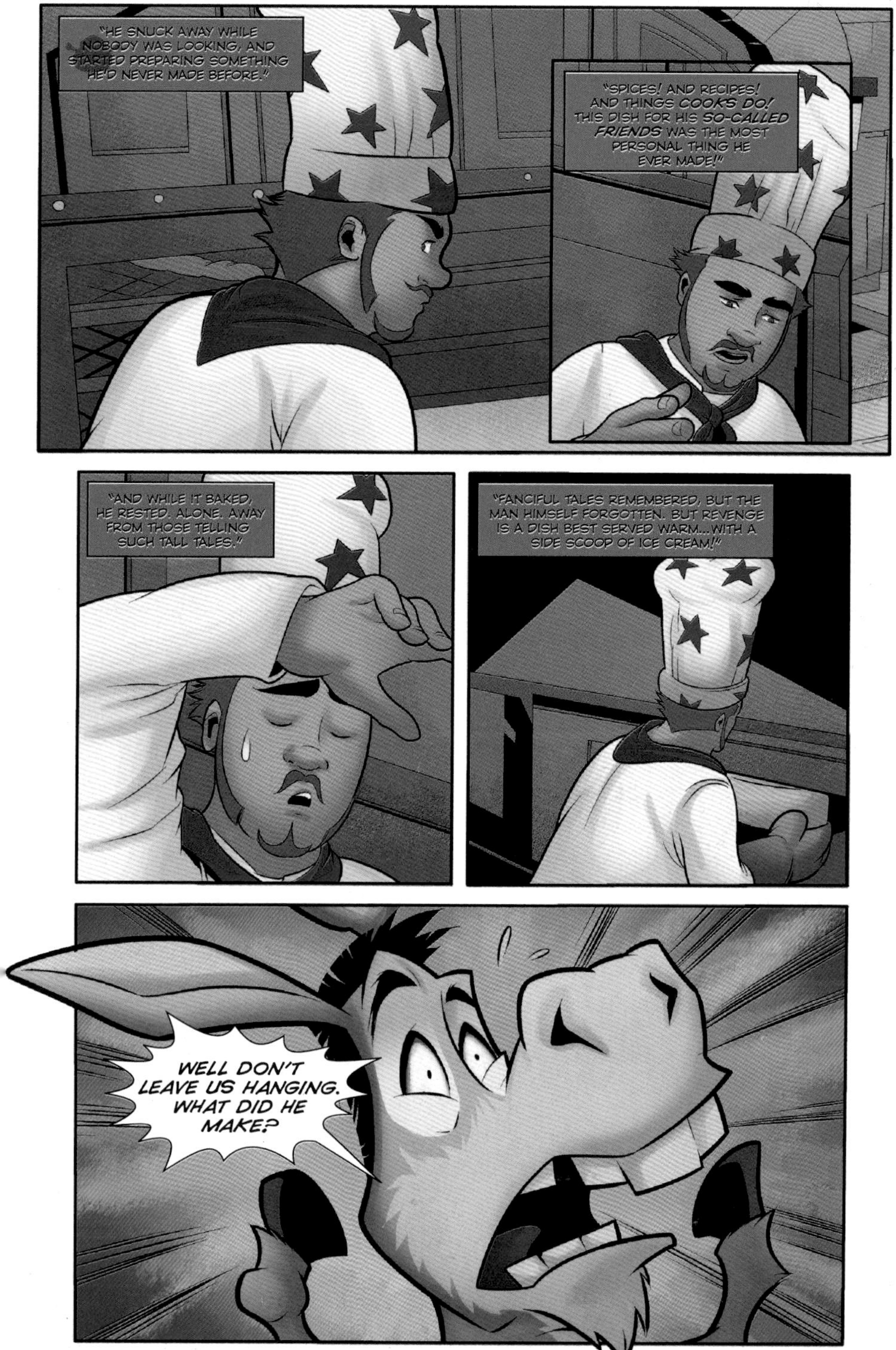
"HE SNUCK AWAY WHILE NOBODY WAS LOOKING, AND STARTED PREPARING SOMETHING HE'D NEVER MADE BEFORE."
"SPICES! AND RECIPES! AND THINGS COOKS DO! THIS DISH FOR HIS SO-CALLED FRIENDS WAS THE MOST PERSONAL THING HE EVER MADE!"
"AND WHILE IT BAKED, HE RESTED. ALONE. AWAY FROM THOSE TELLING SUCH TALL TALES."
"FANCIFUL TALES REMEMBERED, BUT THE MAN HIMSELF FORGOTTEN. BUT REVENGE IS A DISH BEST SERVED WARM...WITH A SIDE SCOOP OF ICE CREAM!"
WELL DON'T LEAVE US HANGING. WHAT DID HE MAKE?

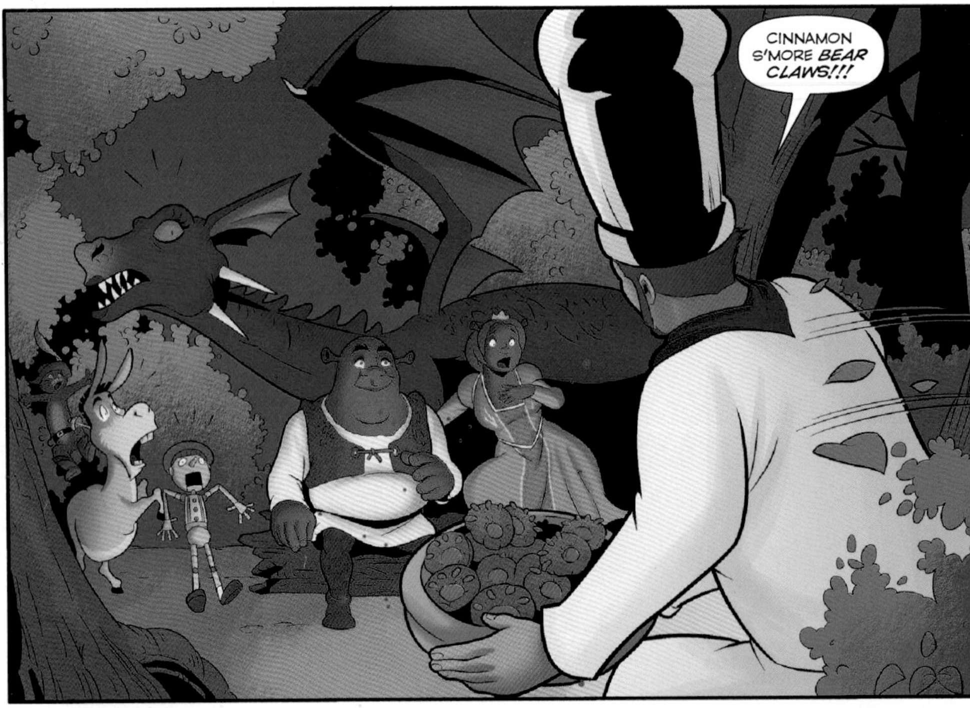
CINNAMON S'MORE *BEAR CLAWS!!!*

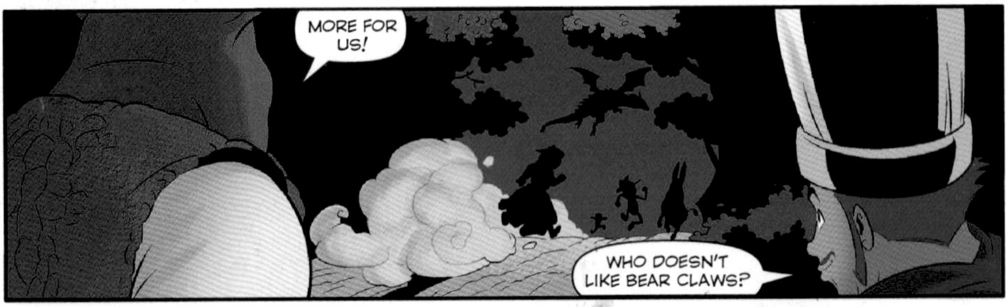
MORE FOR US!
WHO DOESN'T LIKE BEAR CLAWS?

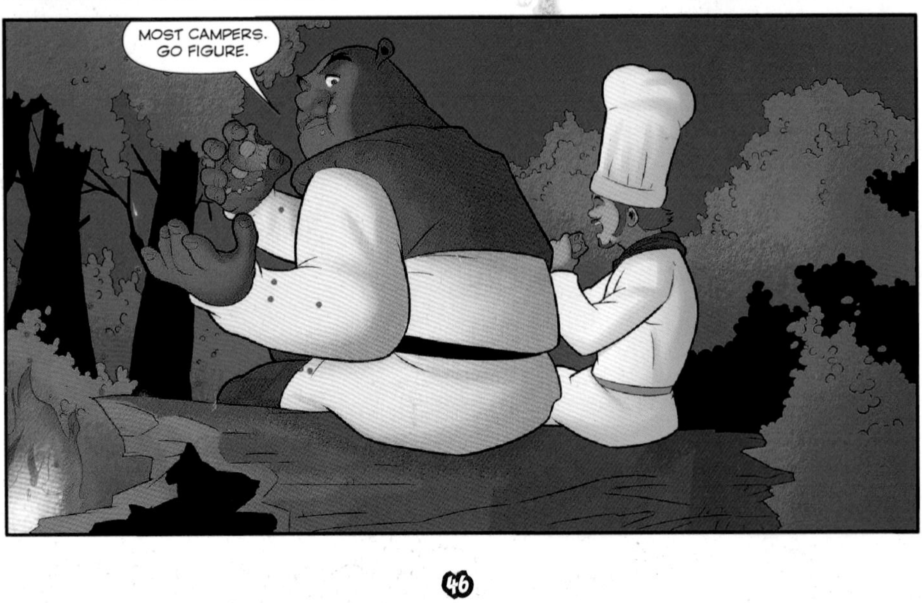
MOST CAMPERS. GO FIGURE.

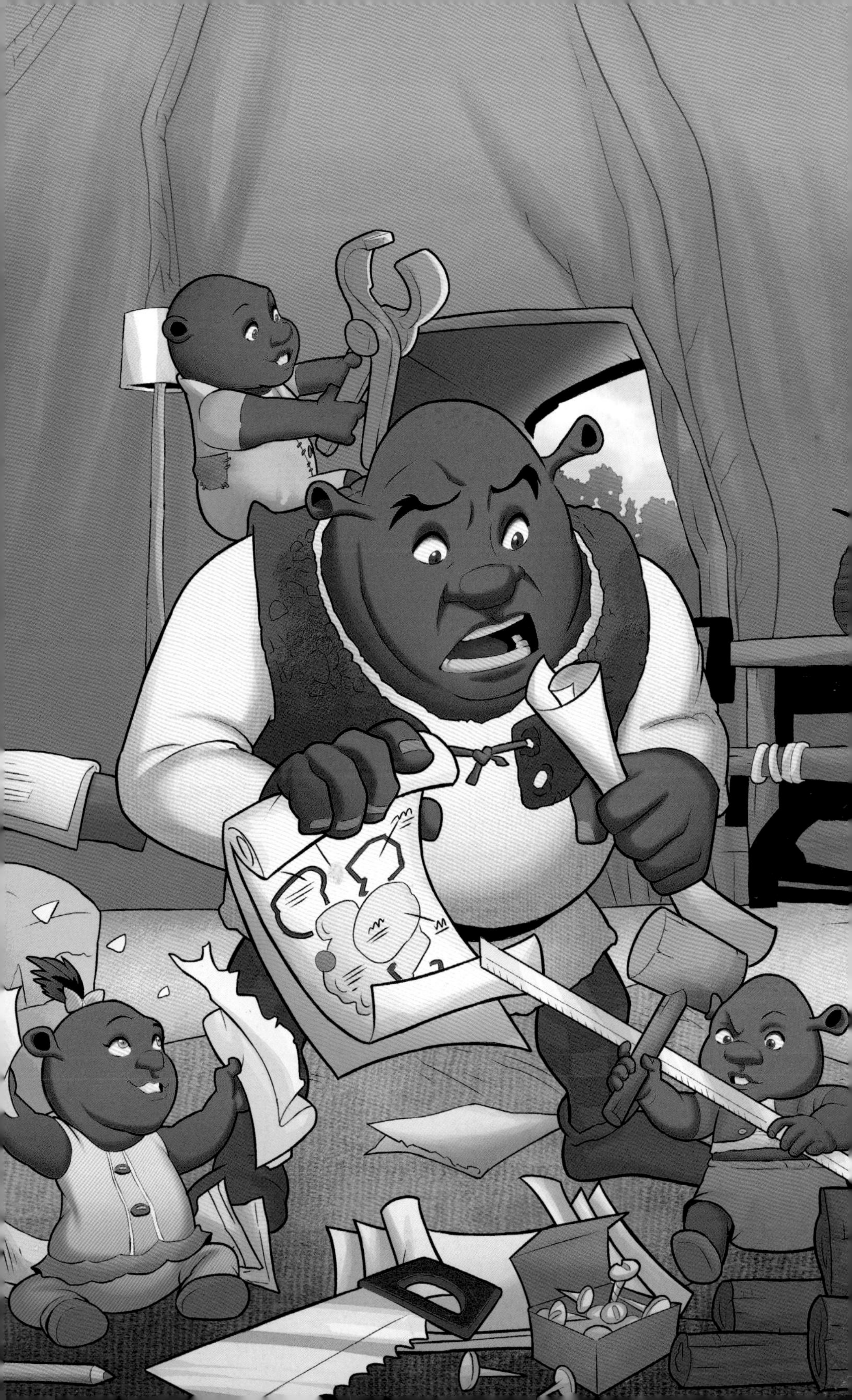

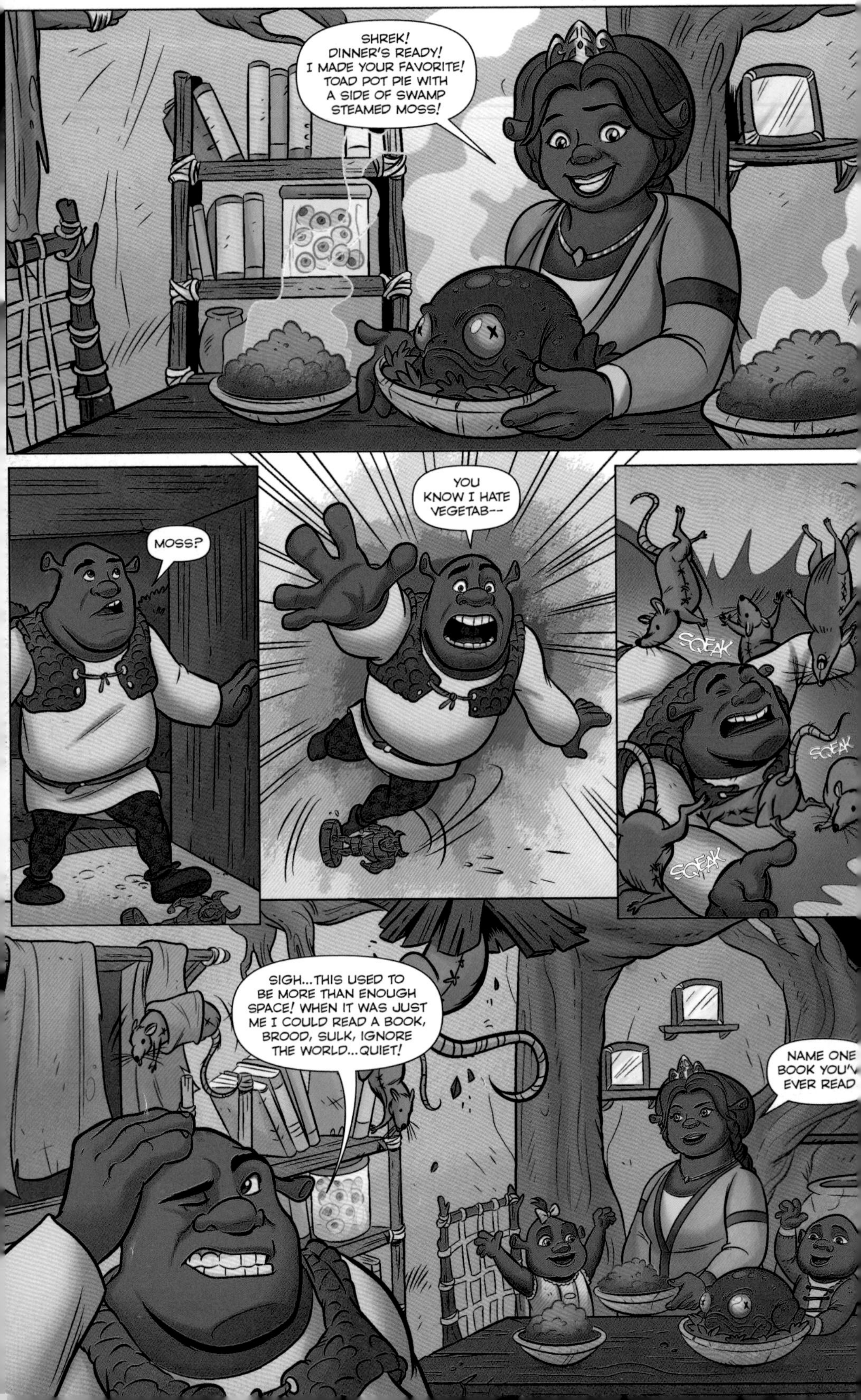

SHREK! DINNER'S READY! I MADE YOUR FAVORITE! TOAD POT PIE WITH A SIDE OF SWAMP STEAMED MOSS!
MOSS?
YOU KNOW I HATE VEGETAB--
SQEAK
SQEAK
SQEAK
SIGH...THIS USED TO BE MORE THAN ENOUGH SPACE! WHEN IT WAS JUST ME I COULD READ A BOOK, BROOD, SULK, IGNORE THE WORLD...QUIET!
NAME ONE BOOK YOU'V EVER READ

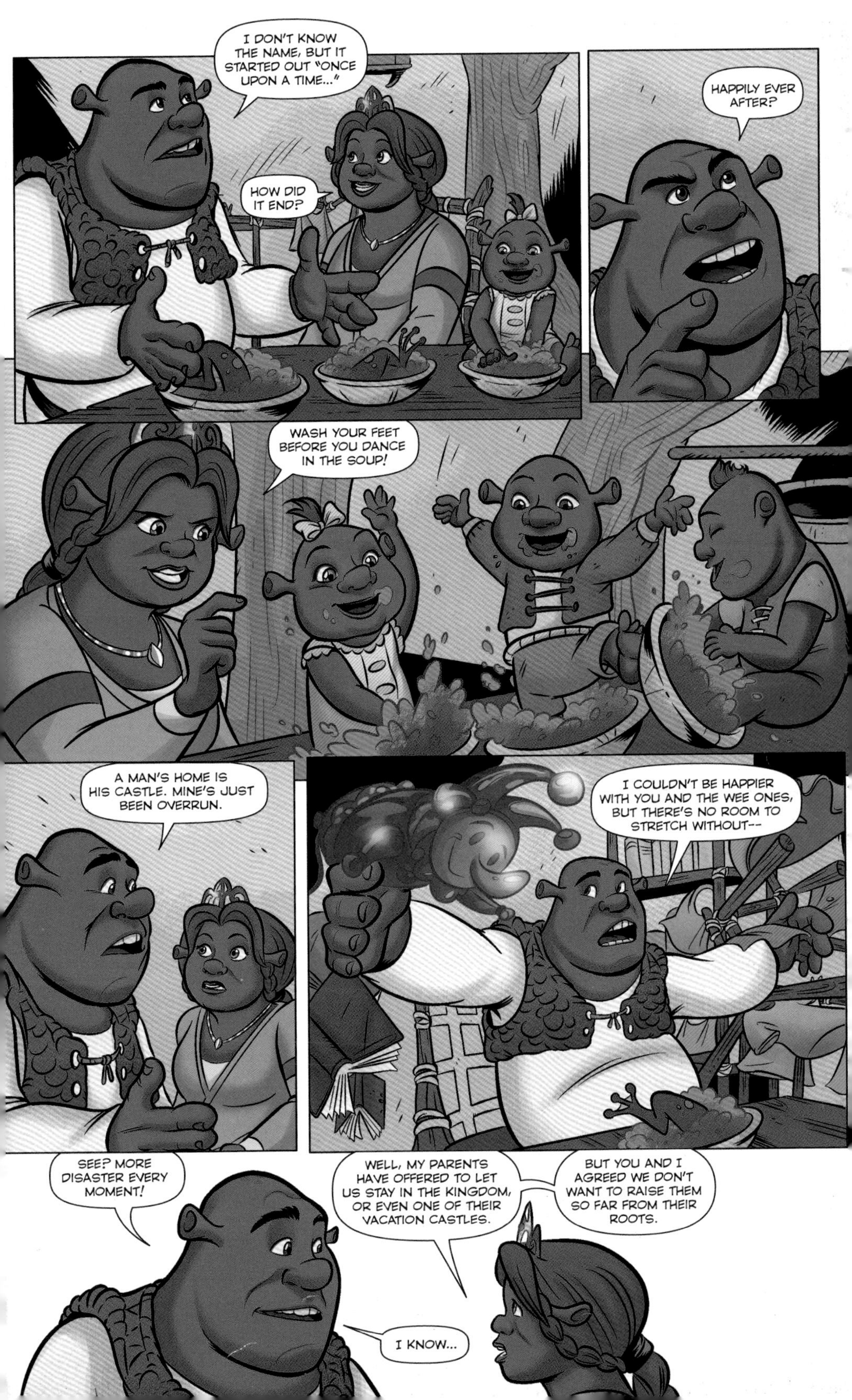
I DON'T KNOW THE NAME, BUT IT STARTED OUT "ONCE UPON A TIME..."
HOW DID IT END?
HAPPILY EVER AFTER?
WASH YOUR FEET BEFORE YOU DANCE IN THE SOUP!
A MAN'S HOME IS HIS CASTLE. MINE'S JUST BEEN OVERRUN.
I COULDN'T BE HAPPIER WITH YOU AND THE WEE ONES, BUT THERE'S NO ROOM TO STRETCH WITHOUT--
SEE? MORE DISASTER EVERY MOMENT!
WELL, MY PARENTS HAVE OFFERED TO LET US STAY IN THE KINGDOM, OR EVEN ONE OF THEIR VACATION CASTLES.
BUT YOU AND I AGREED WE DON'T WANT TO RAISE THEM SO FAR FROM THEIR ROOTS.
I KNOW...

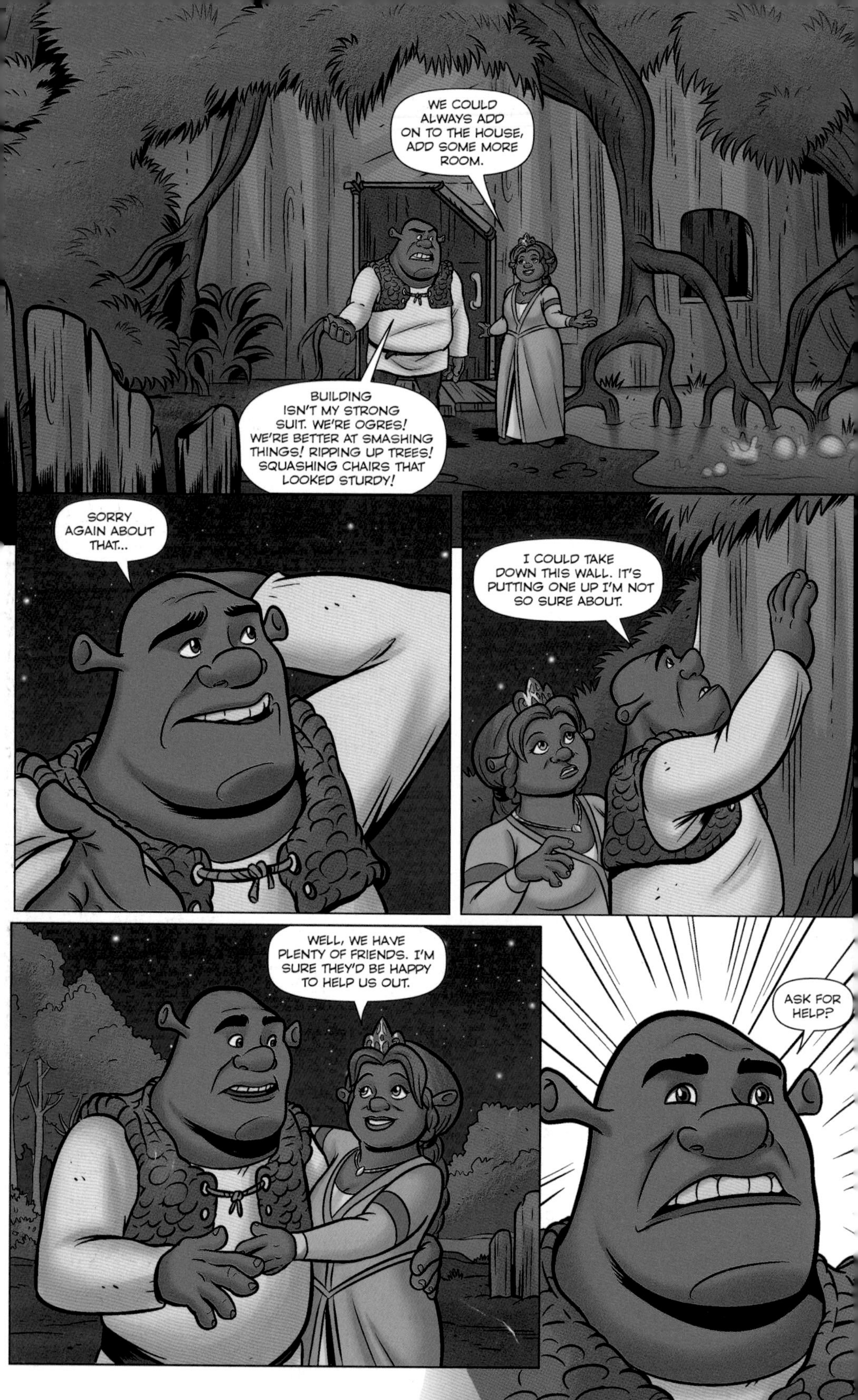
WE COULD ALWAYS ADD ON TO THE HOUSE, ADD SOME MORE ROOM.
BUILDING ISN'T MY STRONG SUIT. WE'RE OGRES! WE'RE BETTER AT SMASHING THINGS! RIPPING UP TREES! SQUASHING CHAIRS THAT LOOKED STURDY!
SORRY AGAIN ABOUT THAT...
I COULD TAKE DOWN THIS WALL. IT'S PUTTING ONE UP I'M NOT SO SURE ABOUT.
WELL, WE HAVE PLENTY OF FRIENDS. I'M SURE THEY'D BE HAPPY TO HELP US OUT.
ASK FOR HELP?

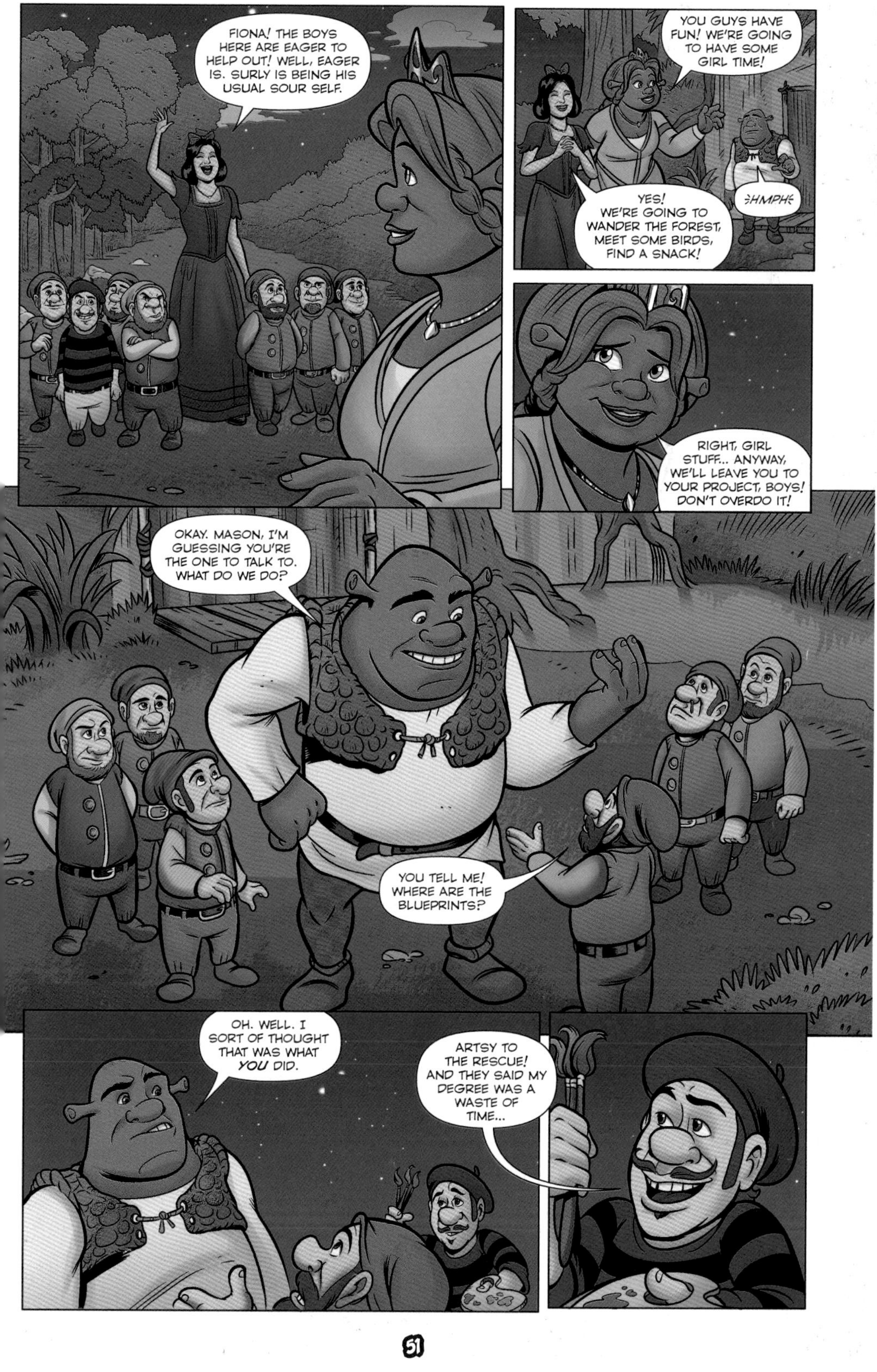
FIONA! THE BOYS HERE ARE EAGER TO HELP OUT! WELL, EAGER IS. SURLY IS BEING HIS USUAL SOUR SELF.
YOU GUYS HAVE FUN! WE'RE GOING TO HAVE SOME GIRL TIME!
YES! WE'RE GOING TO WANDER THE FOREST, MEET SOME BIRDS, FIND A SNACK!
HMPH
RIGHT, GIRL STUFF... ANYWAY, WE'LL LEAVE YOU TO YOUR PROJECT, BOYS! DON'T OVERDO IT!
OKAY. MASON, I'M GUESSING YOU'RE THE ONE TO TALK TO. WHAT DO WE DO?
YOU TELL ME! WHERE ARE THE BLUEPRINTS?
OH. WELL. I SORT OF THOUGHT THAT WAS WHAT *YOU* DID.
ARTSY TO THE RESCUE! AND THEY SAID MY DEGREE WAS A WASTE OF TIME...

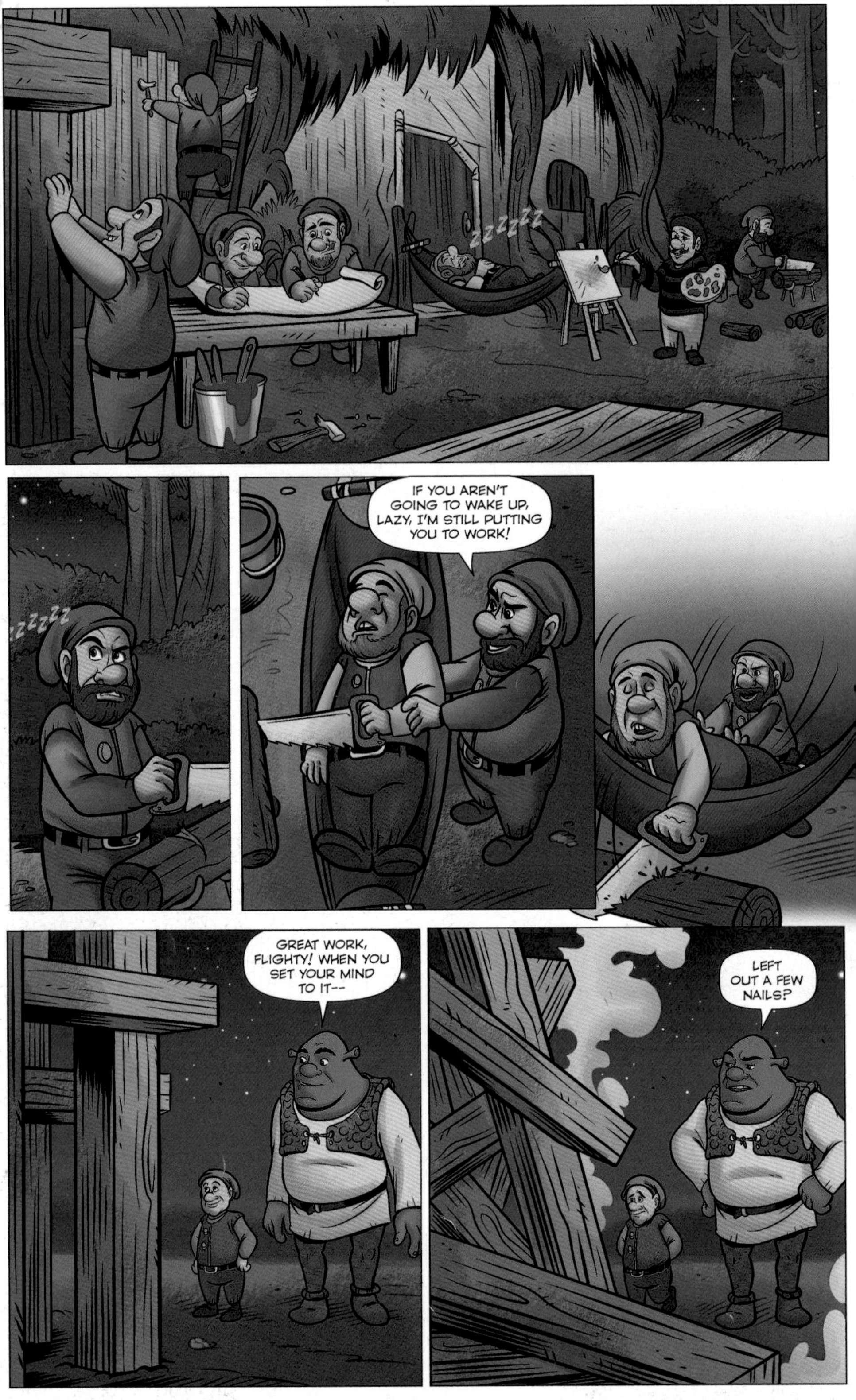

ZZZZZZ
ZZZZZZ
IF YOU AREN'T GOING TO WAKE UP, LAZY, I'M STILL PUTTING YOU TO WORK!
GREAT WORK, FLIGHTY! WHEN YOU SET YOUR MIND TO IT--
LEFT OUT A FEW NAILS?

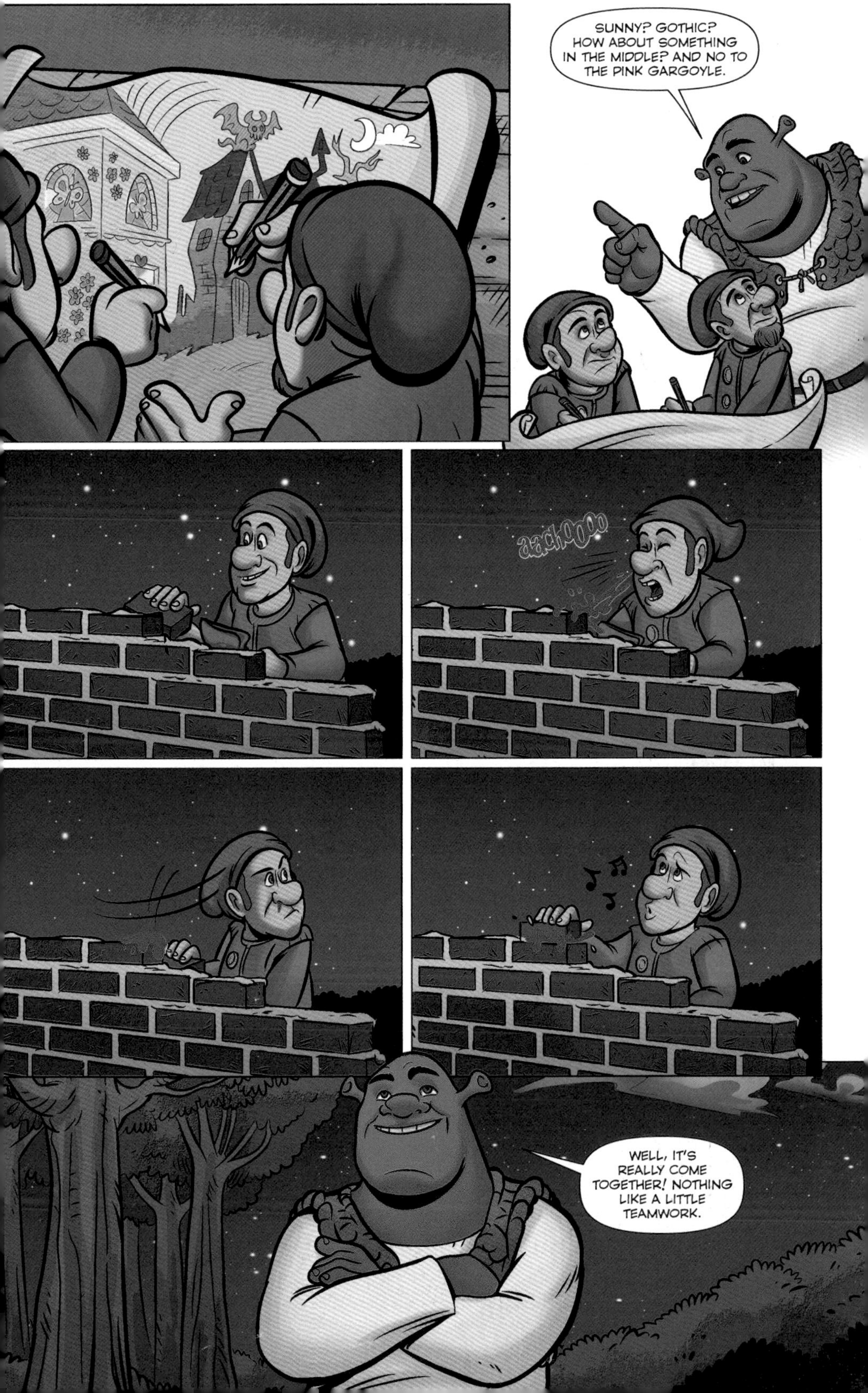
SUNNY? GOTHIC? HOW ABOUT SOMETHING IN THE MIDDLE? AND NO TO THE PINK GARGOYLE.
aachOOOO
WELL, IT'S REALLY COME TOGETHER! NOTHING LIKE A LITTLE TEAMWORK.

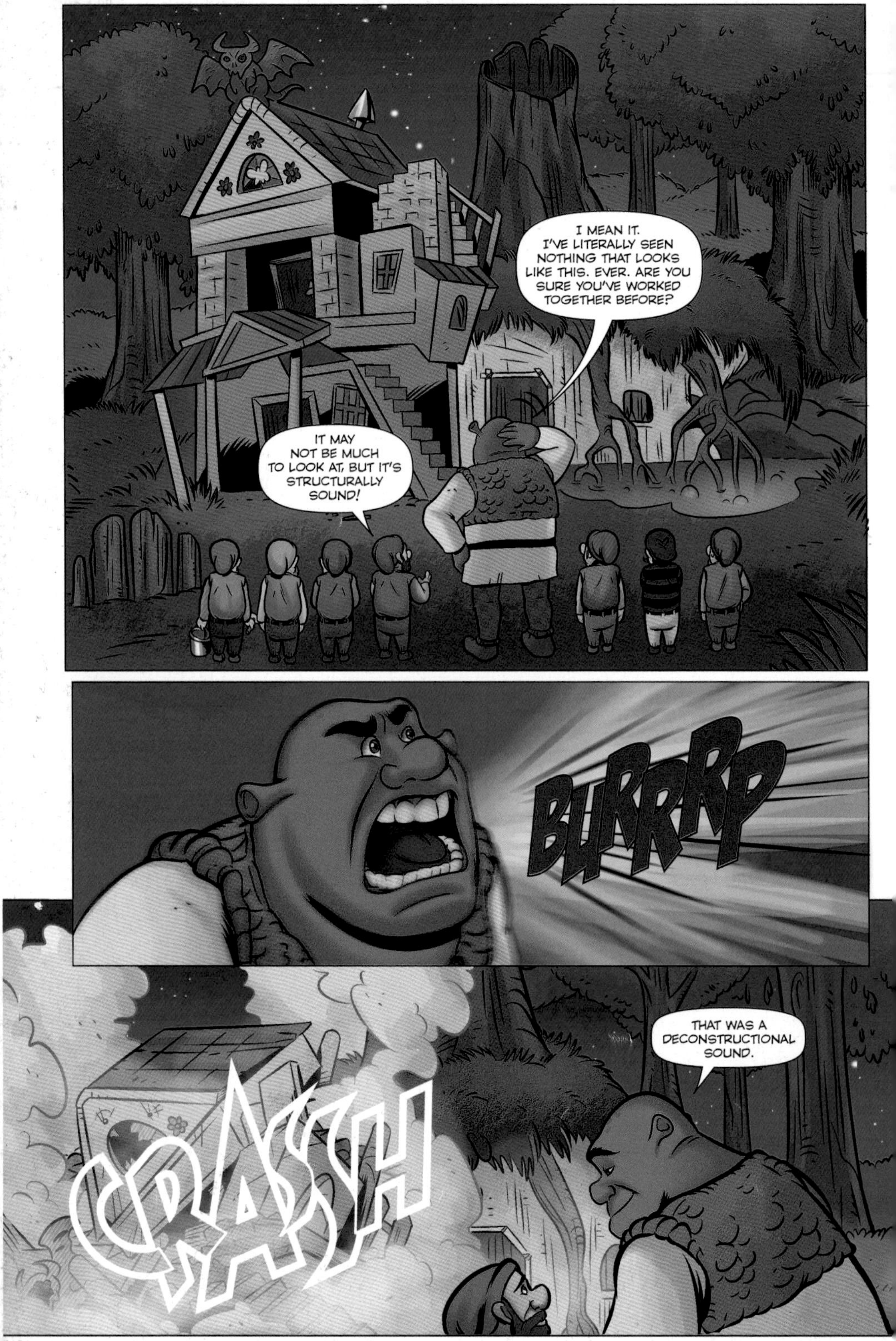
I MEAN IT. I'VE LITERALLY SEEN NOTHING THAT LOOKS LIKE THIS. EVER. ARE YOU SURE YOU'VE WORKED TOGETHER BEFORE?
IT MAY NOT BE MUCH TO LOOK AT, BUT IT'S STRUCTURALLY SOUND!
BURRRP
CRASH
THAT WAS A DECONSTRUCTIONAL SOUND.

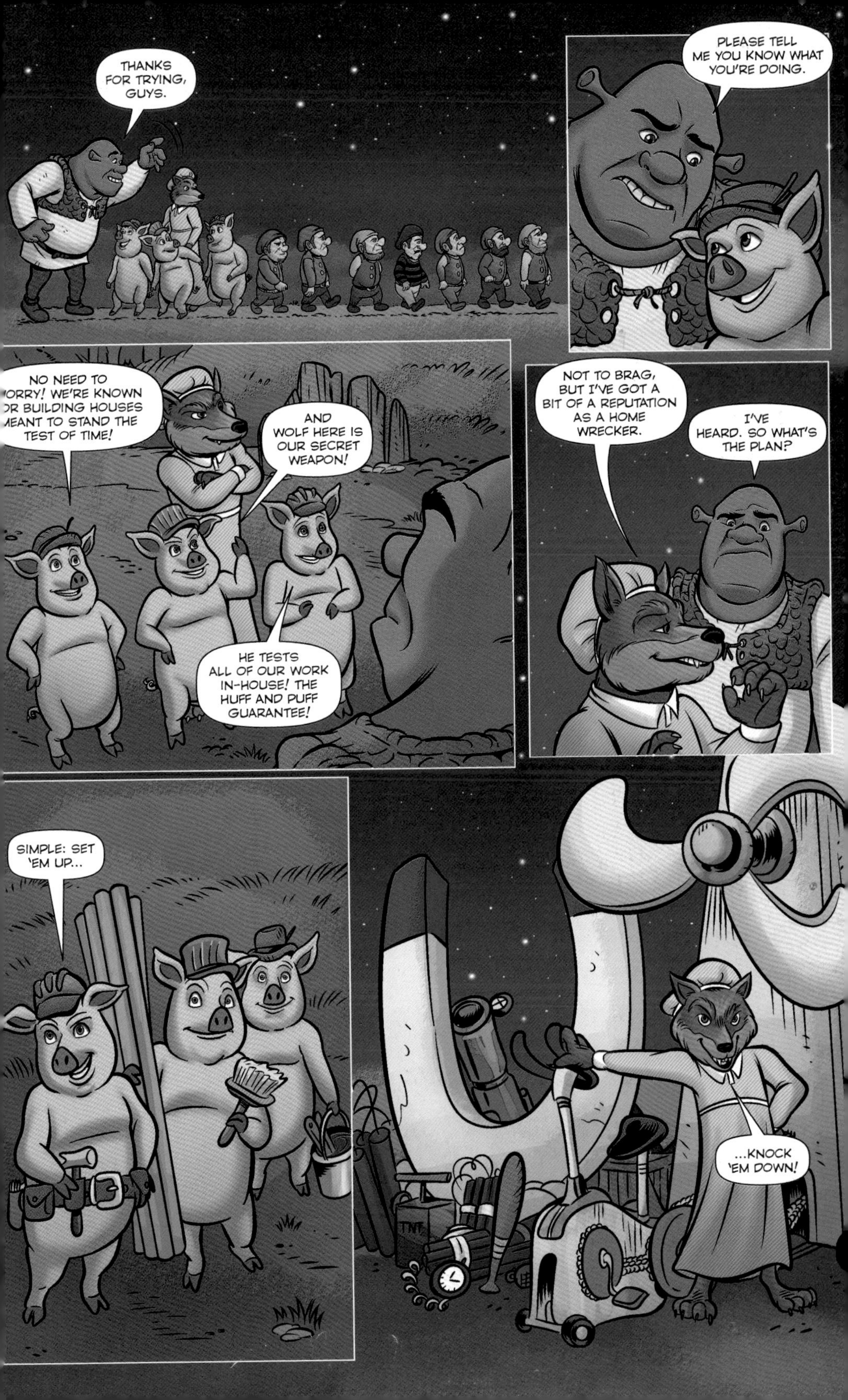
THANKS FOR TRYING, GUYS.
PLEASE TELL ME YOU KNOW WHAT YOU'RE DOING.
NO NEED TO WORRY! WE'RE KNOWN FOR BUILDING HOUSES MEANT TO STAND THE TEST OF TIME!
AND WOLF HERE IS OUR SECRET WEAPON!
HE TESTS ALL OF OUR WORK IN-HOUSE! THE HUFF AND PUFF GUARANTEE!
NOT TO BRAG, BUT I'VE GOT A BIT OF A REPUTATION AS A HOME WRECKER.
I'VE HEARD. SO WHAT'S THE PLAN?
SIMPLE: SET 'EM UP...
...KNOCK 'EM DOWN!
TNT

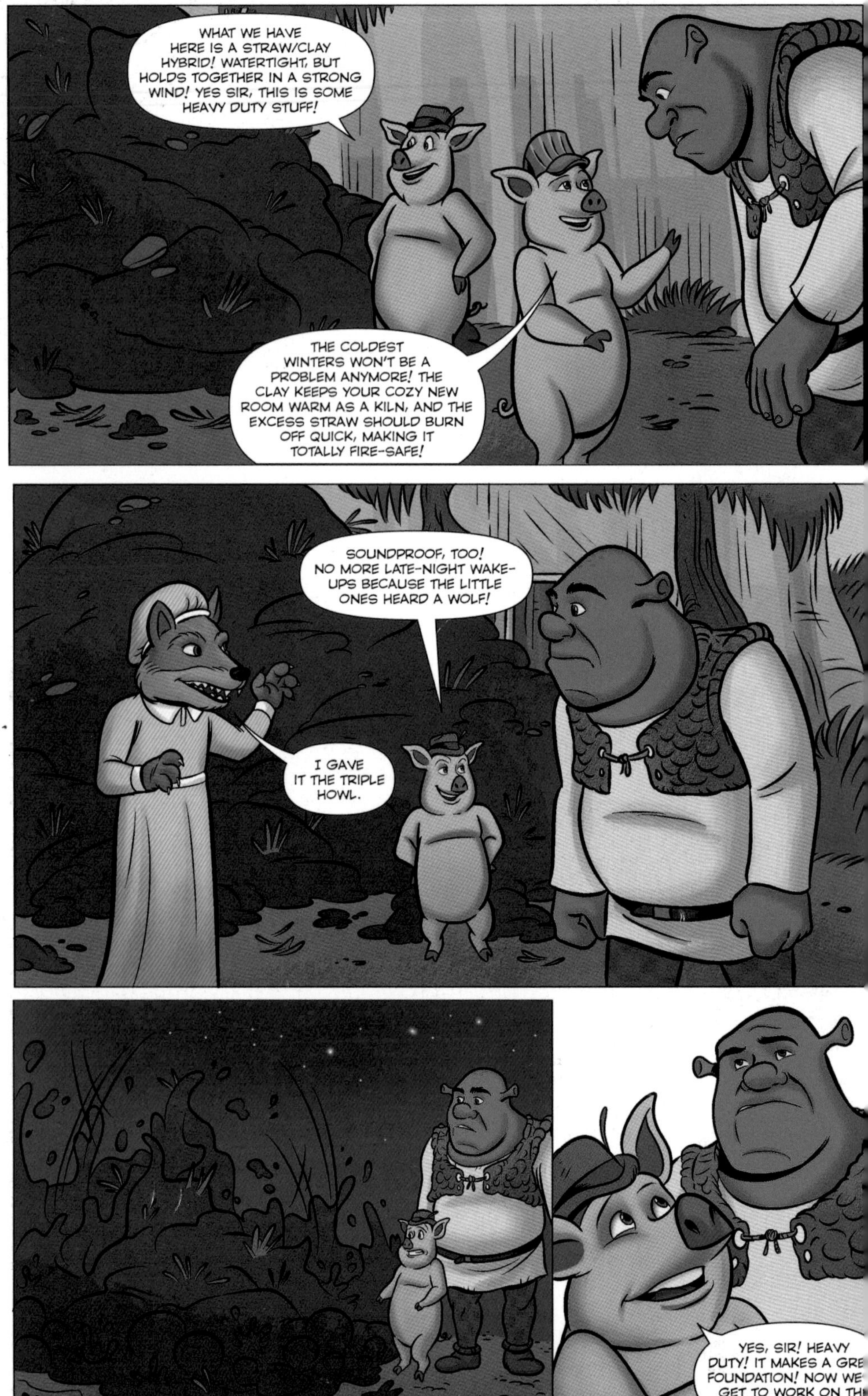

WHAT WE HAVE HERE IS A STRAW/CLAY HYBRID! WATERTIGHT, BUT HOLDS TOGETHER IN A STRONG WIND! YES SIR, THIS IS SOME HEAVY DUTY STUFF!
THE COLDEST WINTERS WON'T BE A PROBLEM ANYMORE! THE CLAY KEEPS YOUR COZY NEW ROOM WARM AS A KILN, AND THE EXCESS STRAW SHOULD BURN OFF QUICK, MAKING IT TOTALLY FIRE-SAFE!
SOUNDPROOF, TOO! NO MORE LATE-NIGHT WAKE-UPS BECAUSE THE LITTLE ONES HEARD A WOLF!
I GAVE IT THE TRIPLE HOWL.
YES, SIR! HEAVY DUTY! IT MAKES A GRE
FOUNDATION! NOW WE
GET TO WORK ON TH
REAL ADDITION!

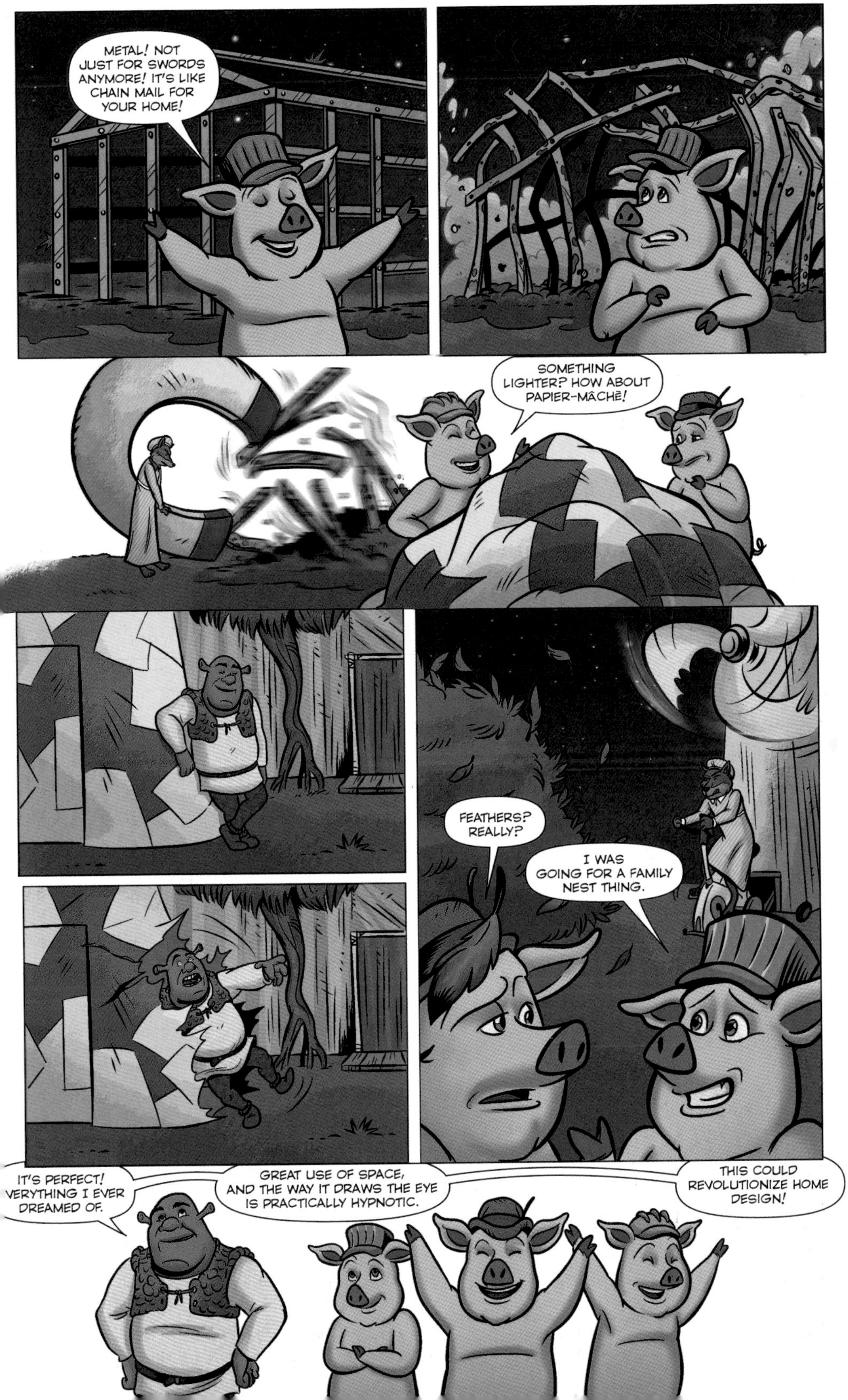
METAL! NOT JUST FOR SWORDS ANYMORE! IT'S LIKE CHAIN MAIL FOR YOUR HOME!
SOMETHING LIGHTER? HOW ABOUT PAPIER-MÂCHÉ!
FEATHERS? REALLY?
I WAS GOING FOR A FAMILY NEST THING.
IT'S PERFECT! VERYTHING I EVER DREAMED OF.
GREAT USE OF SPACE, AND THE WAY IT DRAWS THE EYE IS PRACTICALLY HYPNOTIC.
THIS COULD REVOLUTIONIZE HOME DESIGN!

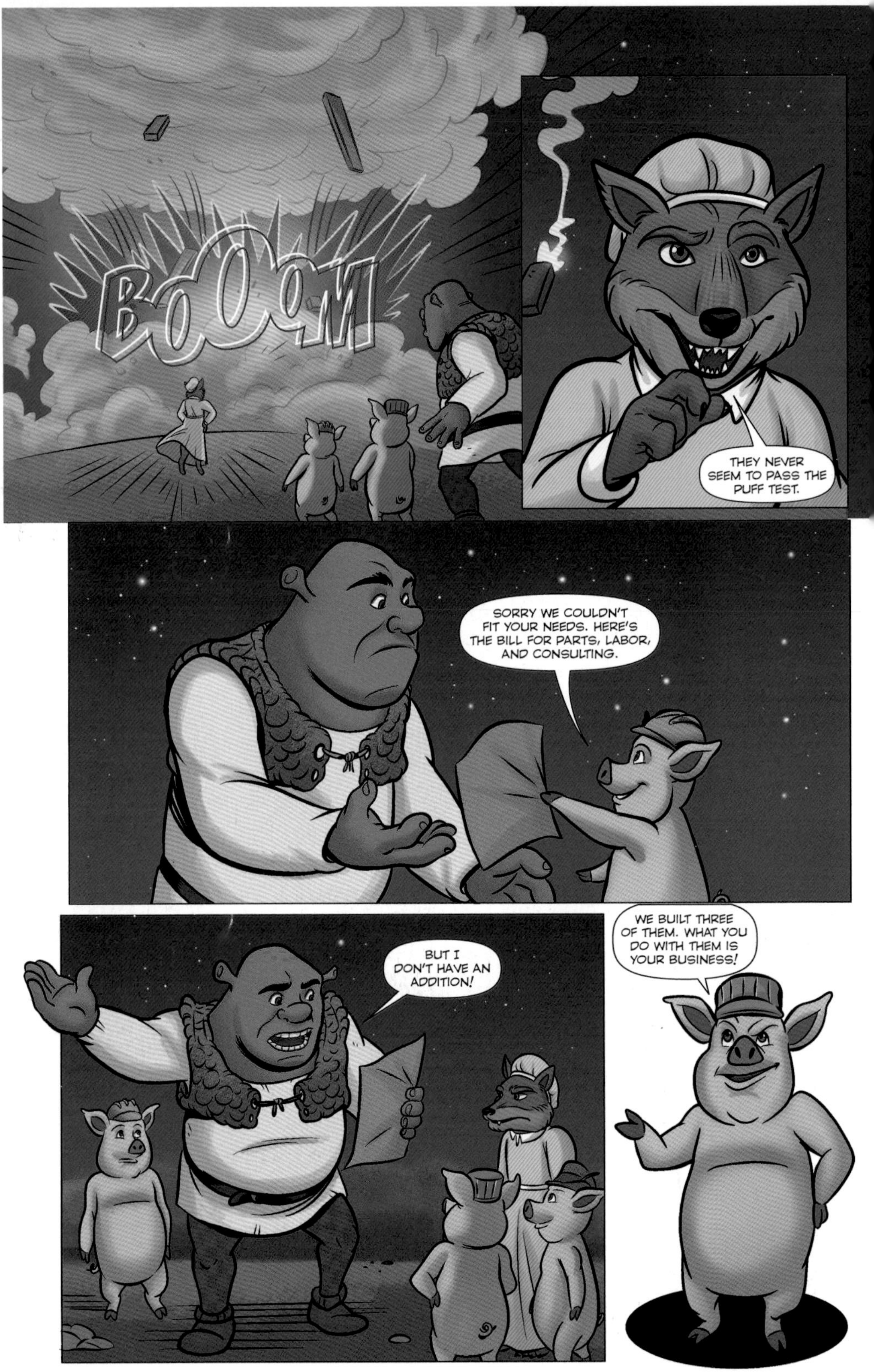
BOOOM
THEY NEVER SEEM TO PASS THE PUFF TEST.
SORRY WE COULDN'T FIT YOUR NEEDS. HERE'S THE BILL FOR PARTS, LABOR, AND CONSULTING.
BUT I DON'T HAVE AN ADDITION!
WE BUILT THREE OF THEM. WHAT YOU DO WITH THEM IS YOUR BUSINESS!

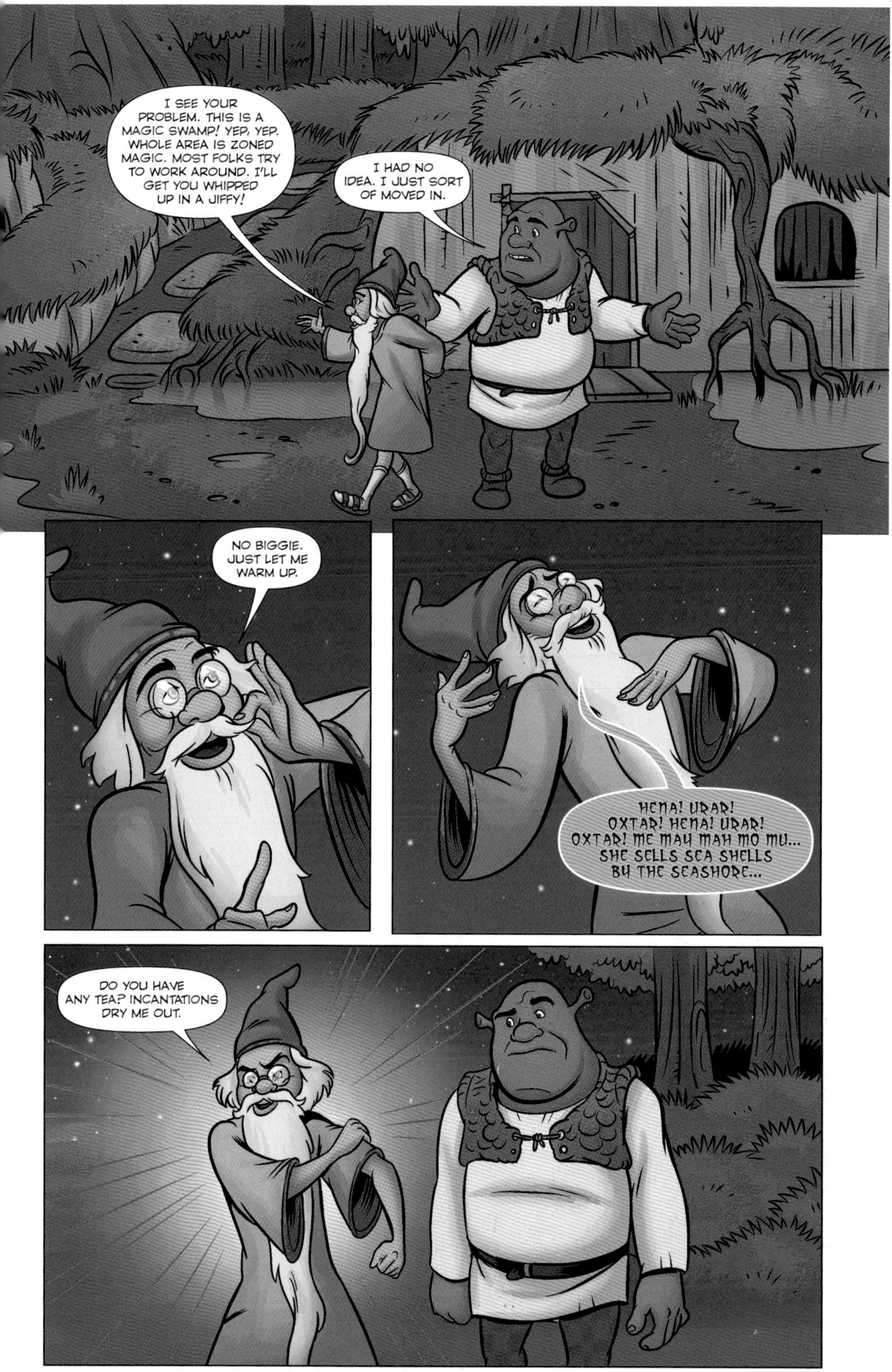
I SEE YOUR PROBLEM. THIS IS A MAGIC SWAMP! YEP, YEP. WHOLE AREA IS ZONED MAGIC. MOST FOLKS TRY TO WORK AROUND. I'LL GET YOU WHIPPED UP IN A JIFFY!
I HAD NO IDEA. I JUST SORT OF MOVED IN.
NO BIGGIE. JUST LET ME WARM UP.
HENA! URAR! OXTAR! HENA! URAR! OXTAR! ME MAY MAH MO MU... SHE SELLS SEA SHELLS BY THE SEASHORE...
DO YOU HAVE ANY TEA? INCANTATIONS DRY ME OUT.

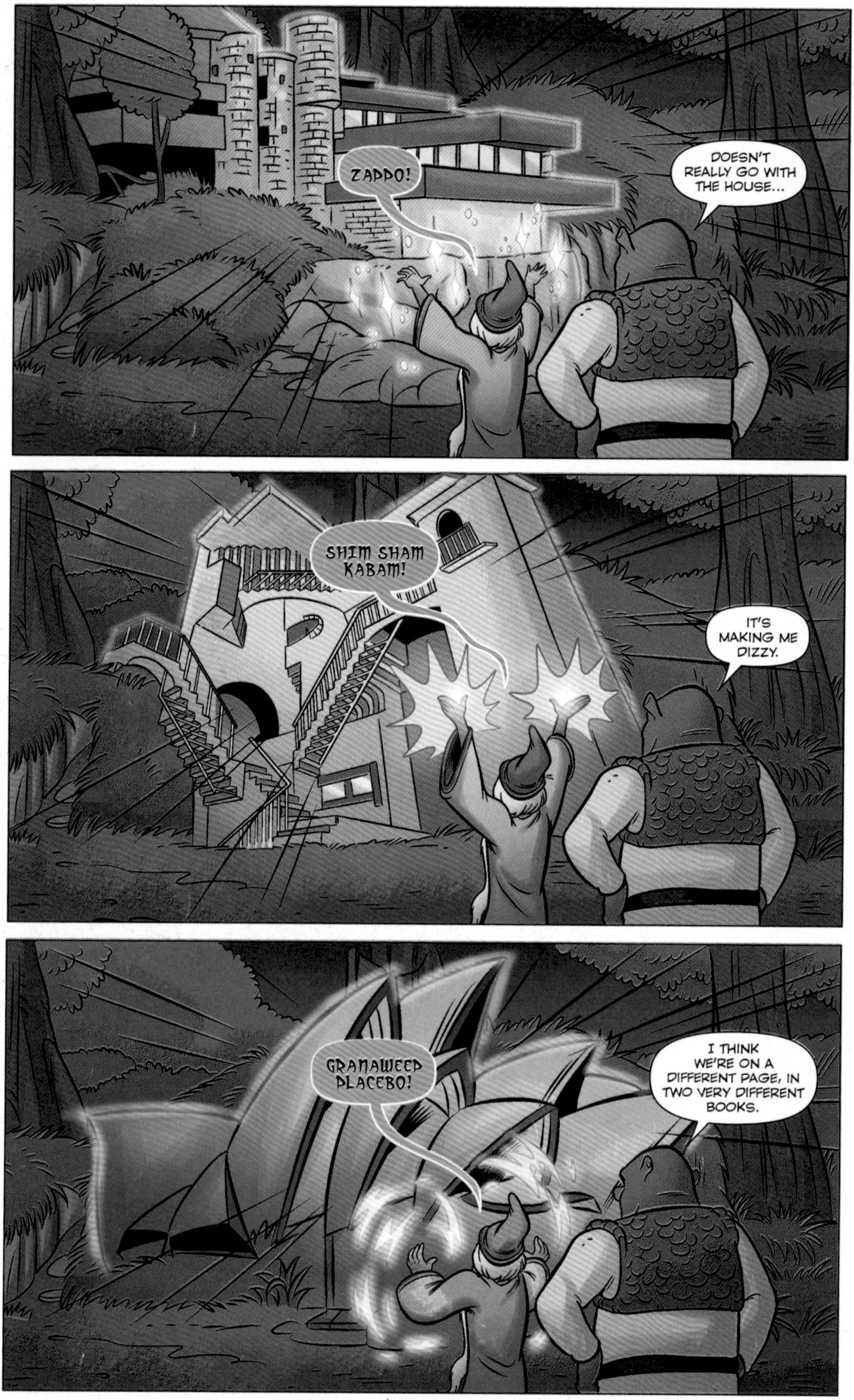
ZAPPO!
DOESN'T REALLY GO WITH THE HOUSE...
SHIM SHAM KABAM!
IT'S MAKING ME DIZZY.
GRANAWEED PLACEBO!
I THINK WE'RE ON A DIFFERENT PAGE, IN TWO VERY DIFFERENT BOOKS.

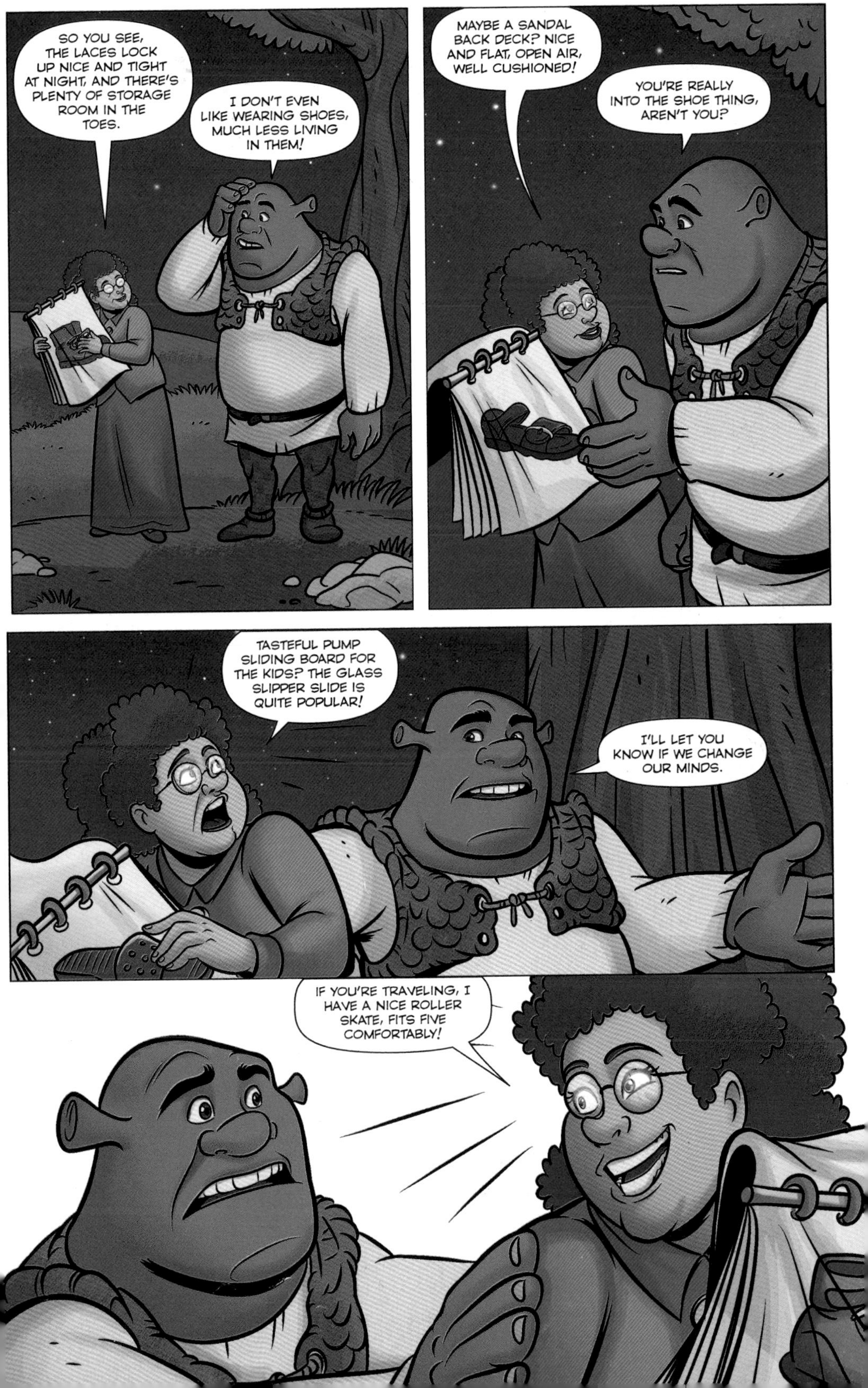
SO YOU SEE, THE LACES LOCK UP NICE AND TIGHT AT NIGHT, AND THERE'S PLENTY OF STORAGE ROOM IN THE TOES.
I DON'T EVEN LIKE WEARING SHOES, MUCH LESS LIVING IN THEM!
MAYBE A SANDAL BACK DECK? NICE AND FLAT, OPEN AIR, WELL CUSHIONED!
YOU'RE REALLY INTO THE SHOE THING, AREN'T YOU?
TASTEFUL PUMP SLIDING BOARD FOR THE KIDS? THE GLASS SLIPPER SLIDE IS QUITE POPULAR!
I'LL LET YOU KNOW IF WE CHANGE OUR MINDS.
IF YOU'RE TRAVELING, I HAVE A NICE ROLLER SKATE, FITS FIVE COMFORTABLY!

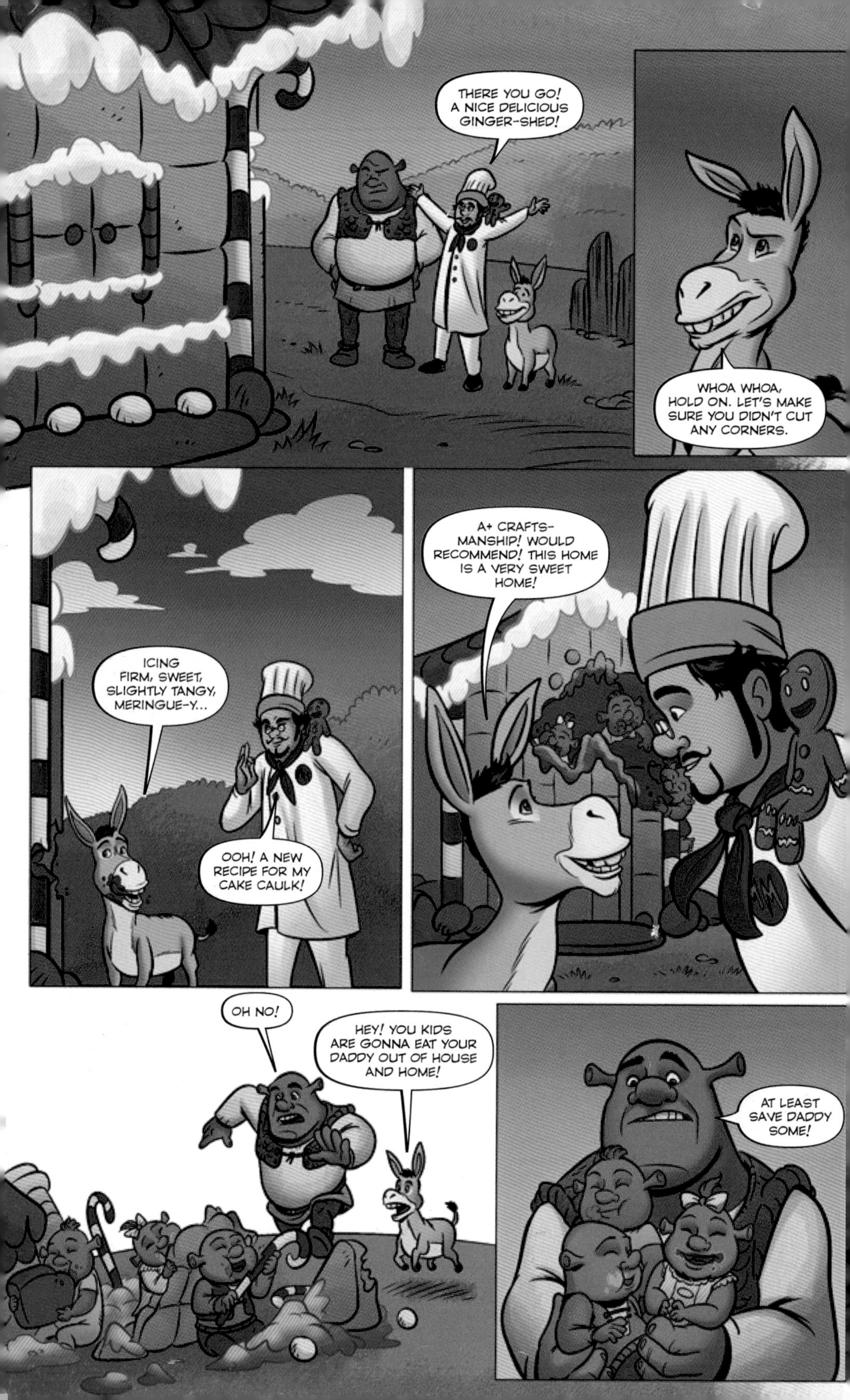

THERE YOU GO! A NICE DELICIOUS GINGER-SHED!
WHOA WHOA, HOLD ON. LET'S MAKE SURE YOU DIDN'T CUT ANY CORNERS.
ICING FIRM, SWEET, SLIGHTLY TANGY, MERINGUE-Y...
OOH! A NEW RECIPE FOR MY CAKE CAULK!
A+ CRAFTS-MANSHIP! WOULD RECOMMEND! THIS HOME IS A VERY SWEET HOME!
OH NO!
HEY! YOU KIDS ARE GONNA EAT YOUR DADDY OUT OF HOUSE AND HOME!
AT LEAST SAVE DADDY SOME!

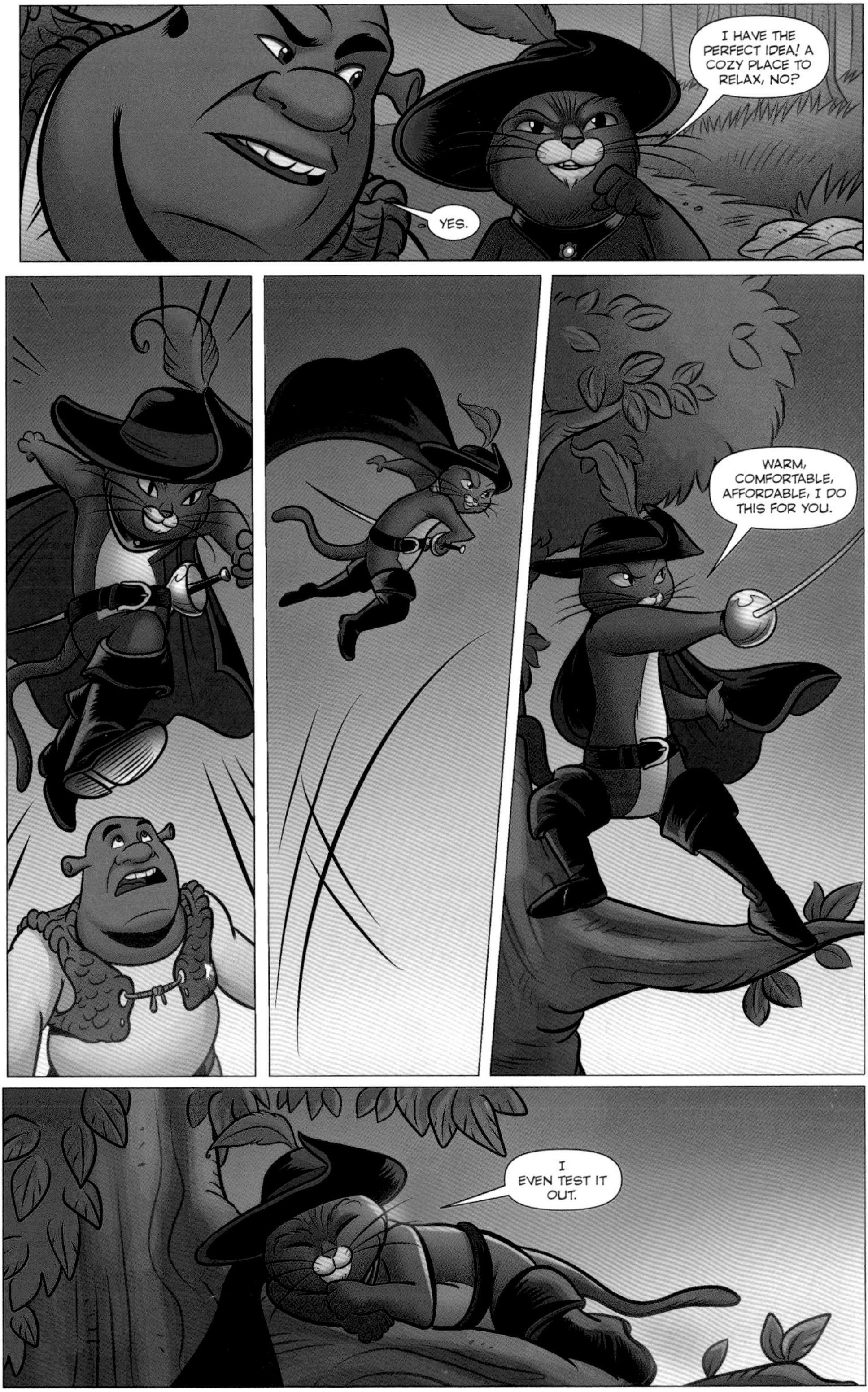
I HAVE THE PERFECT IDEA! A COZY PLACE TO RELAX, NO?
YES.
WARM, COMFORTABLE, AFFORDABLE, I DO THIS FOR YOU.
I EVEN TEST IT OUT.

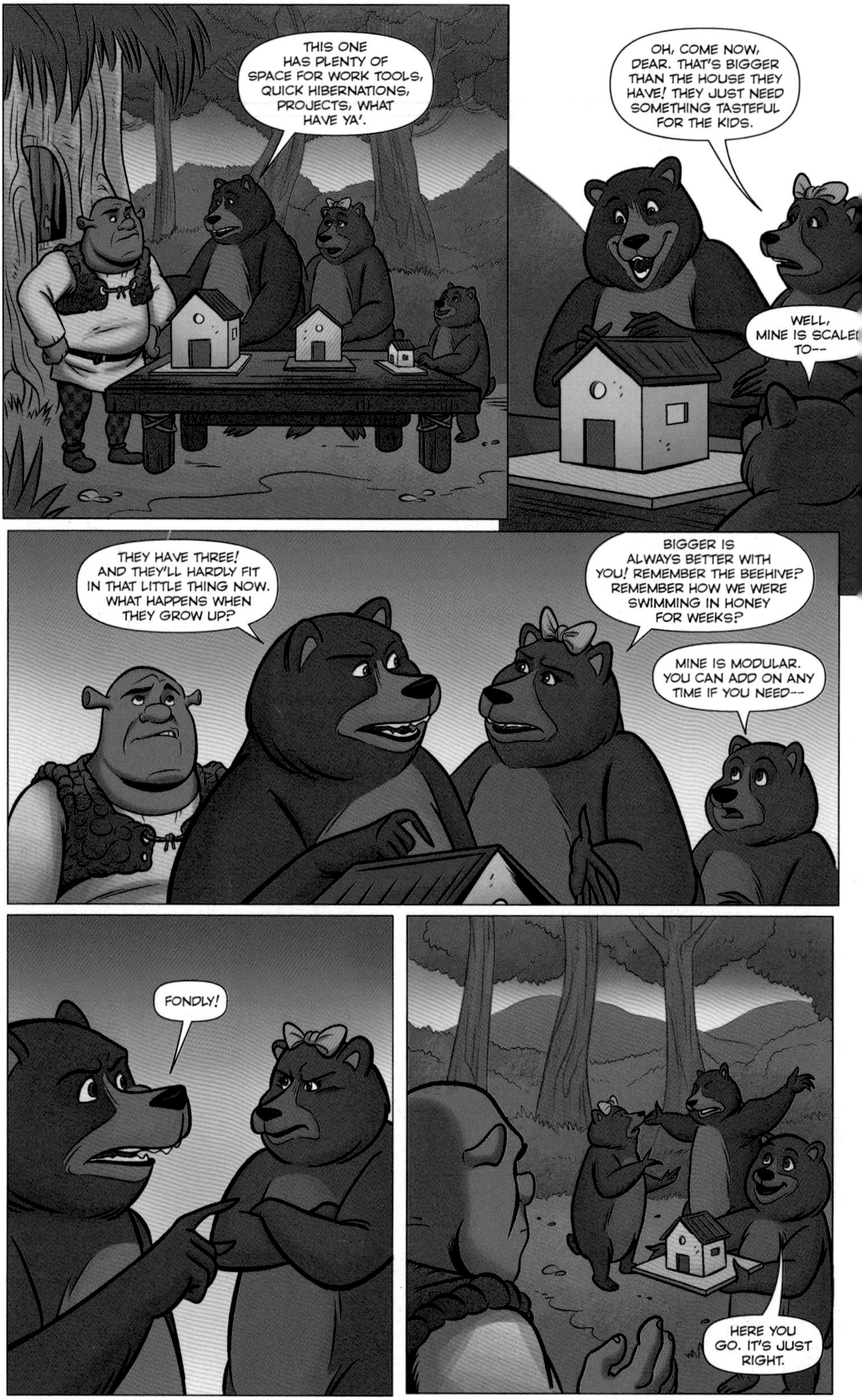
THIS ONE HAS PLENTY OF SPACE FOR WORK TOOLS, QUICK HIBERNATIONS, PROJECTS, WHAT HAVE YA'.
OH, COME NOW, DEAR. THAT'S BIGGER THAN THE HOUSE THEY HAVE! THEY JUST NEED SOMETHING TASTEFUL FOR THE KIDS.
WELL, MINE IS SCALED TO--
THEY HAVE THREE! AND THEY'LL HARDLY FIT IN THAT LITTLE THING NOW. WHAT HAPPENS WHEN THEY GROW UP?
BIGGER IS ALWAYS BETTER WITH YOU! REMEMBER THE BEEHIVE? REMEMBER HOW WE WERE SWIMMING IN HONEY FOR WEEKS?
MINE IS MODULAR. YOU CAN ADD ON ANY TIME IF YOU NEED--
FONDLY!
HERE YOU GO. IT'S JUST RIGHT.

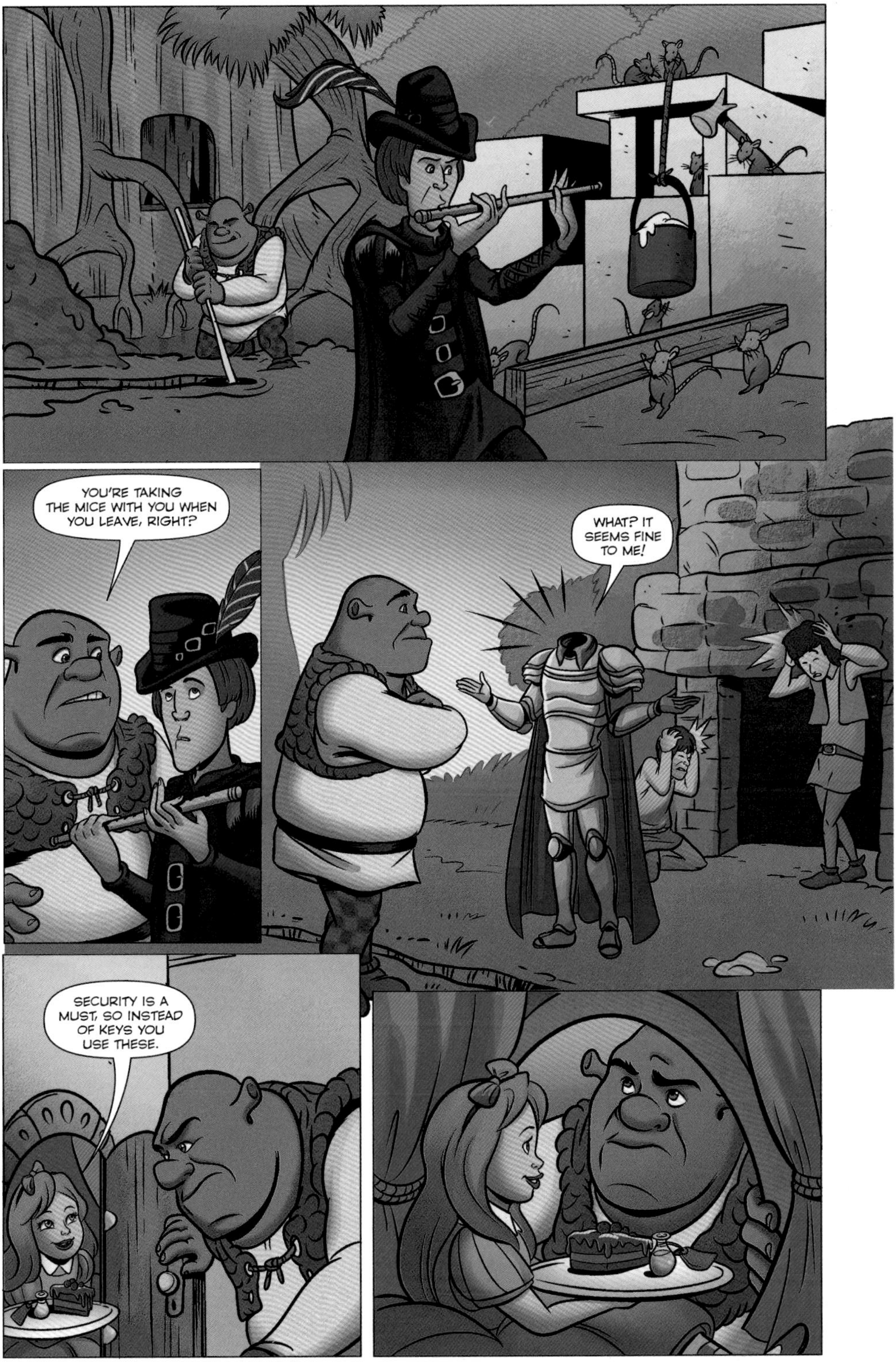
YOU'RE TAKING THE MICE WITH YOU WHEN YOU LEAVE, RIGHT?
WHAT? IT SEEMS FINE TO ME!
SECURITY IS A MUST, SO INSTEAD OF KEYS YOU USE THESE.

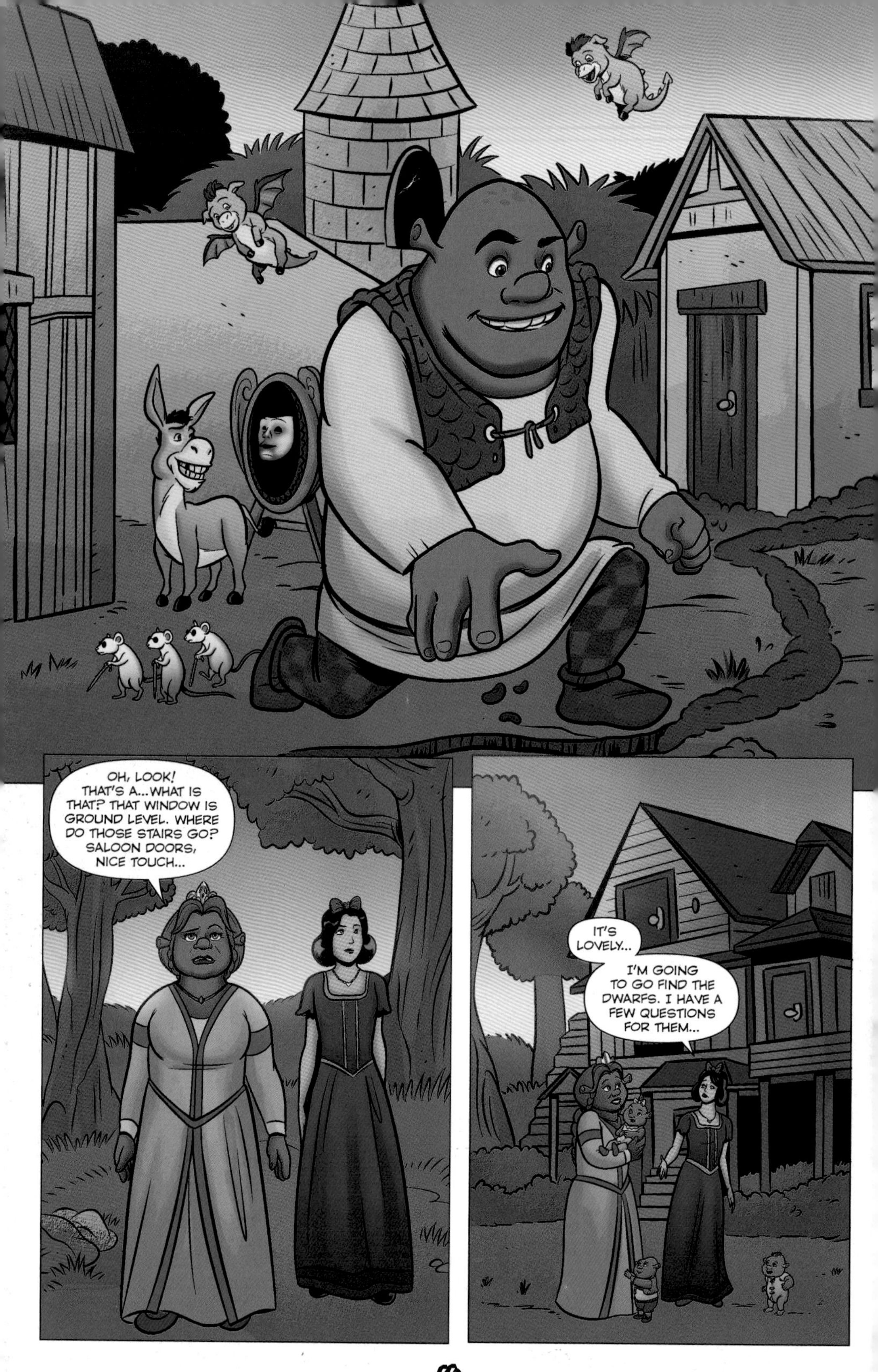
OH, LOOK! THAT'S A...WHAT IS THAT? THAT WINDOW IS GROUND LEVEL. WHERE DO THOSE STAIRS GO? SALOON DOORS, NICE TOUCH...
IT'S LOVELY...
I'M GOING TO GO FIND THE DWARFS. I HAVE A FEW QUESTIONS FOR THEM...

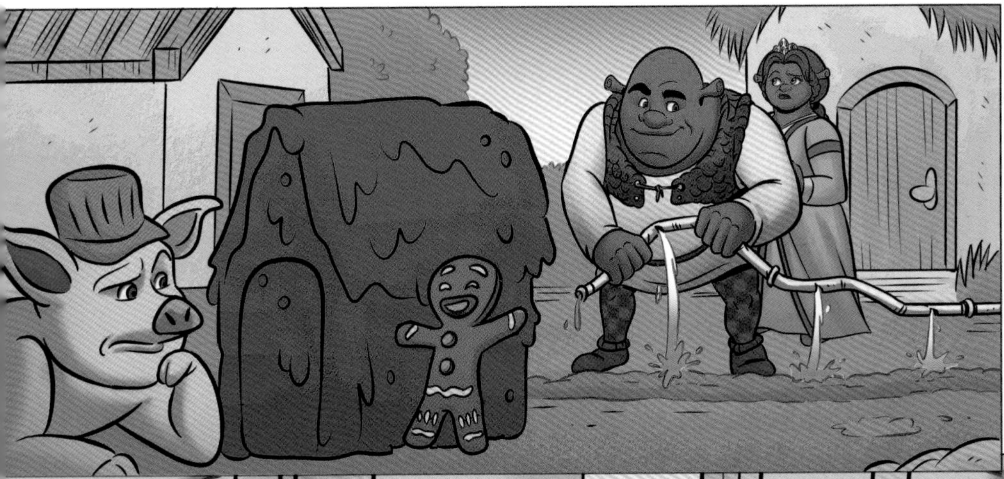

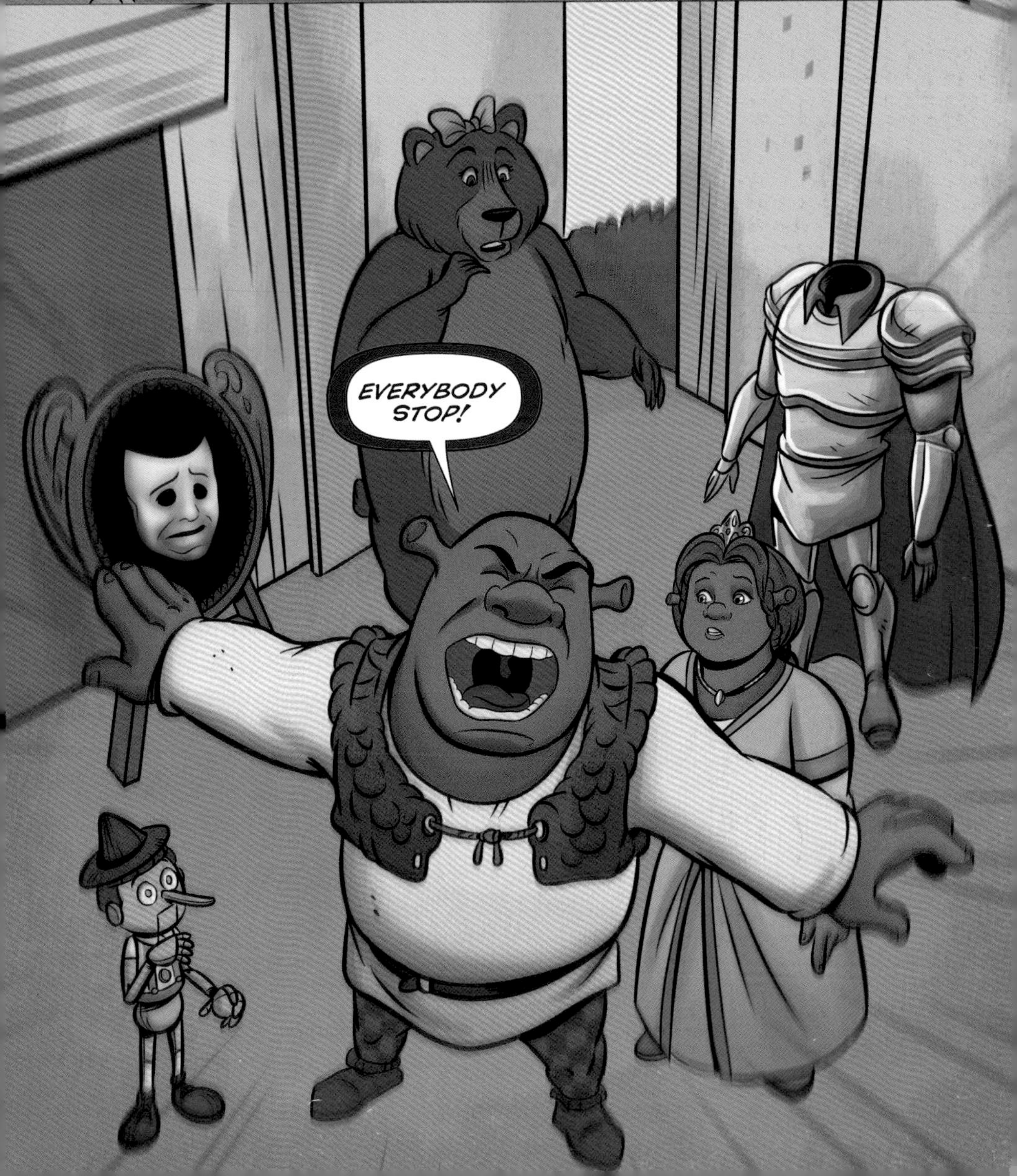
EVERYBODY STOP!

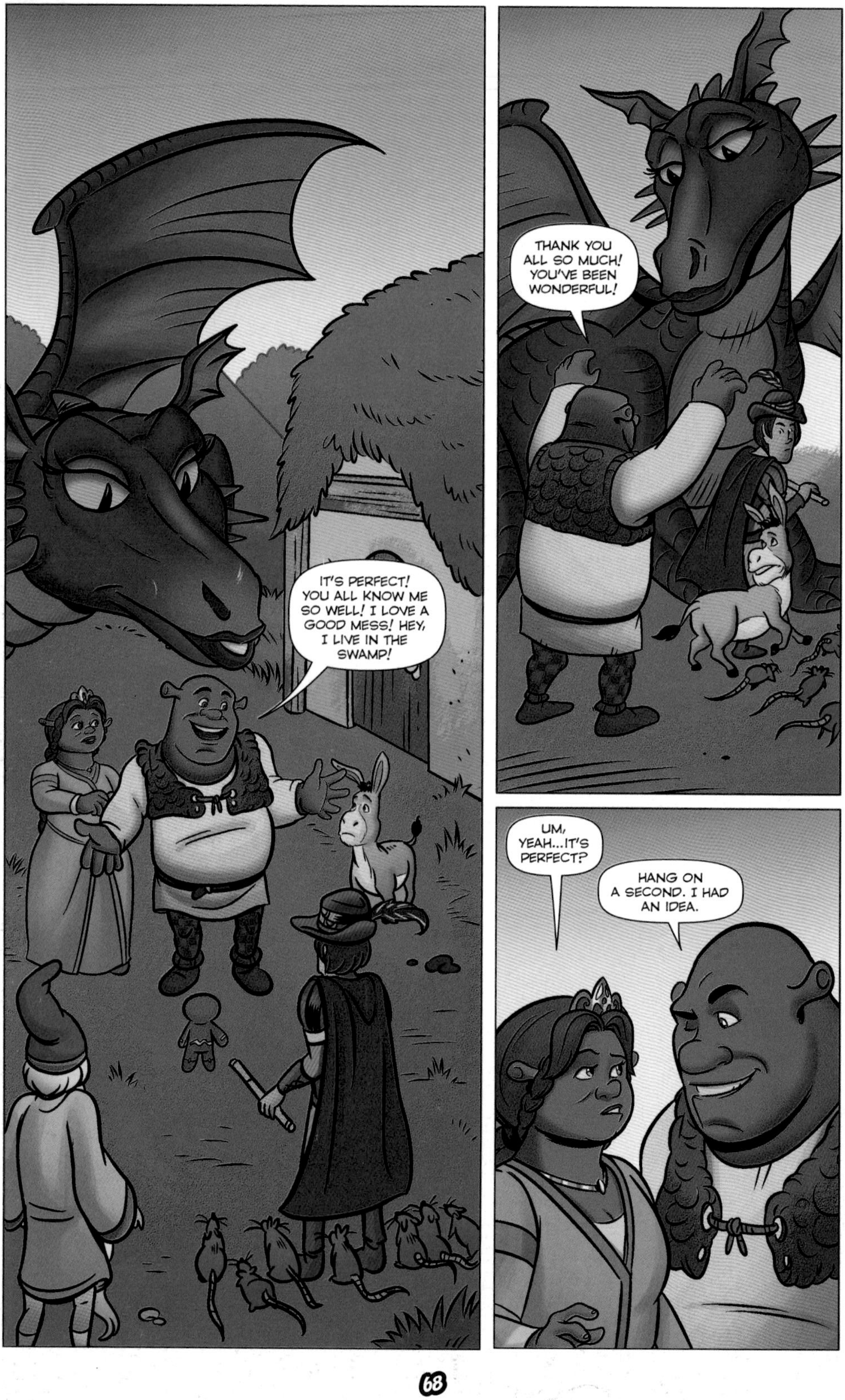
IT'S PERFECT! YOU ALL KNOW ME SO WELL! I LOVE A GOOD MESS! HEY, I LIVE IN THE SWAMP!
THANK YOU ALL SO MUCH! YOU'VE BEEN WONDERFUL!
UM, YEAH...IT'S PERFECT?
HANG ON A SECOND. I HAD AN IDEA.

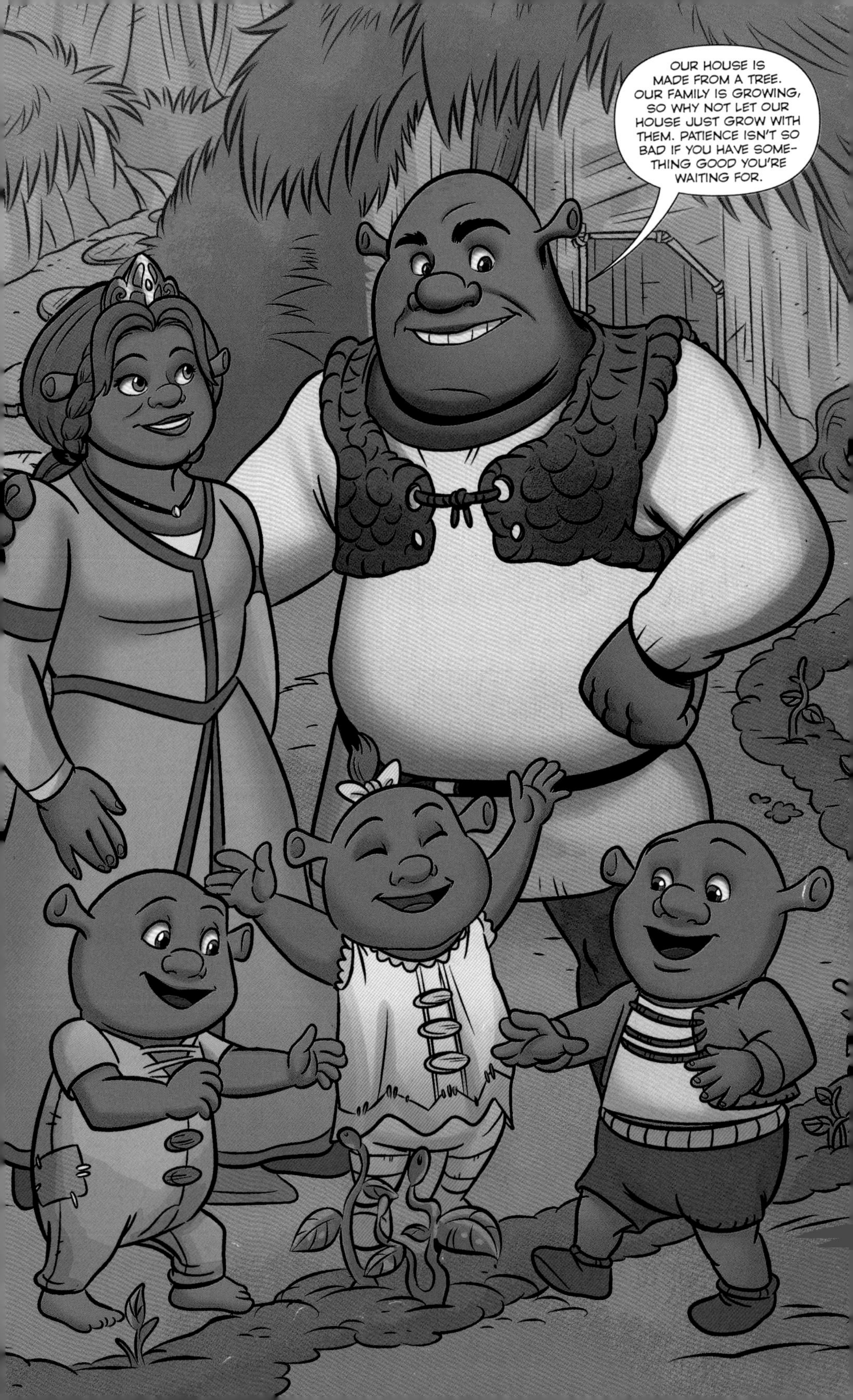
OUR HOUSE IS MADE FROM A TREE. OUR FAMILY IS GROWING, SO WHY NOT LET OUR HOUSE JUST GROW WITH THEM. PATIENCE ISN'T SO BAD IF YOU HAVE SOME-THING GOOD YOU'RE WAITING FOR.

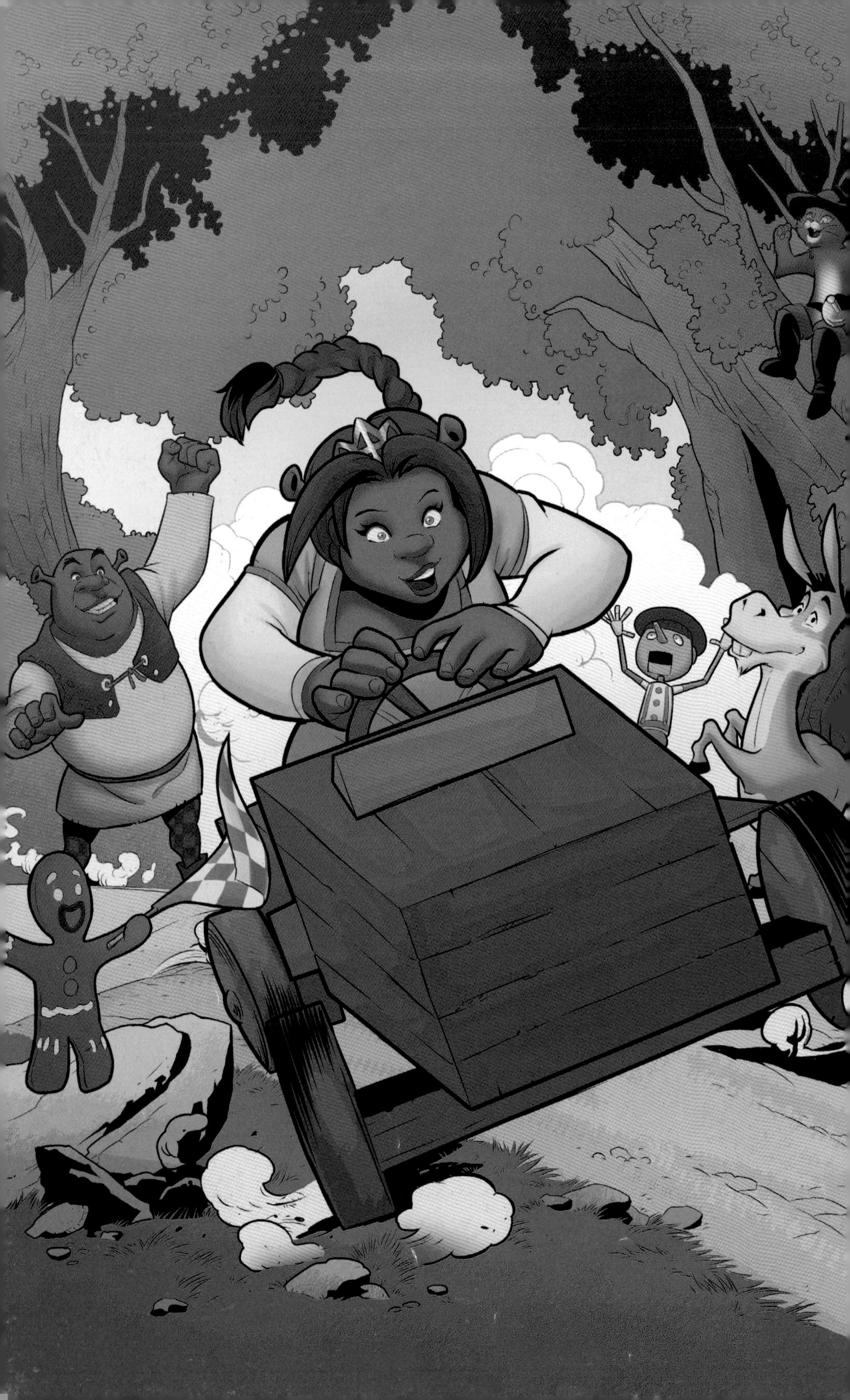

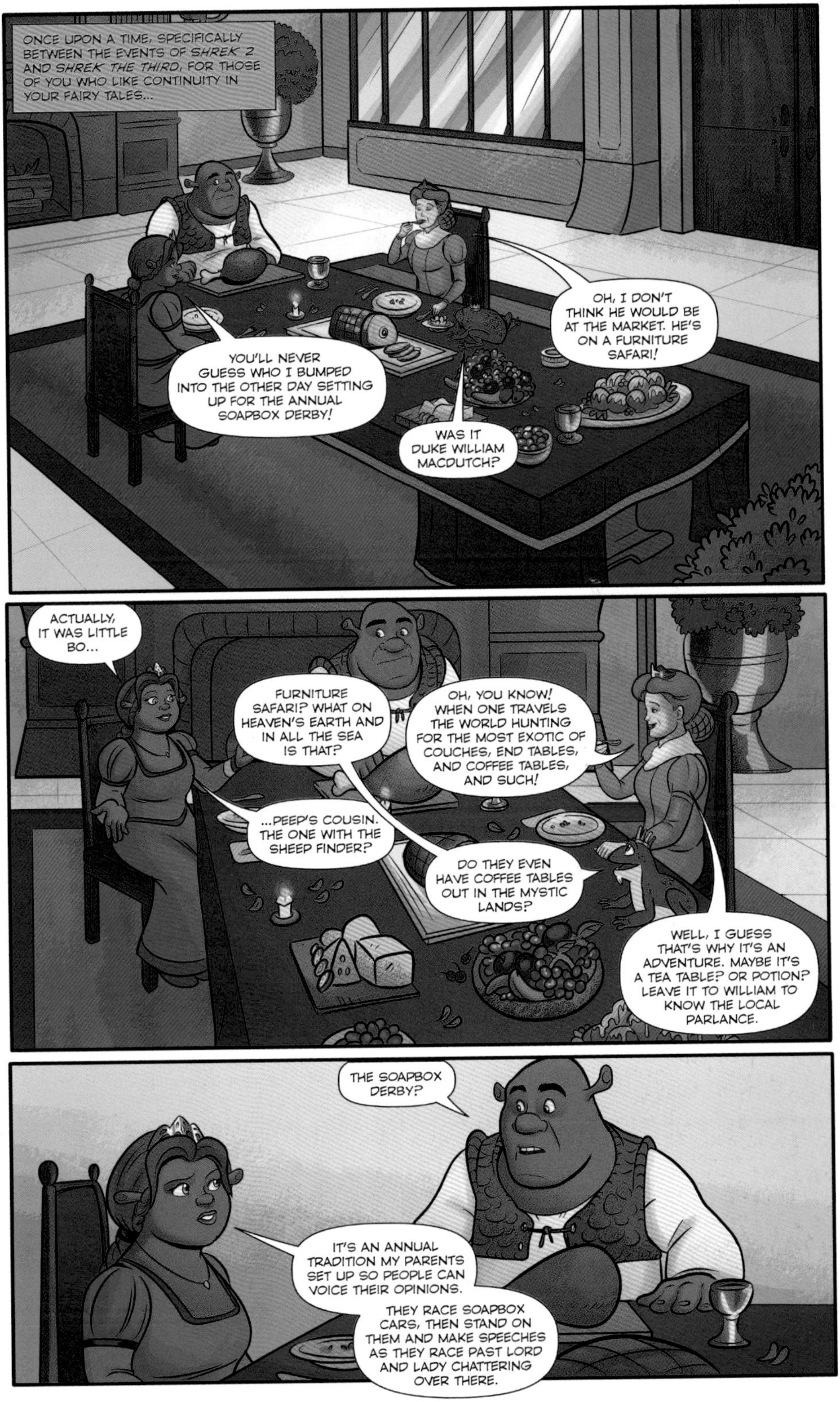
ONCE UPON A TIME, SPECIFICALLY BETWEEN THE EVENTS OF *SHREK 2* AND *SHREK THE THIRD*, FOR THOSE OF YOU WHO LIKE CONTINUITY IN YOUR FAIRY TALES...
YOU'LL NEVER GUESS WHO I BUMPED INTO THE OTHER DAY SETTING UP FOR THE ANNUAL SOAPBOX DERBY!
WAS IT DUKE WILLIAM MACDUTCH?
OH, I DON'T THINK HE WOULD BE AT THE MARKET. HE'S ON A FURNITURE SAFARI!
ACTUALLY, IT WAS LITTLE BO...
...PEEP'S COUSIN. THE ONE WITH THE SHEEP FINDER?
FURNITURE SAFARI? WHAT ON HEAVEN'S EARTH AND IN ALL THE SEA IS THAT?
OH, YOU KNOW! WHEN ONE TRAVELS THE WORLD HUNTING FOR THE MOST EXOTIC OF COUCHES, END TABLES, AND COFFEE TABLES, AND SUCH!
DO THEY EVEN HAVE COFFEE TABLES OUT IN THE MYSTIC LANDS?
WELL, I GUESS THAT'S WHY IT'S AN ADVENTURE. MAYBE IT'S A TEA TABLE? OR POTION? LEAVE IT TO WILLIAM TO KNOW THE LOCAL PARLANCE.
THE SOAPBOX DERBY?
IT'S AN ANNUAL TRADITION MY PARENTS SET UP SO PEOPLE CAN VOICE THEIR OPINIONS.
THEY RACE SOAPBOX CARS, THEN STAND ON THEM AND MAKE SPEECHES AS THEY RACE PAST LORD AND LADY CHATTERING OVER THERE.

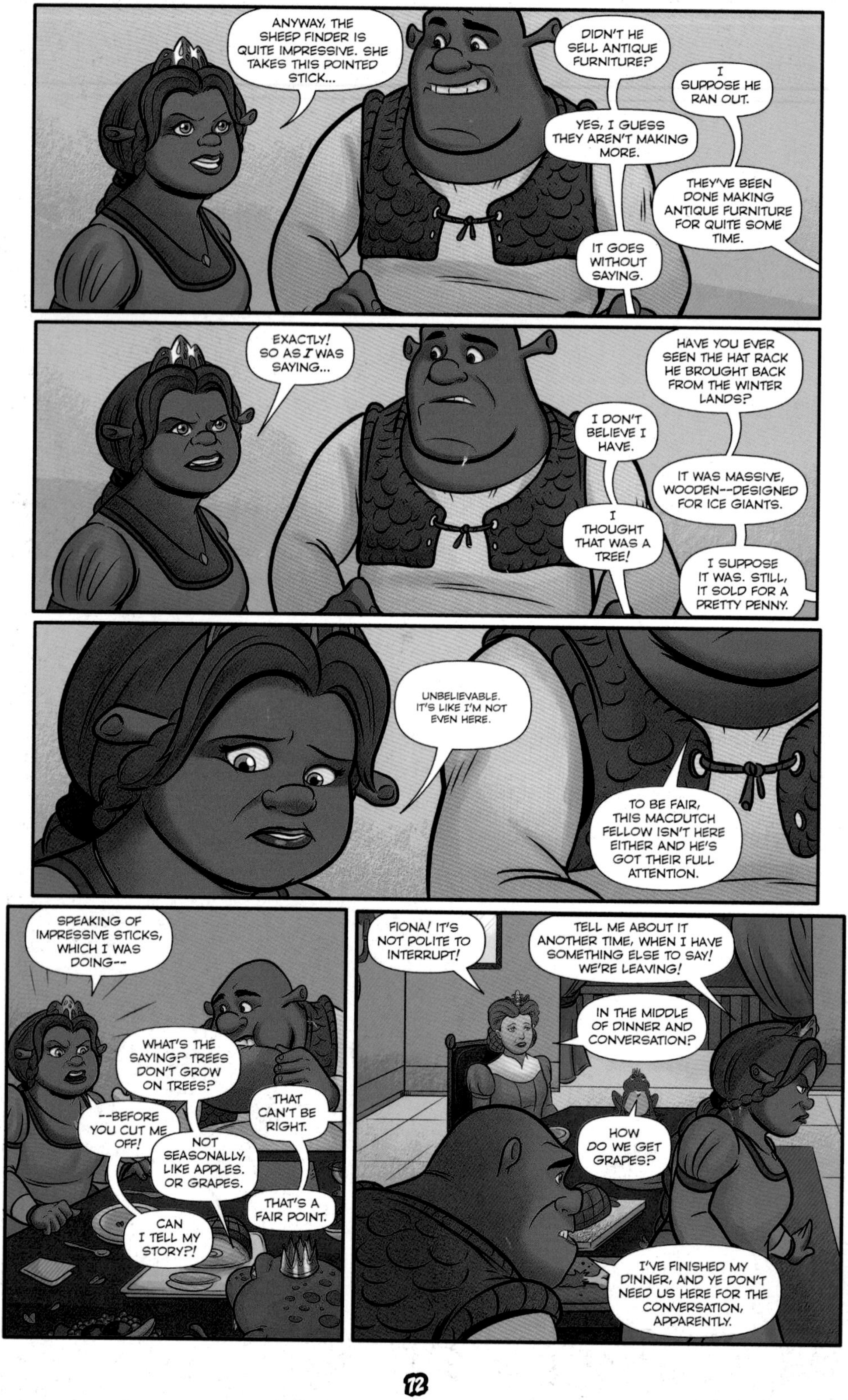
ANYWAY, THE SHEEP FINDER IS QUITE IMPRESSIVE. SHE TAKES THIS POINTED STICK...
DIDN'T HE SELL ANTIQUE FURNITURE?
I SUPPOSE HE RAN OUT.
YES, I GUESS THEY AREN'T MAKING MORE.
THEY'VE BEEN DONE MAKING ANTIQUE FURNITURE FOR QUITE SOME TIME.
IT GOES WITHOUT SAYING.
EXACTLY! SO AS I WAS SAYING...
HAVE YOU EVER SEEN THE HAT RACK HE BROUGHT BACK FROM THE WINTER LANDS?
I DON'T BELIEVE I HAVE.
IT WAS MASSIVE, WOODEN--DESIGNED FOR ICE GIANTS.
I THOUGHT THAT WAS A TREE!
I SUPPOSE IT WAS. STILL, IT SOLD FOR A PRETTY PENNY.
UNBELIEVABLE. IT'S LIKE I'M NOT EVEN HERE.
TO BE FAIR, THIS MACDUTCH FELLOW ISN'T HERE EITHER AND HE'S GOT THEIR FULL ATTENTION.
SPEAKING OF IMPRESSIVE STICKS, WHICH I WAS DOING--
WHAT'S THE SAYING? TREES DON'T GROW ON TREES?
--BEFORE YOU CUT ME OFF!
THAT CAN'T BE RIGHT.
NOT SEASONALLY, LIKE APPLES. OR GRAPES.
THAT'S A FAIR POINT.
CAN I TELL MY STORY?!
FIONA! IT'S NOT POLITE TO INTERRUPT!
TELL ME ABOUT IT ANOTHER TIME, WHEN I HAVE SOMETHING ELSE TO SAY! WE'RE LEAVING!
IN THE MIDDLE OF DINNER AND CONVERSATION?
HOW DO WE GET GRAPES?
I'VE FINISHED MY DINNER, AND YE DON'T NEED US HERE FOR THE CONVERSATION, APPARENTLY.

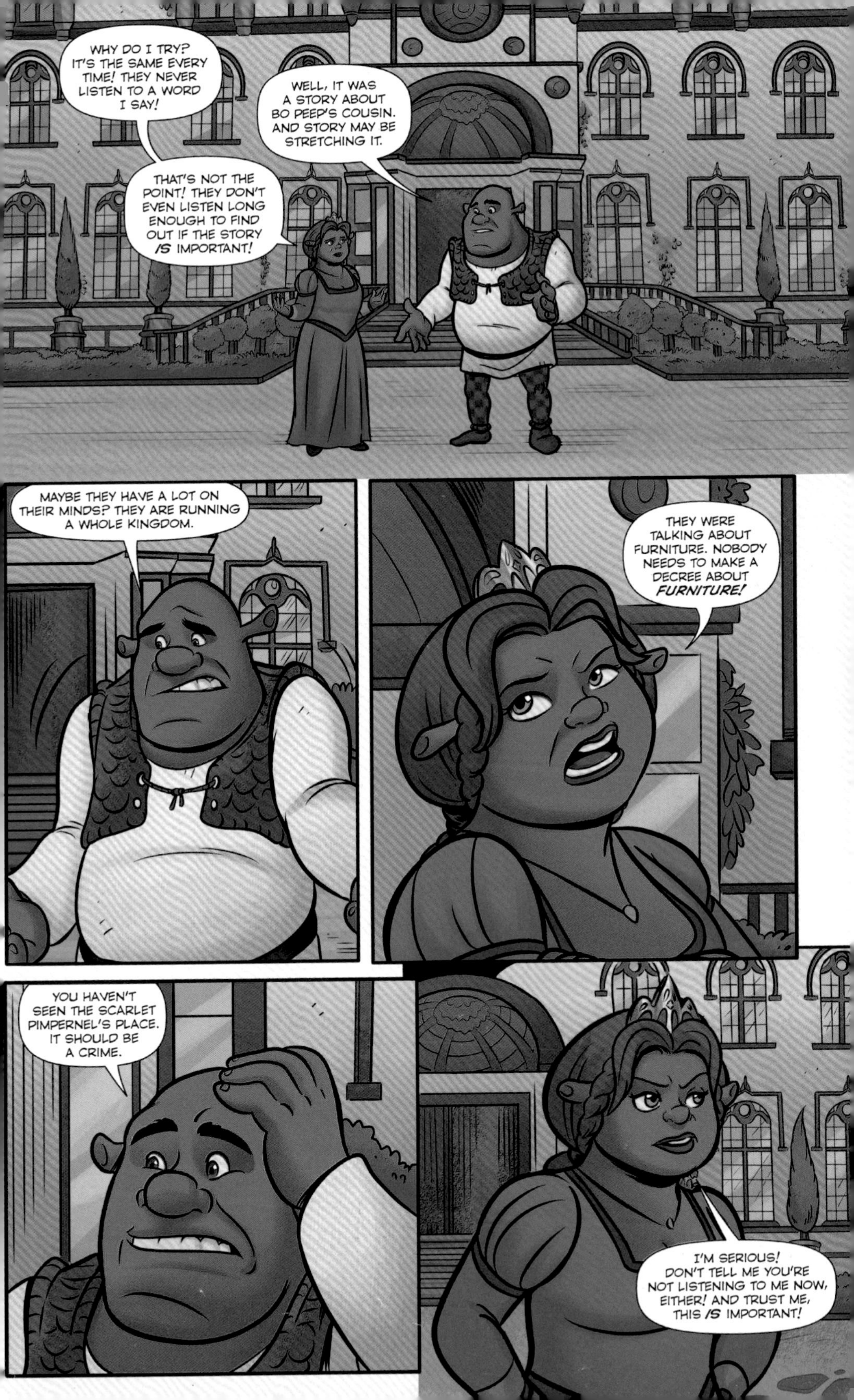
WHY DO I TRY? IT'S THE SAME EVERY TIME! THEY NEVER LISTEN TO A WORD I SAY!
WELL, IT WAS A STORY ABOUT BO PEEP'S COUSIN. AND STORY MAY BE STRETCHING IT.
THAT'S NOT THE POINT! THEY DON'T EVEN LISTEN LONG ENOUGH TO FIND OUT IF THE STORY *IS* IMPORTANT!
MAYBE THEY HAVE A LOT ON THEIR MINDS? THEY ARE RUNNING A WHOLE KINGDOM.
THEY WERE TALKING ABOUT FURNITURE. NOBODY NEEDS TO MAKE A DECREE ABOUT *FURNITURE!*
YOU HAVEN'T SEEN THE SCARLET PIMPERNEL'S PLACE. IT SHOULD BE A CRIME.
I'M SERIOUS! DON'T TELL ME YOU'RE NOT LISTENING TO ME NOW, EITHER! AND TRUST ME, THIS *IS* IMPORTANT!

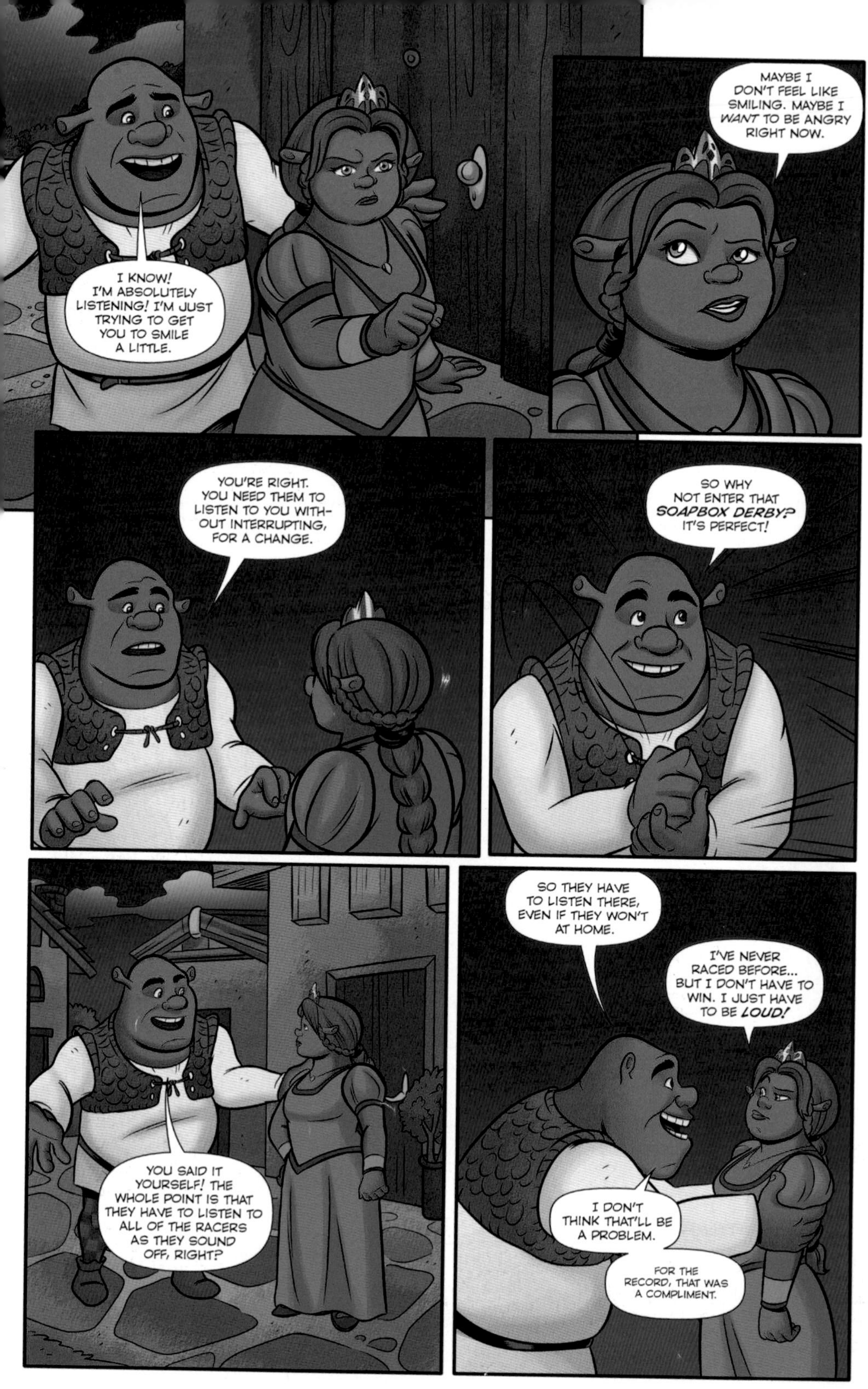
I KNOW! I'M ABSOLUTELY LISTENING! I'M JUST TRYING TO GET YOU TO SMILE A LITTLE.
MAYBE I DON'T FEEL LIKE SMILING. MAYBE I WANT TO BE ANGRY RIGHT NOW.
YOU'RE RIGHT. YOU NEED THEM TO LISTEN TO YOU WITH-OUT INTERRUPTING, FOR A CHANGE.
SO WHY NOT ENTER THAT SOAPBOX DERBY? IT'S PERFECT!
YOU SAID IT YOURSELF! THE WHOLE POINT IS THAT THEY HAVE TO LISTEN TO ALL OF THE RACERS AS THEY SOUND OFF, RIGHT?
SO THEY HAVE TO LISTEN THERE, EVEN IF THEY WON'T AT HOME.
I'VE NEVER RACED BEFORE... BUT I DON'T HAVE TO WIN. I JUST HAVE TO BE LOUD!
I DON'T THINK THAT'LL BE A PROBLEM.
FOR THE RECORD, THAT WAS A COMPLIMENT.

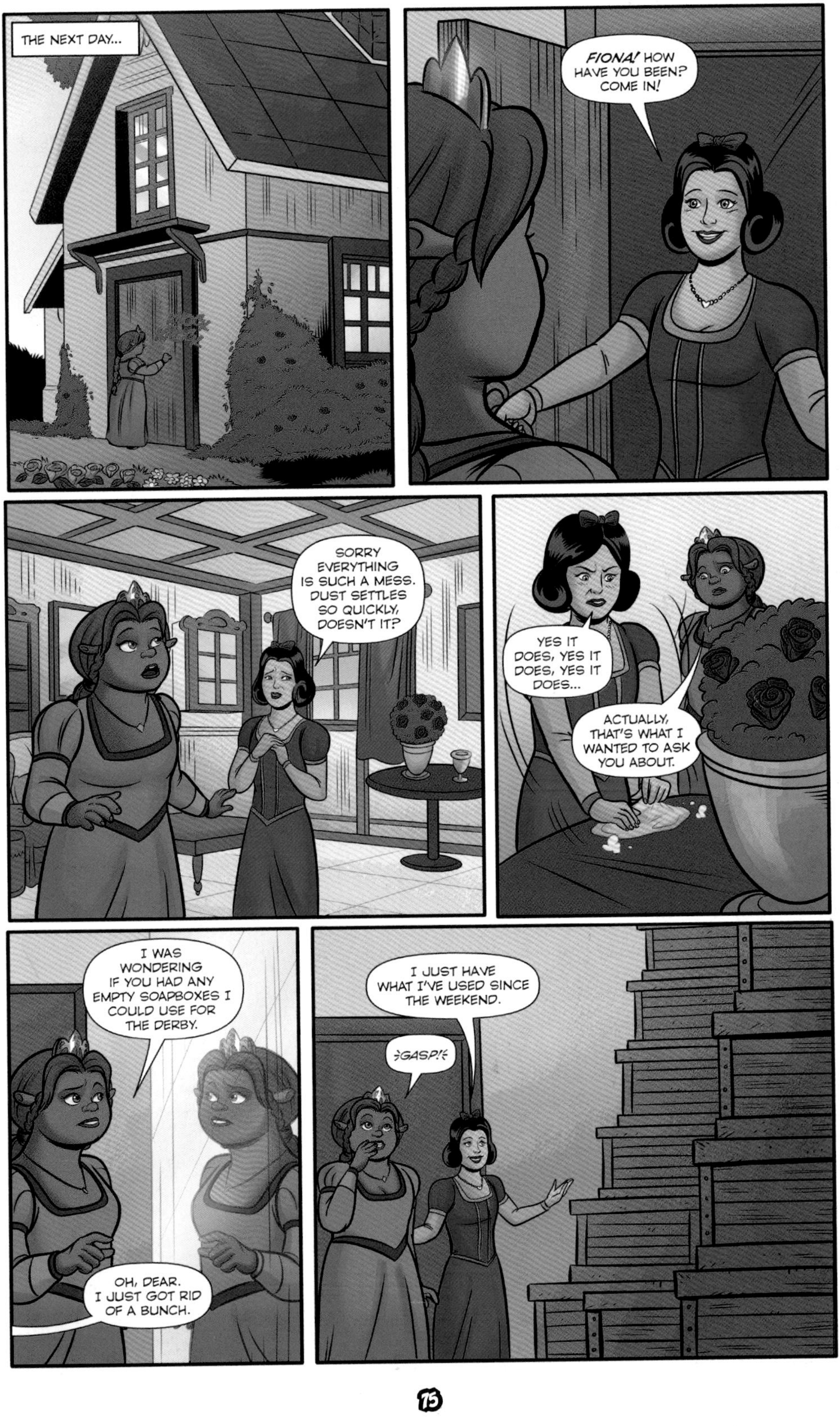
THE NEXT DAY...
FIONA! HOW HAVE YOU BEEN? COME IN!
SORRY EVERYTHING IS SUCH A MESS. DUST SETTLES SO QUICKLY, DOESN'T IT?
YES IT DOES, YES IT DOES, YES IT DOES...
ACTUALLY, THAT'S WHAT I WANTED TO ASK YOU ABOUT.
I WAS WONDERING IF YOU HAD ANY EMPTY SOAPBOXES I COULD USE FOR THE DERBY.
OH, DEAR. I JUST GOT RID OF A BUNCH.
I JUST HAVE WHAT I'VE USED SINCE THE WEEKEND.
GASP!

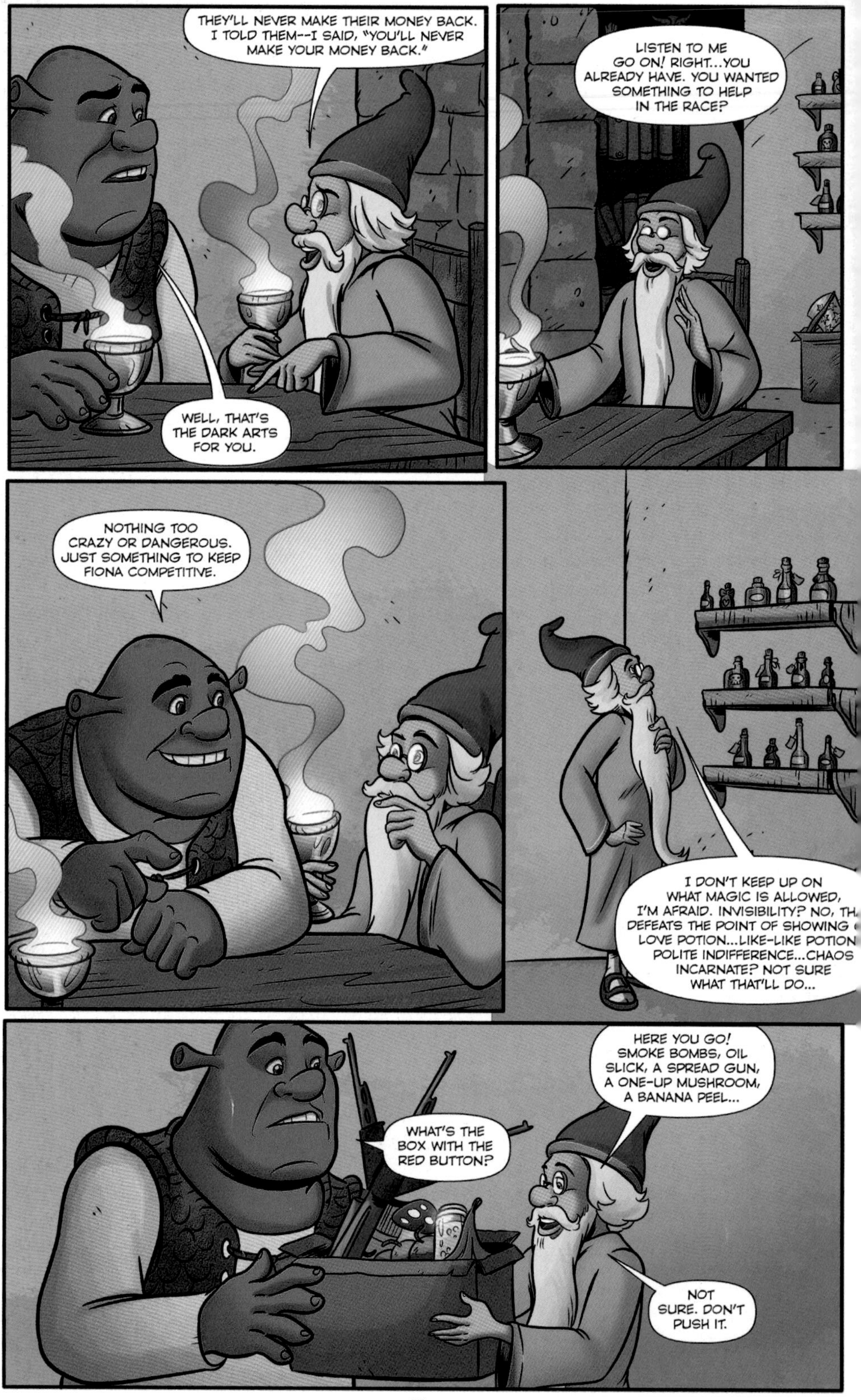
THEY'LL NEVER MAKE THEIR MONEY BACK. I TOLD THEM--I SAID, "YOU'LL NEVER MAKE YOUR MONEY BACK."
WELL, THAT'S THE DARK ARTS FOR YOU.
LISTEN TO ME GO ON! RIGHT...YOU ALREADY HAVE. YOU WANTED SOMETHING TO HELP IN THE RACE?
NOTHING TOO CRAZY OR DANGEROUS. JUST SOMETHING TO KEEP FIONA COMPETITIVE.
I DON'T KEEP UP ON WHAT MAGIC IS ALLOWED, I'M AFRAID. INVISIBILITY? NO, TH
DEFEATS THE POINT OF SHOWING
LOVE POTION...LIKE-LIKE POTION
POLITE INDIFFERENCE...CHAOS INCARNATE? NOT SURE WHAT THAT'LL DO...
HERE YOU GO! SMOKE BOMBS, OIL SLICK, A SPREAD GUN, A ONE-UP MUSHROOM, A BANANA PEEL...
WHAT'S THE BOX WITH THE RED BUTTON?
NOT SURE. DON'T PUSH IT.

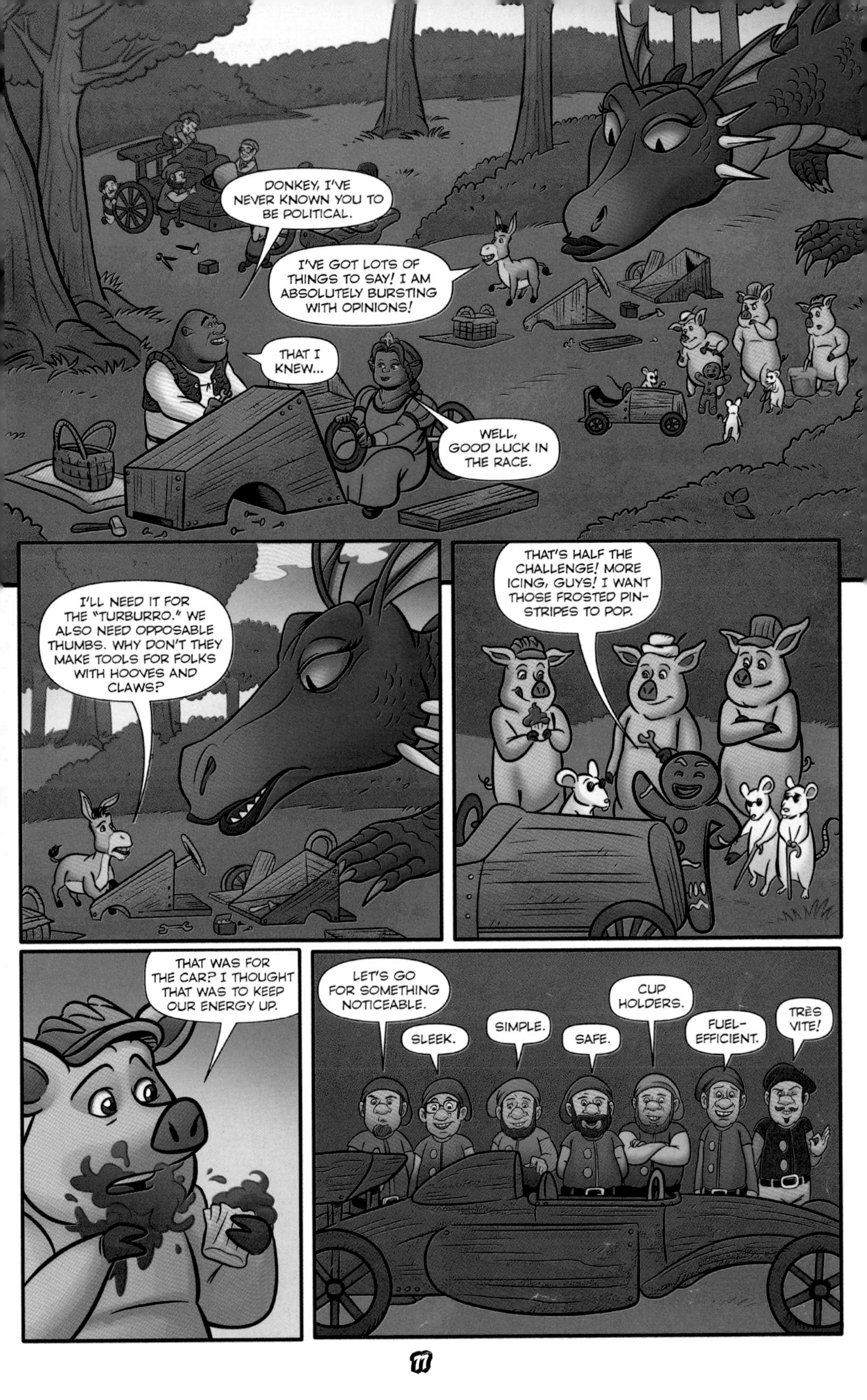
DONKEY, I'VE NEVER KNOWN YOU TO BE POLITICAL.
I'VE GOT LOTS OF THINGS TO SAY! I AM ABSOLUTELY BURSTING WITH OPINIONS!
THAT I KNEW...
WELL, GOOD LUCK IN THE RACE.
I'LL NEED IT FOR THE "TURBURRO." WE ALSO NEED OPPOSABLE THUMBS. WHY DON'T THEY MAKE TOOLS FOR FOLKS WITH HOOVES AND CLAWS?
THAT'S HALF THE CHALLENGE! MORE ICING, GUYS! I WANT THOSE FROSTED PIN-STRIPES TO POP.
THAT WAS FOR THE CAR? I THOUGHT THAT WAS TO KEEP OUR ENERGY UP.
LET'S GO FOR SOMETHING NOTICEABLE.
SLEEK.
SIMPLE.
SAFE.
CUP HOLDERS.
FUEL-EFFICIENT.
TRÈS VITE!

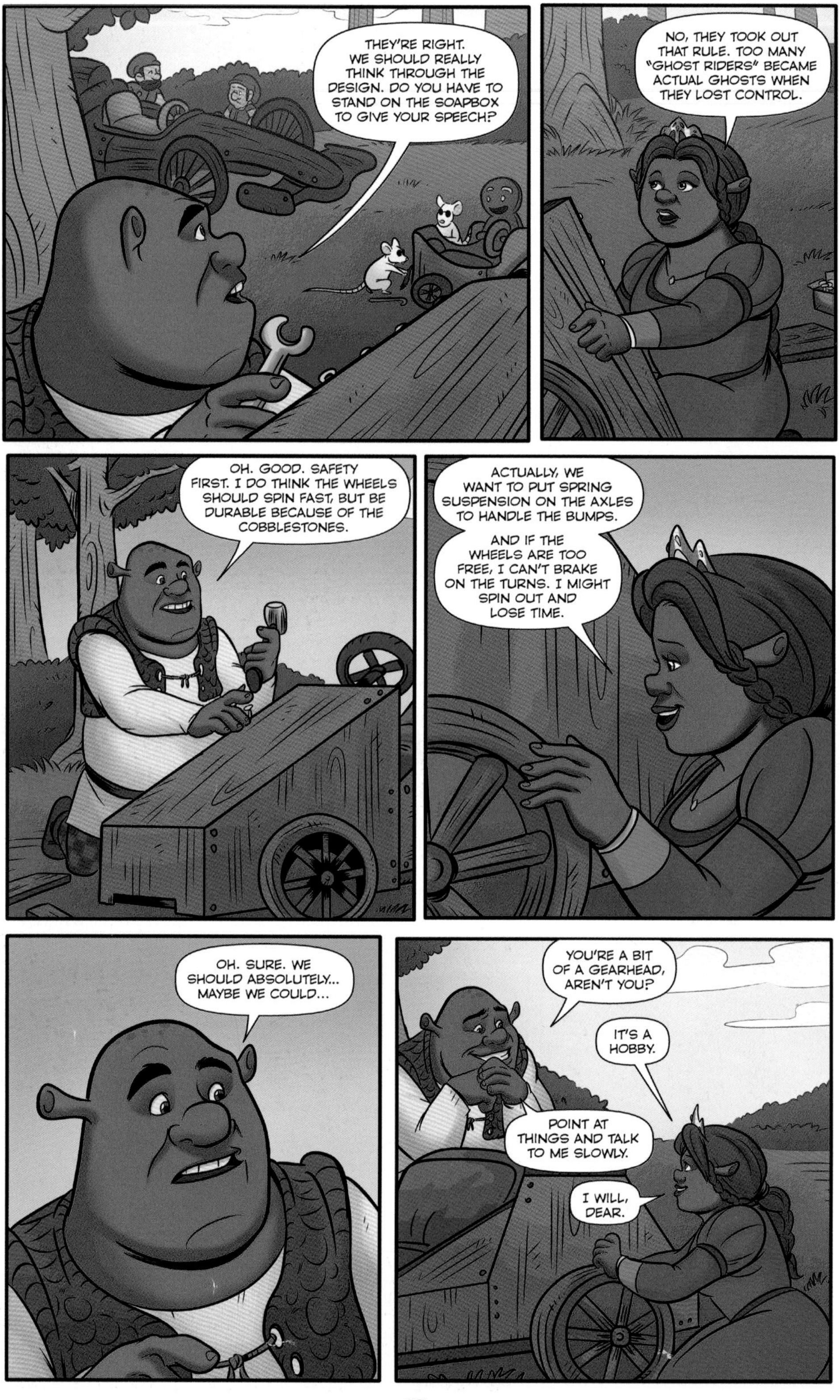
THEY'RE RIGHT. WE SHOULD REALLY THINK THROUGH THE DESIGN. DO YOU HAVE TO STAND ON THE SOAPBOX TO GIVE YOUR SPEECH?
NO, THEY TOOK OUT THAT RULE. TOO MANY "GHOST RIDERS" BECAME ACTUAL GHOSTS WHEN THEY LOST CONTROL.
OH. GOOD. SAFETY FIRST. I DO THINK THE WHEELS SHOULD SPIN FAST, BUT BE DURABLE BECAUSE OF THE COBBLESTONES.
ACTUALLY, WE WANT TO PUT SPRING SUSPENSION ON THE AXLES TO HANDLE THE BUMPS.
AND IF THE WHEELS ARE TOO FREE, I CAN'T BRAKE ON THE TURNS. I MIGHT SPIN OUT AND LOSE TIME.
OH. SURE. WE SHOULD ABSOLUTELY... MAYBE WE COULD...
YOU'RE A BIT OF A GEARHEAD, AREN'T YOU?
IT'S A HOBBY.
POINT AT THINGS AND TALK TO ME SLOWLY.
I WILL, DEAR.

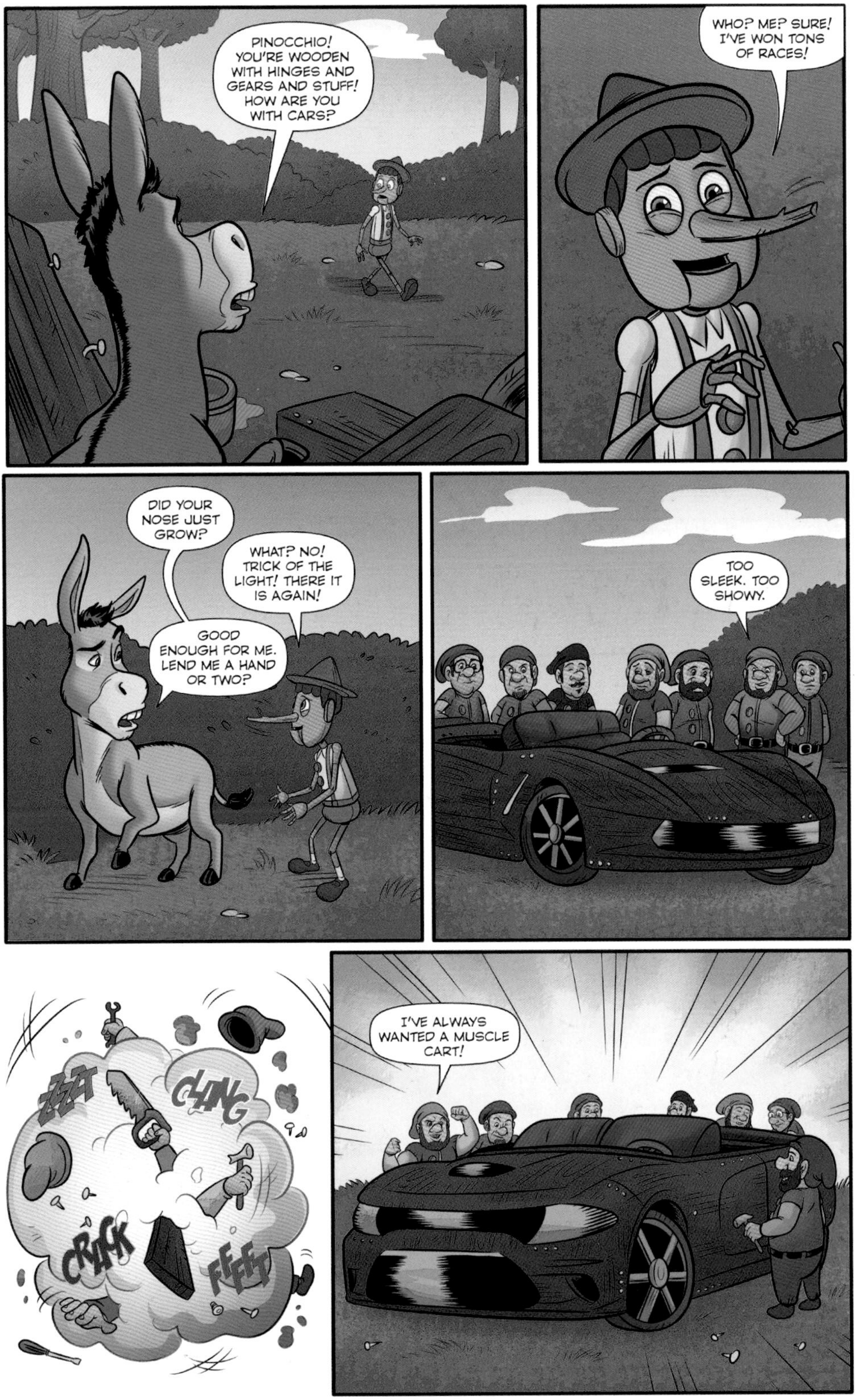
PINOCCHIO! YOU'RE WOODEN WITH HINGES AND GEARS AND STUFF! HOW ARE YOU WITH CARS?
WHO? ME? SURE! I'VE WON TONS OF RACES!
DID YOUR NOSE JUST GROW?
WHAT? NO! TRICK OF THE LIGHT! THERE IT IS AGAIN!
GOOD ENOUGH FOR ME. LEND ME A HAND OR TWO?
TOO SLEEK. TOO SHOWY.
ZZZT
CLANG
CRICK
FFFFT
I'VE ALWAYS WANTED A MUSCLE CART!

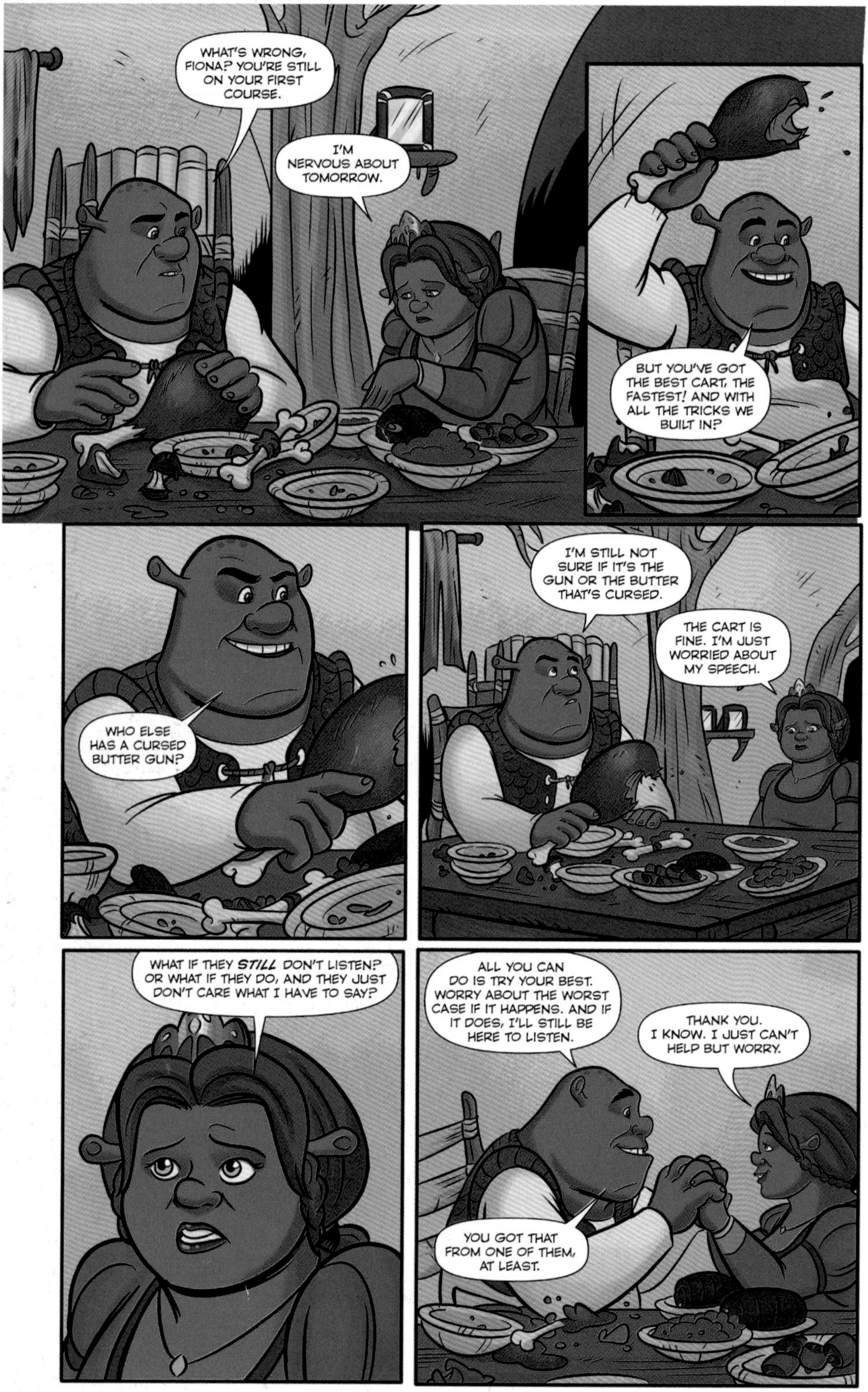
WHAT'S WRONG, FIONA? YOU'RE STILL ON YOUR FIRST COURSE.
I'M NERVOUS ABOUT TOMORROW.
BUT YOU'VE GOT THE BEST CART, THE FASTEST! AND WITH ALL THE TRICKS WE BUILT IN?
WHO ELSE HAS A CURSED BUTTER GUN?
I'M STILL NOT SURE IF IT'S THE GUN OR THE BUTTER THAT'S CURSED.
THE CART IS FINE. I'M JUST WORRIED ABOUT MY SPEECH.
WHAT IF THEY *STILL* DON'T LISTEN? OR WHAT IF THEY DO, AND THEY JUST DON'T CARE WHAT I HAVE TO SAY?
ALL YOU CAN DO IS TRY YOUR BEST. WORRY ABOUT THE WORST CASE IF IT HAPPENS. AND IF IT DOES, I'LL STILL BE HERE TO LISTEN.
THANK YOU. I KNOW. I JUST CAN'T HELP BUT WORRY.
YOU GOT THAT FROM ONE OF THEM, AT LEAST.

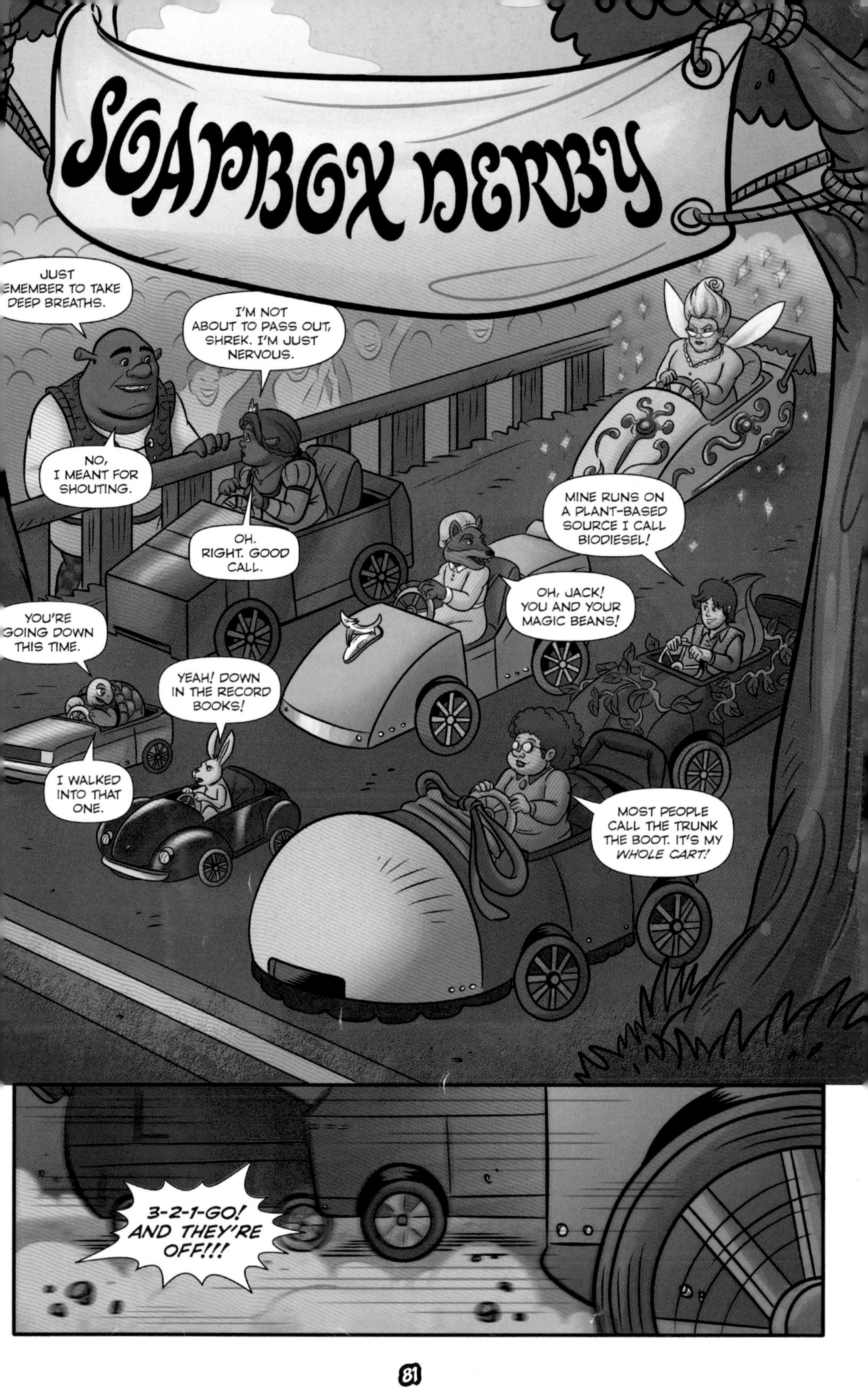
SOAPBOX DERBY
JUST
EMEMBER TO TAKE
DEEP BREATHS.
I'M NOT ABOUT TO PASS OUT, SHREK. I'M JUST NERVOUS.
NO, I MEANT FOR SHOUTING.
OH. RIGHT. GOOD CALL.
MINE RUNS ON A PLANT-BASED SOURCE I CALL BIODIESEL!
OH, JACK! YOU AND YOUR MAGIC BEANS!
YOU'RE
GOING DOWN THIS TIME.
YEAH! DOWN IN THE RECORD BOOKS!
I WALKED INTO THAT ONE.
MOST PEOPLE CALL THE TRUNK THE BOOT. IT'S MY *WHOLE CART!*
3-2-1-GO! AND THEY'RE OFF!!!

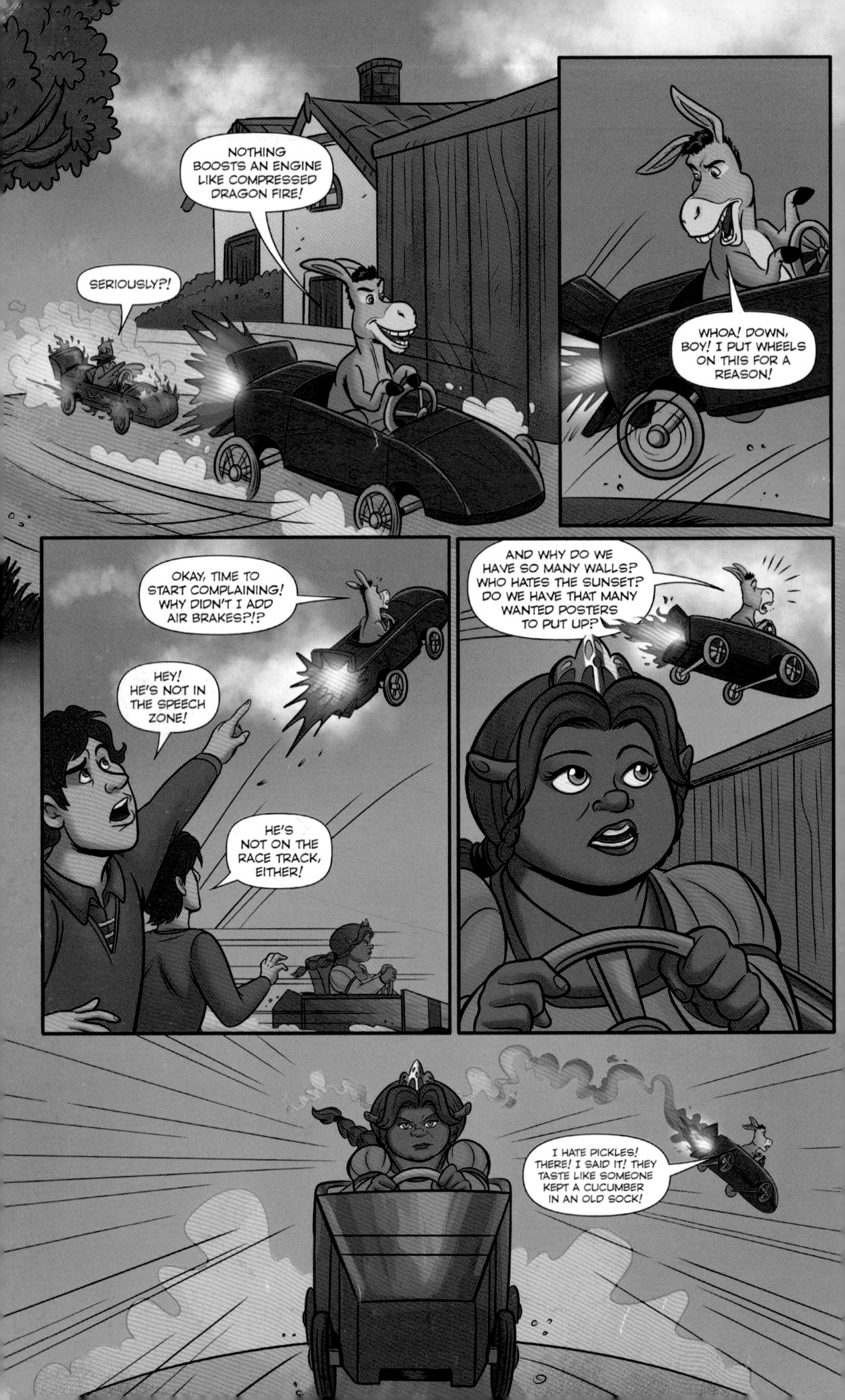
NOTHING BOOSTS AN ENGINE LIKE COMPRESSED DRAGON FIRE!
SERIOUSLY?!
WHOA! DOWN, BOY! I PUT WHEELS ON THIS FOR A REASON!
OKAY, TIME TO START COMPLAINING! WHY DIDN'T I ADD AIR BRAKES?!?
HEY! HE'S NOT IN THE SPEECH ZONE!
HE'S NOT ON THE RACE TRACK, EITHER!
AND WHY DO WE HAVE SO MANY WALLS? WHO HATES THE SUNSET? DO WE HAVE THAT MANY WANTED POSTERS TO PUT UP?
I HATE PICKLES! THERE! I SAID IT! THEY TASTE LIKE SOMEONE KEPT A CUCUMBER IN AN OLD SOCK!

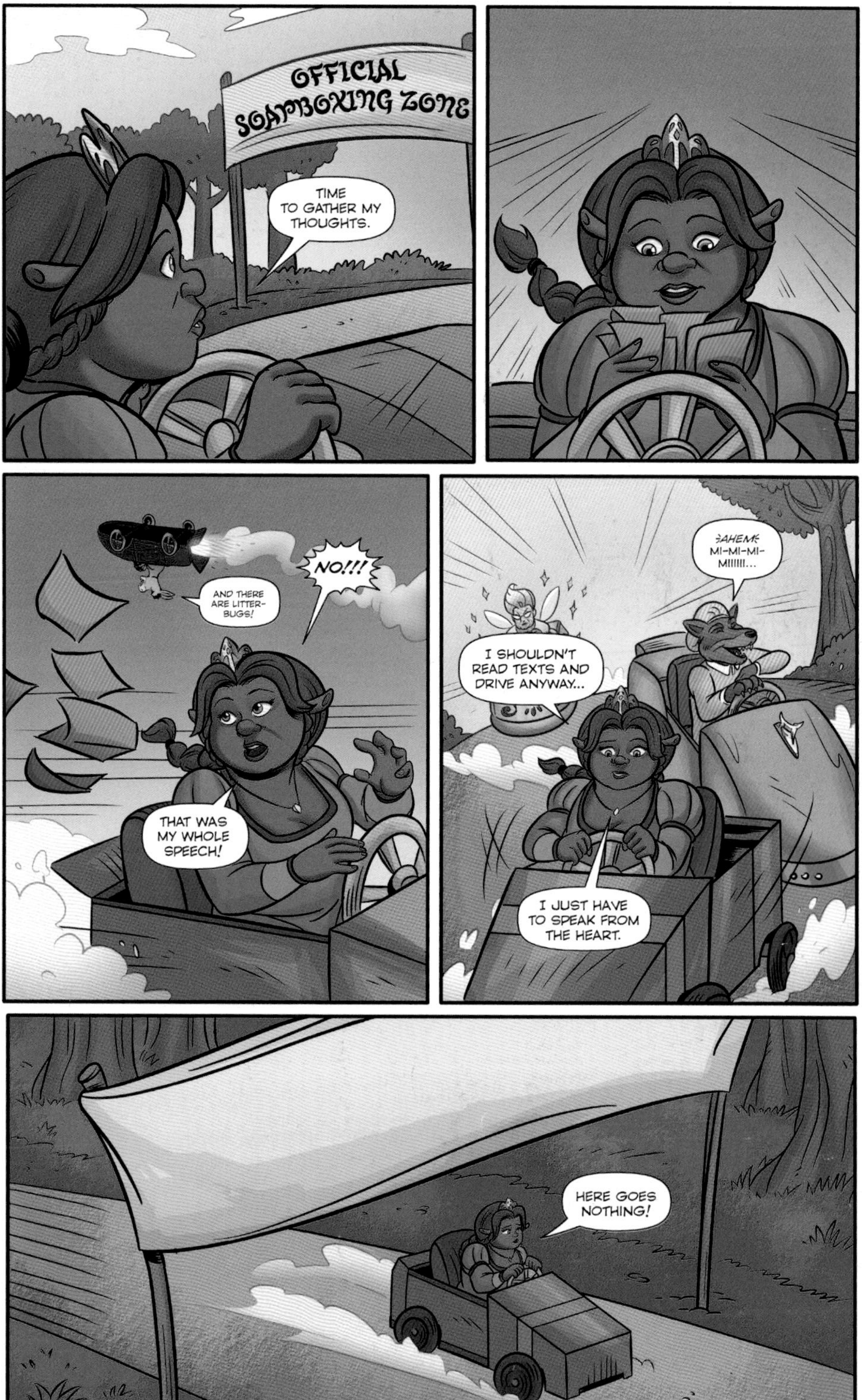
OFFICIAL SOAPBOXING ZONE
TIME TO GATHER MY THOUGHTS.
NO!!!
AND THERE ARE LITTER-BUGS!
THAT WAS MY WHOLE SPEECH!
AHEM
MI-MI-MI-MIIIIII...
I SHOULDN'T READ TEXTS AND DRIVE ANYWAY...
I JUST HAVE TO SPEAK FROM THE HEART.
HERE GOES NOTHING!

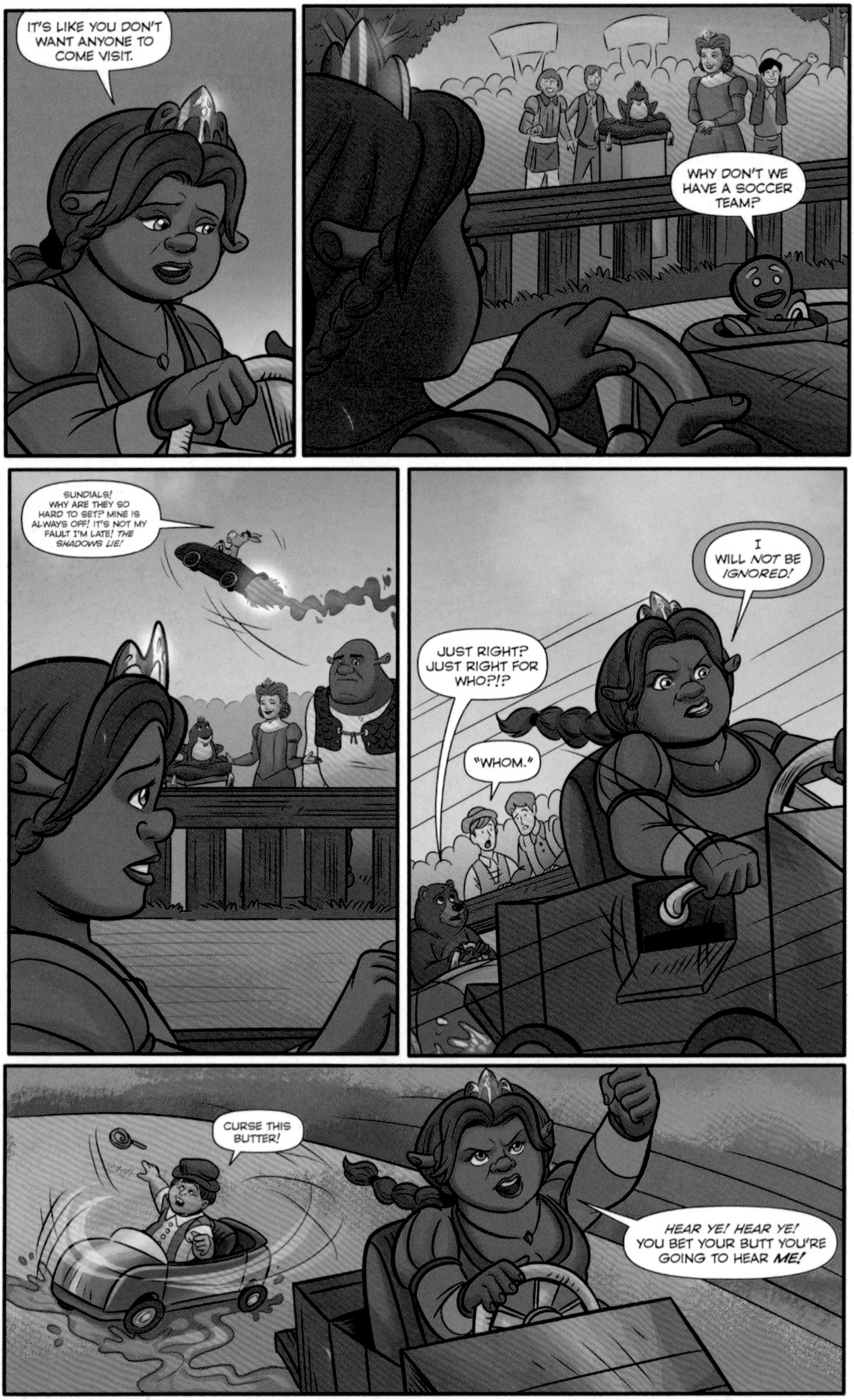
IT'S LIKE YOU DON'T WANT ANYONE TO COME VISIT.
WHY DON'T WE HAVE A SOCCER TEAM?
SUNDIALS! WHY ARE THEY SO HARD TO SET? MINE IS ALWAYS OFF! IT'S NOT MY FAULT I'M LATE! *THE SHADOWS LIE!*
I WILL *NOT* BE *IGNORED!*
JUST RIGHT? JUST RIGHT FOR WHO?!?
"WHOM."
CURSE THIS BUTTER!
HEAR YE! HEAR YE! YOU BET YOUR BUTT YOU'RE GOING TO HEAR ***ME!***

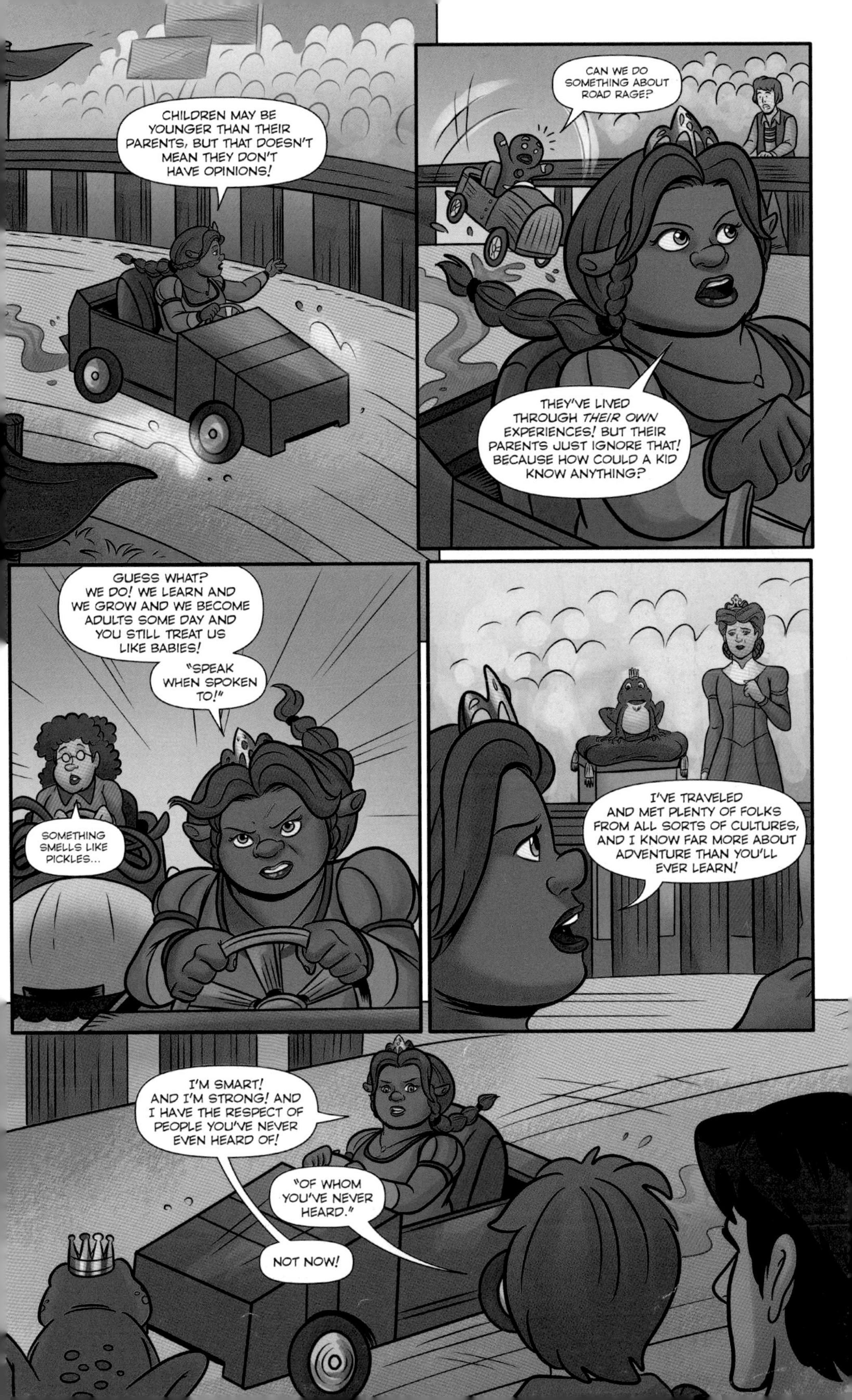
CHILDREN MAY BE YOUNGER THAN THEIR PARENTS, BUT THAT DOESN'T MEAN THEY DON'T HAVE OPINIONS!
CAN WE DO SOMETHING ABOUT ROAD RAGE?
THEY'VE LIVED THROUGH *THEIR OWN* EXPERIENCES! BUT THEIR PARENTS JUST IGNORE THAT! BECAUSE HOW COULD A KID KNOW ANYTHING?
GUESS WHAT? WE DO! WE LEARN AND WE GROW AND WE BECOME ADULTS SOME DAY AND YOU STILL TREAT US LIKE BABIES!
"SPEAK WHEN SPOKEN TO!"
SOMETHING SMELLS LIKE PICKLES...
I'VE TRAVELED AND MET PLENTY OF FOLKS FROM ALL SORTS OF CULTURES, AND I KNOW FAR MORE ABOUT ADVENTURE THAN YOU'LL EVER LEARN!
I'M SMART! AND I'M STRONG! AND I HAVE THE RESPECT OF PEOPLE YOU'VE NEVER EVEN HEARD OF!
"OF WHOM YOU'VE NEVER HEARD."
NOT NOW!

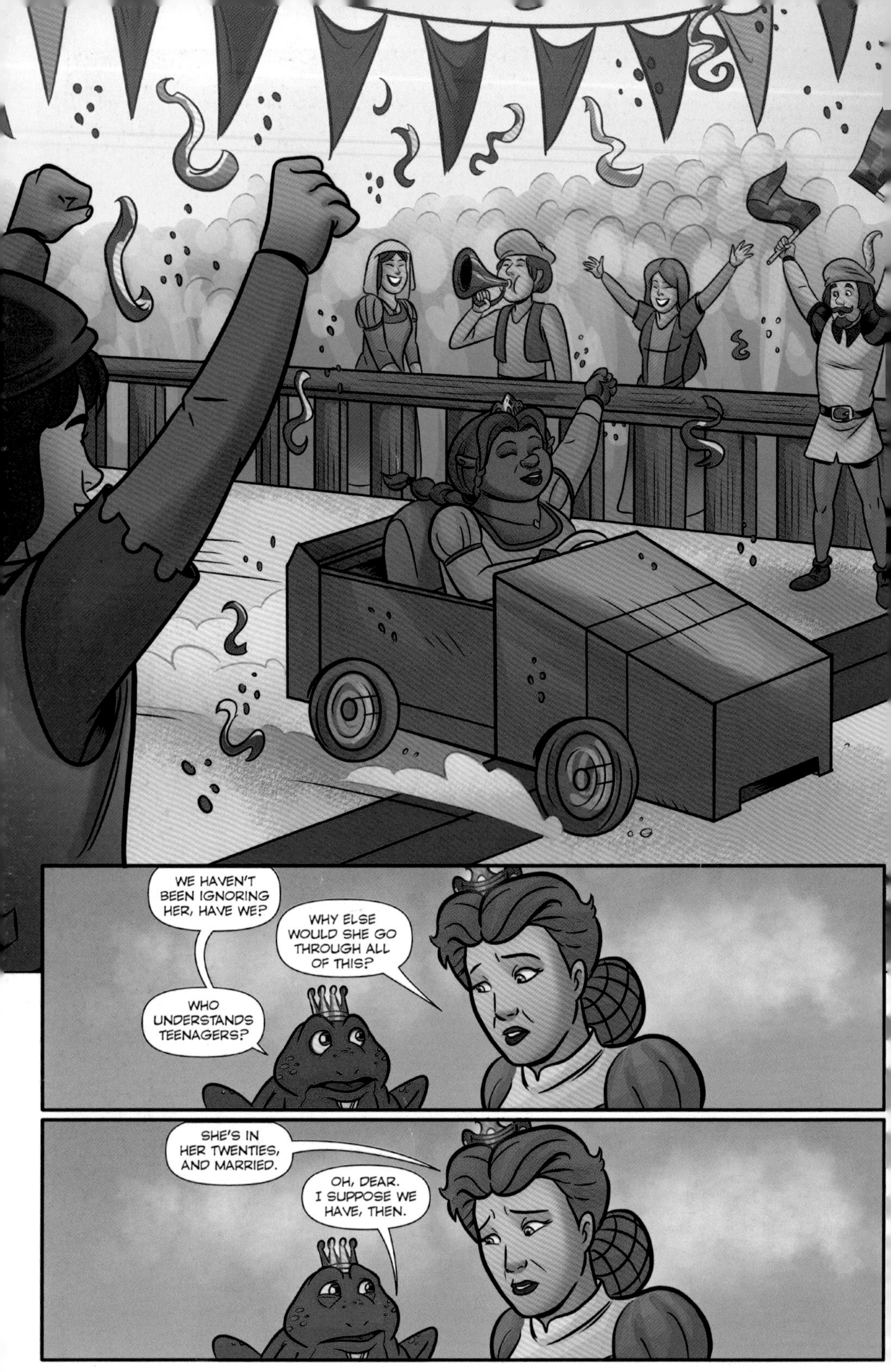
WE HAVEN'T BEEN IGNORING HER, HAVE WE?
WHY ELSE WOULD SHE GO THROUGH ALL OF THIS?
WHO UNDERSTANDS TEENAGERS?
SHE'S IN HER TWENTIES, AND MARRIED.
OH, DEAR. I SUPPOSE WE HAVE, THEN.

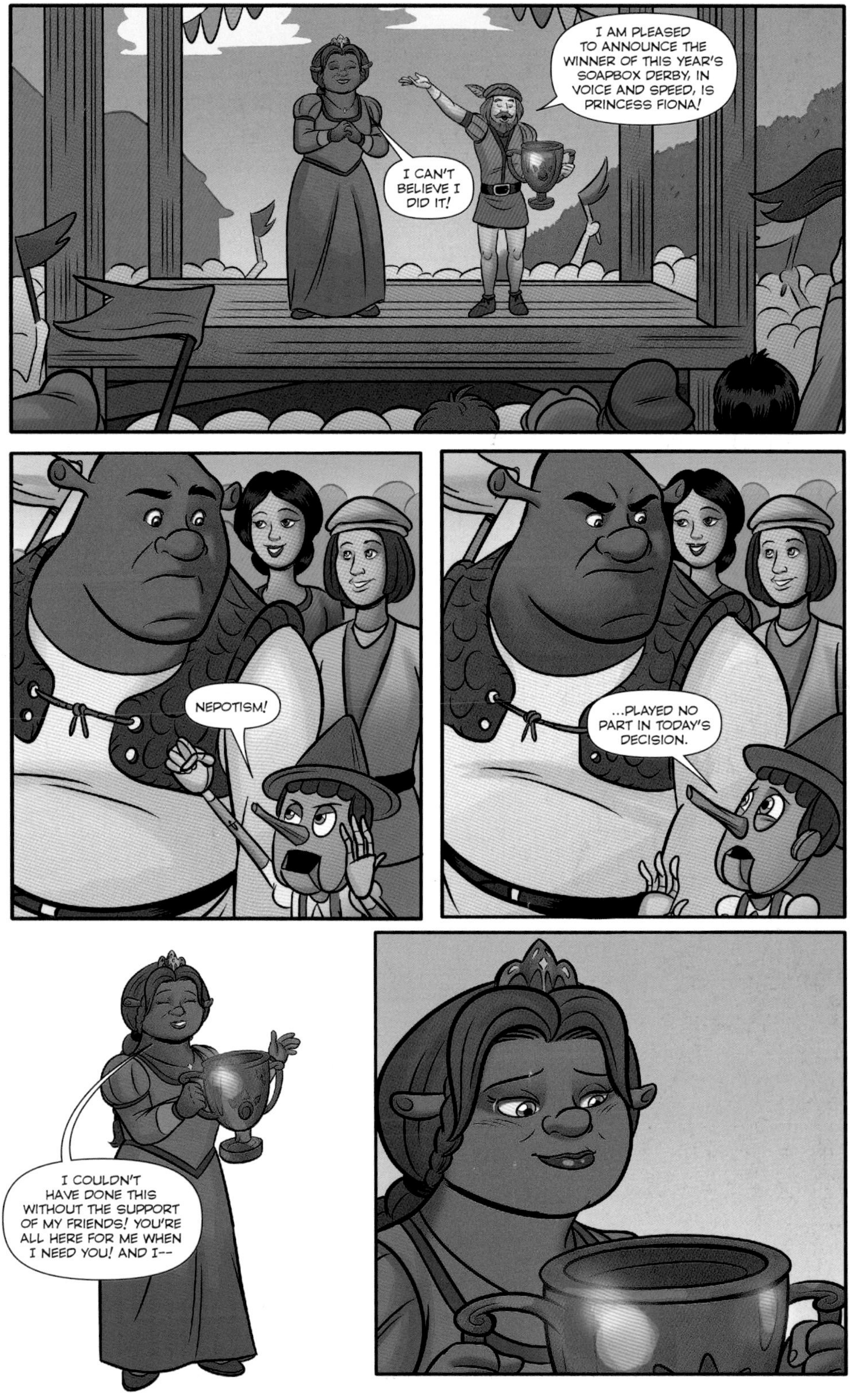
I AM PLEASED TO ANNOUNCE THE WINNER OF THIS YEAR'S SOAPBOX DERBY, IN VOICE AND SPEED, IS PRINCESS FIONA!
I CAN'T BELIEVE I DID IT!
NEPOTISM!
...PLAYED NO PART IN TODAY'S DECISION.
I COULDN'T HAVE DONE THIS WITHOUT THE SUPPORT OF MY FRIENDS! YOU'RE ALL HERE FOR ME WHEN I NEED YOU! AND I--

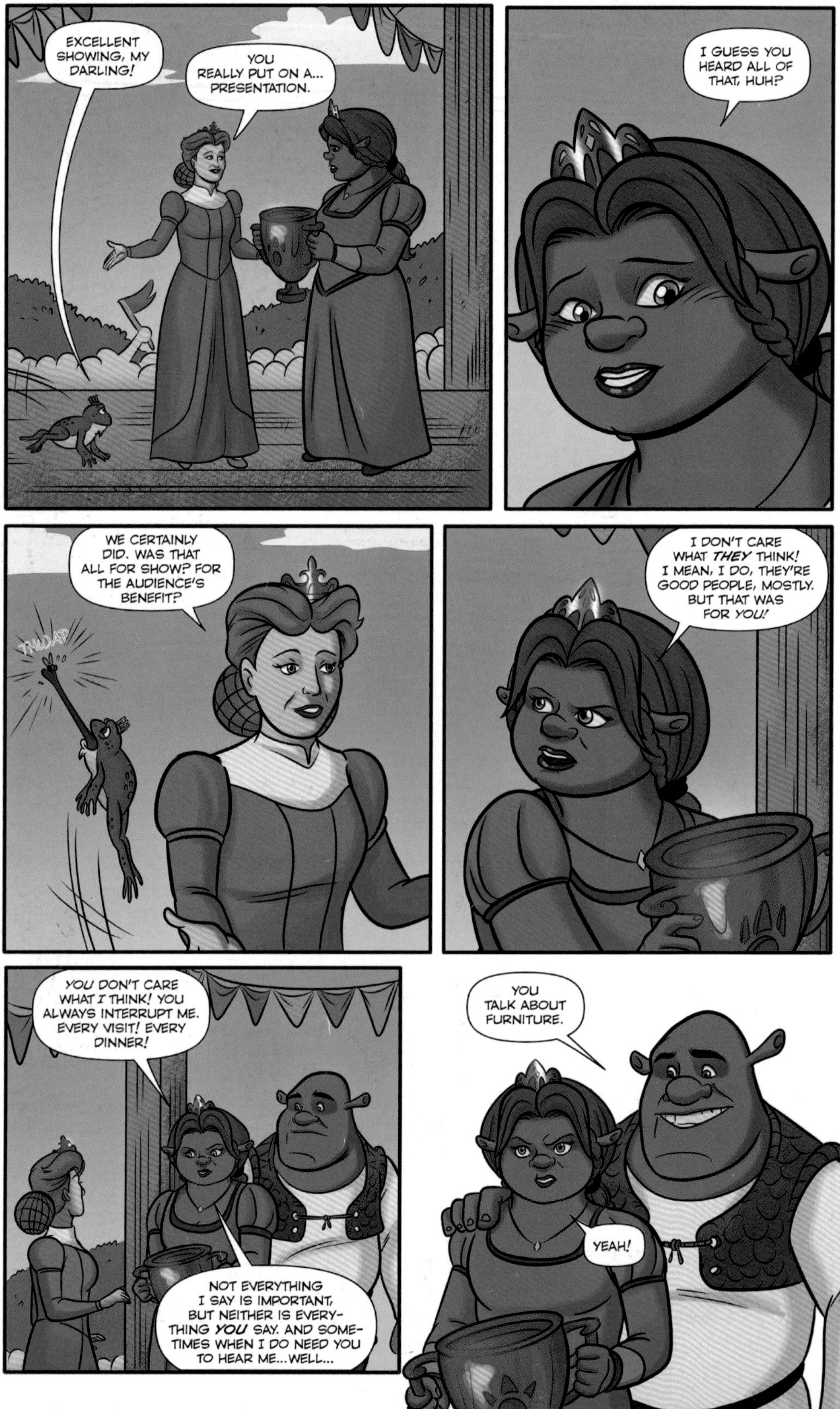

EXCELLENT SHOWING, MY DARLING!
YOU REALLY PUT ON A... PRESENTATION.
I GUESS YOU HEARD ALL OF THAT, HUH?
WE CERTAINLY DID. WAS THAT ALL FOR SHOW? FOR THE AUDIENCE'S BENEFIT?
THWAP
I DON'T CARE WHAT *THEY* THINK! I MEAN, I DO, THEY'RE GOOD PEOPLE, MOSTLY. BUT THAT WAS FOR *YOU!*
YOU DON'T CARE WHAT *I* THINK! YOU ALWAYS INTERRUPT ME. EVERY VISIT! EVERY DINNER!
NOT EVERYTHING I SAY IS IMPORTANT, BUT NEITHER IS EVERY-THING *YOU* SAY. AND SOME-TIMES WHEN I DO NEED YOU TO HEAR ME...WELL...
YOU TALK ABOUT FURNITURE.
YEAH!

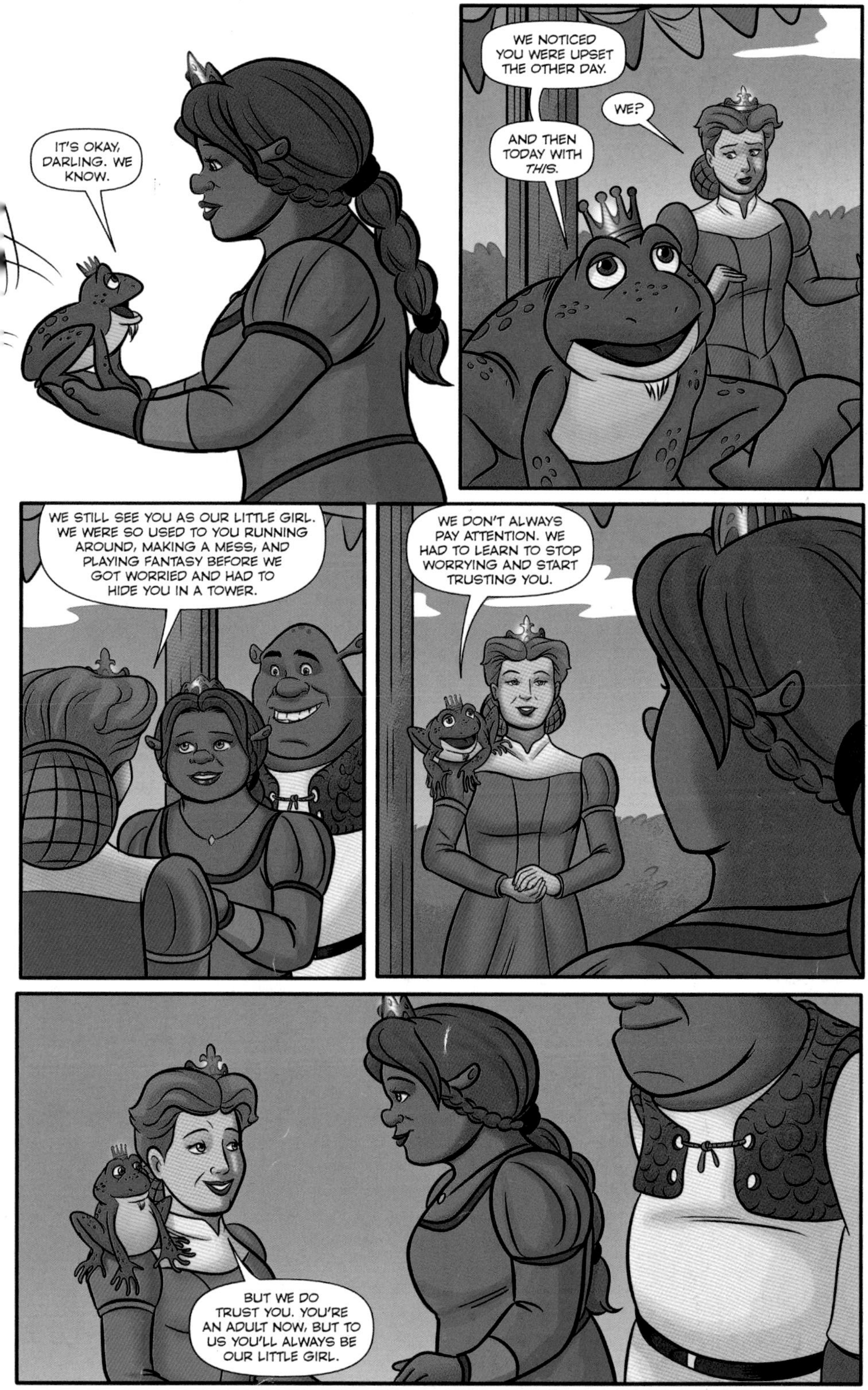
IT'S OKAY, DARLING. WE KNOW.
WE NOTICED YOU WERE UPSET THE OTHER DAY.
AND THEN TODAY WITH *THIS*.
WE?
WE STILL SEE YOU AS OUR LITTLE GIRL. WE WERE SO USED TO YOU RUNNING AROUND, MAKING A MESS, AND PLAYING FANTASY BEFORE WE GOT WORRIED AND HAD TO HIDE YOU IN A TOWER.
WE DON'T ALWAYS PAY ATTENTION. WE HAD TO LEARN TO STOP WORRYING AND START TRUSTING YOU.
BUT WE DO TRUST YOU. YOU'RE AN ADULT NOW, BUT TO US YOU'LL ALWAYS BE OUR LITTLE GIRL.

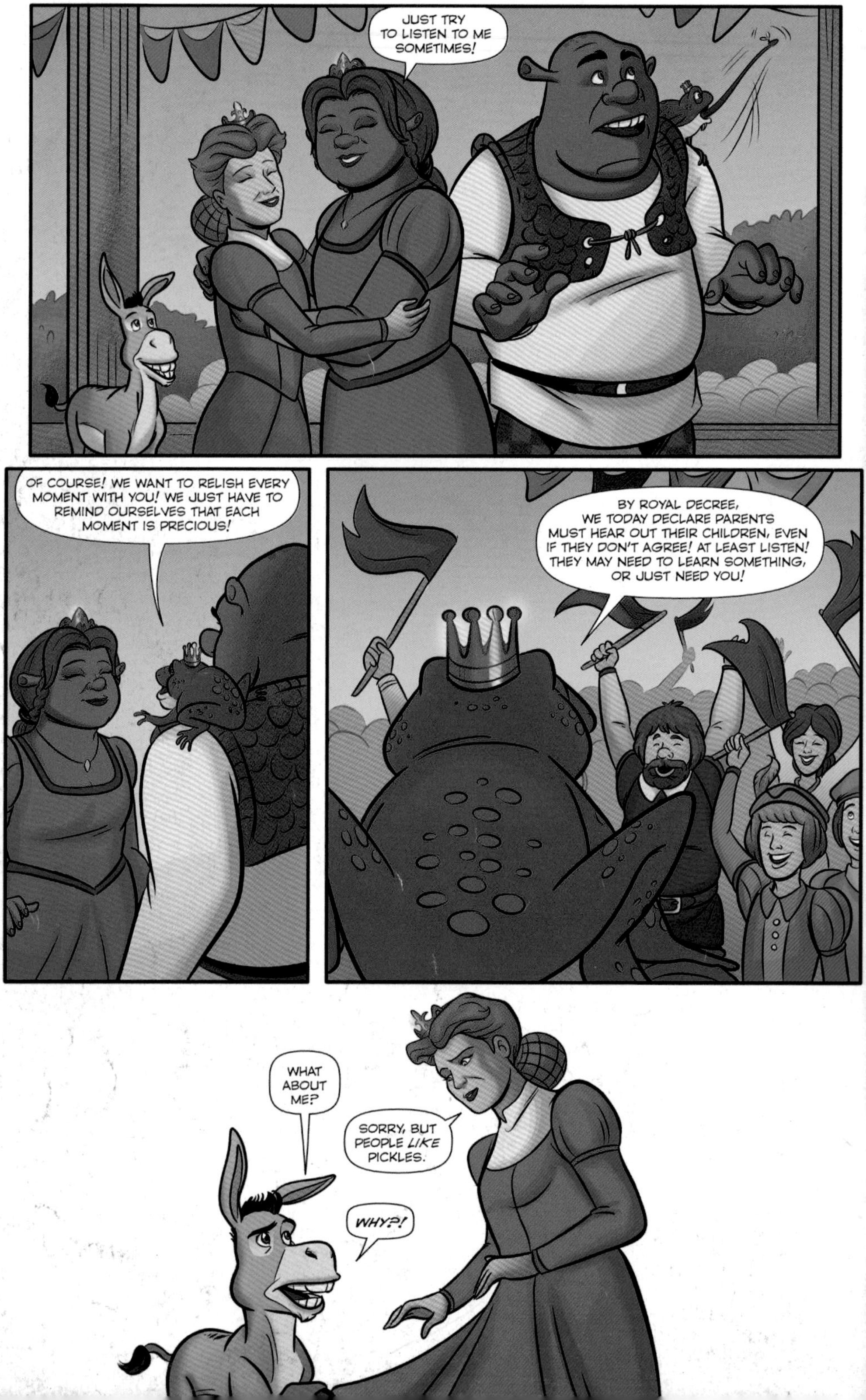
JUST TRY TO LISTEN TO ME SOMETIMES!
OF COURSE! WE WANT TO RELISH EVERY MOMENT WITH YOU! WE JUST HAVE TO REMIND OURSELVES THAT EACH MOMENT IS PRECIOUS!
BY ROYAL DECREE, WE TODAY DECLARE PARENTS MUST HEAR OUT THEIR CHILDREN, EVEN IF THEY DON'T AGREE! AT LEAST LISTEN! THEY MAY NEED TO LEARN SOMETHING, OR JUST NEED YOU!
WHAT ABOUT ME?
SORRY, BUT PEOPLE *LIKE* PICKLES.
WHY?!

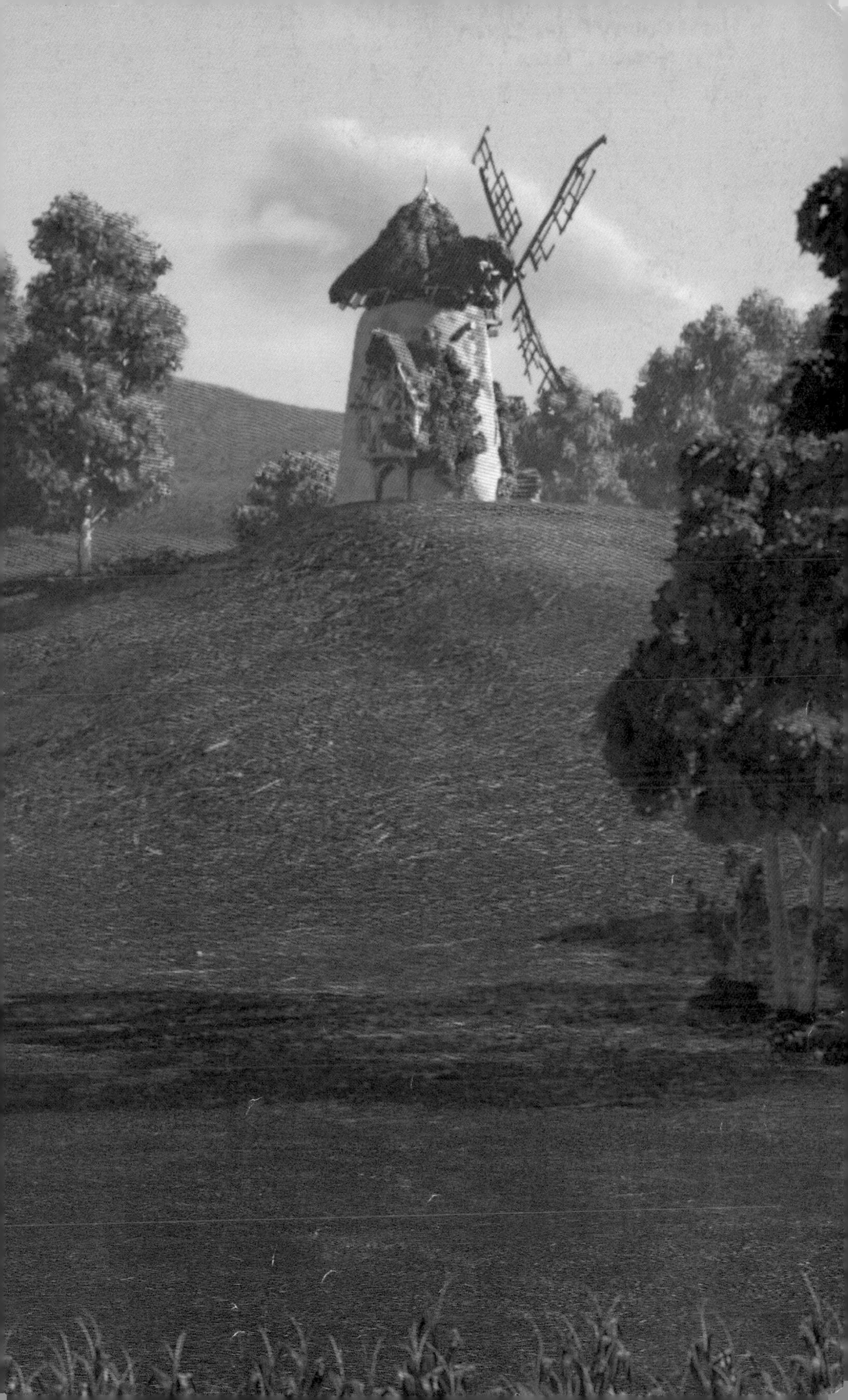

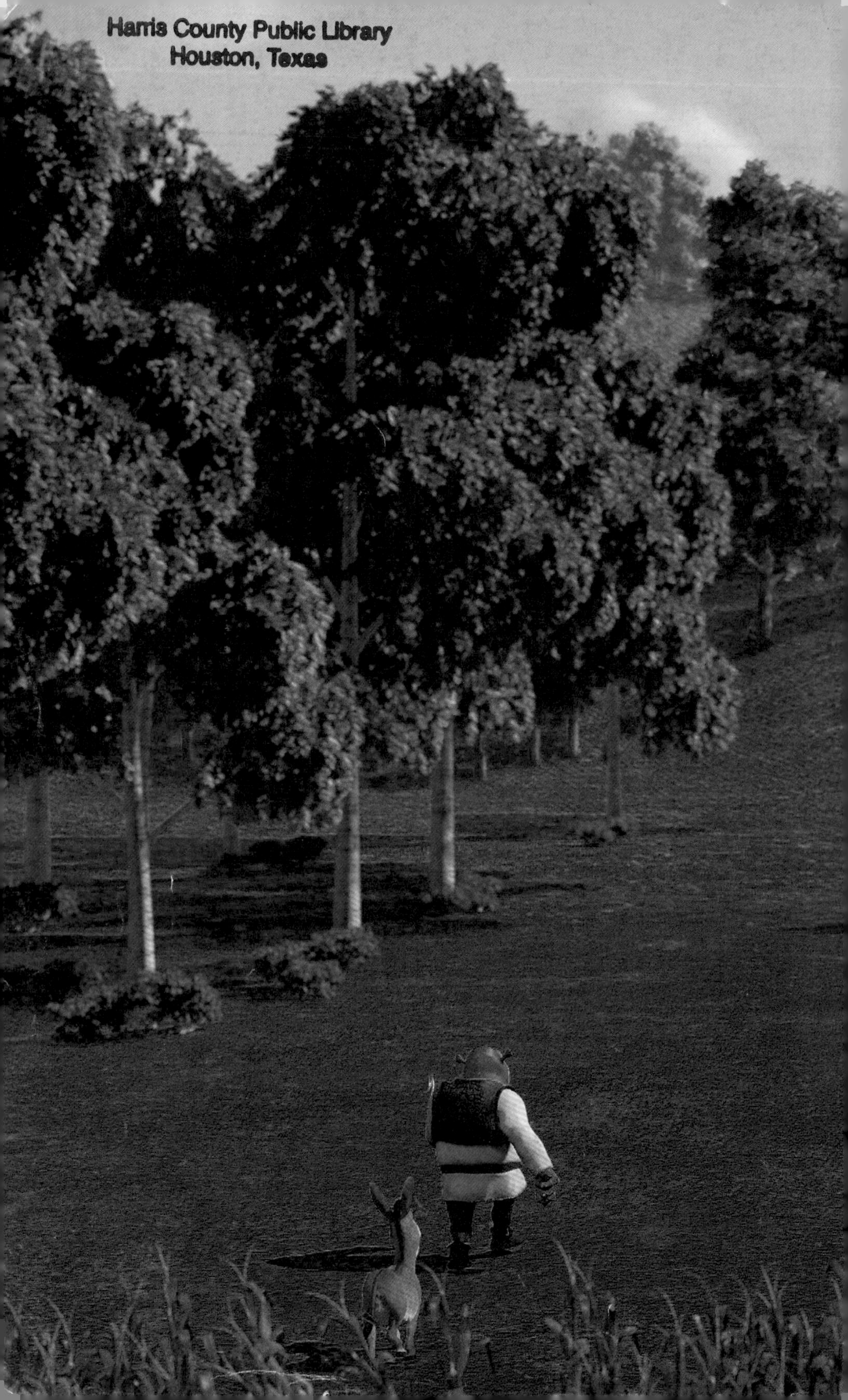